Advance Praise

"Whitney Boyd is Canada's answer to Sophie Kinsella! *Tanned, Toned and Totally Faking It* is a terrific read, from start to finish. Her characters are funny, fresh, sometimes flawed, but always believable."

~Deborrah Olson, honorable mention recipient for the 2010 Brenda Strathern Late Bloomers Writing Prize, sponsored by The Calgary Foundation.

"*Tanned, Toned, and Totally Faking It* is an enjoyable romp through the enviable life of a pop princess….with one added challenge: Mikayla Rivers has transformed from college student to superstar overnight. Filled with star-studded cameo appearances from the likes of David Letterman, Nick Lachey, Ellen and Lindsay Lohan, Boyd's debut novel accurately portrays the unquenchable appetite of today's celebrity-obsessed public.

"If you've ever wanted to slip into Jessica Simpson's life vicariously, this is the book for you! Recommended usage: slip this rags-to-riches fairytale for grownups into your beach bag between your sunscreen and the latest issue of *People*, and head for sandy shores!"

~Heather Blush, singer/songwriter.

"*Tanned, Toned and Totally Faking It* is a modern *Notting Hill*, told from the celebrity's point of view. Instead of following the struggles of the commoner, dating the celebrity, we follow the celebrity, worried about the commoner.

"I enjoyed that pop star Mikayla is from Calgary, went to the U of C, and visited local Calgary haunts. Too often I see Canadian authors, especially new authors, almost attempt to hide the fact they are Canadian by setting their novels in nameless American locales. Plus, I always like a book that mentions my beloved Calgary Flames in a favourable light.

~Bryan Wright, book reviewer, the CBC Eyeopener in Calgary, AM1010.

"I loved this book! Whitney Boyd does a fantastic job of creating the story of incredibly famous Mikayla Rivers, who is constantly fighting for a balance between her celebrity life, and her private life."

~Steph Hansen, Swing Announcer and Assistant Music Director, Country 105—CKRY FM.

Tanned, Toned and Totally Faking It

Whitney Boyd

WiDō Publishing • Salt Lake City

WiDō Publishing
Salt Lake City, Utah
Copyright © 2012 by Whitney Boyd

All rights reserved. No part of this book may be reproduced or transmitted in any form or by any means, electronic or mechanical, including photocopying, recording, or by any information storage and retrieval system, without the written consent of the publisher.

This book is a work of fiction. Names, characters, places, organizations and incidents either are products of the author's imagination or are used fictitiously. Any resemblance to actual persons, living or dead, events or organizations is entirely coincidental.

Cover photo by Tracy Blowers
Cover design by Don Gee

ISBN: 978-1-937178-12-3
www.widopublishing.com

This book is dedicated to my wonderful husband Stephen

Chapter One

"You'll have to go up two cup sizes." The man peers at me over his black-rimmed, Gucci reading glasses. "If you can get surgery done between now and then, that would be ideal, but if not, we can provide you with inserts. And if your doctor can fit you in, perhaps he can fix your nose while he's at it."

What's wrong with my nose? And my chest?

I self-consciously feel my nose with my right hand. It feels normal. The same as always. It's not misshapen or anything. Just normal. A normal nose.

"Um, I think my nose is fine. I mean, this is just a photo-shoot, right? And I am really grateful that you want me to be the cover of your October issue, but I'm not going to permanently alter my body for it, uh..." I trail off. Crap. I've forgotten his name already.

Joshua? Jeremiah? I think it was a Bible-sounding name. Ezekiel?

I just won't refer to him at all. I'll call him "buddy;" although he doesn't really look like the type who would respond favorably to being called buddy. This guy is posh. And glamorous.

"Now, Mikayla, we at *Celebrity Magazine* have an image to maintain. Hot. Young. Sexy. You fit that perfectly right now. You are the hottest thing in Hollywood, and we need to make sure that you look it on our cover."

The man's voice is humming in a smooth, melodic way, and I am trying hard to listen.

I should be focusing. I'm trying to. It's just that I didn't get much sleep last night. The room was fine, but my bed just didn't feel right.

Focus. What is he saying again?

"So you have a few options. You don't want the nose job, fine. We can airbrush it. So here's what you have to decide on. Implants versus inserts. Wig versus dye. And bikini versus halter. What will it be?" He stops talking and looks at me, his ballpoint pen poised over the notepad lying open on his desk. His eyebrows are drawn together, and he is surveying my body as if I am a piece of meat.

To be honest, it sometimes does feel that way lately. Like the entire world is starving and I am the last morsel of… something. Steak, maybe. No matter where I go, people watch me. Always measuring, always looking for the tiniest bit of fat to cut off, wondering how much money they can make off me.

I pull myself up straighter in the massive leather arm chair. We're in an office at *Celebrity Magazine,* very professional and chic. The walls are a beige-white color and splashed with framed pictures of the celebrities that have graced their magazine's cover over the years. Madonna. Britney Spears. Taylor Swift. That black-haired chick from Pussycat Dolls. Orlando Bloom. Brad Pitt. It's only been six months since my album came out, and already I'm rubbing shoulders with the great ones.

Which is kind of cool to be honest.

And a bit overwhelming.

Okay, don't get distracted, Mikayla.

I push every thought from my mind. Focus. Think of

sunshine and a soft breeze and the ocean.

Although, I kind of have to go to the bathroom at the moment, so maybe thinking of the ocean is not the best idea.

I shift in my chair a bit.

"Look." I clear my throat. "I appreciate this. I do. But I don't think I feel comfortable posing in a bikini. And what's wrong with my hair color? And my breasts? I mean, I don't think I should have to modify myself. Don't my fans want to see the real Mikayla Rivers, not this made up, you know, fake?"

I almost choke on the word "fans." This is unreal. How in the world do I have fans?

The man drums his long, manicured fingers on the gleaming glass-top desk in front of him. He tilts his head and examines me, lifting one eyebrow.

"Mikayla." He speaks in a would-be patient voice. "I have discussed this with your manager. She fully agrees that we need to constantly be improving and developing your image. Wholesome, hometown girl can only work for so long. People need to see a different side of you."

Cheryl. I am definitely going to have a word with her. She's not only my manager, but we grew up together. She was my roommate for a year in college—me, my sister, and Cheryl. I don't know why I agreed to have her manage me in the first place. Rachelle and I were always venting about Cheryl and the latest thing she'd said or done. Like when Rachelle invited her boyfriend over to the apartment and Cheryl hit on him and flirted so outrageously that he ended up leaving early, claiming he felt sick.

And then the times that she made fun of my clothes whenever I dressed up to go on a date. "That's the ugliest shirt I've ever seen," she'd say. "Where'd you get it, the thrift store for the homeless?"

Why in the world did I agree to let her handle my career? It's just that everything happened so fast, and then the whole thing with her mom being old friends with my mother. Cheryl offered to step in, and what with her business degree and our shared history, my mother thought it would be a fantastic idea, and that was it. *My* manager, a decision I regret every day. And yet I can't do anything about it now. Not with that teeny bit of collagen blackmail that Cheryl continues to hold over my head.

I brush back a bit of blonde hair that has somehow escaped my headband.

Okay. Calm down. This is not the place or time to worry about Cheryl.

I flash the man what feels like a winsome smile. "I'll discuss this with Cheryl and get back to you by the end of the day. Is that alright?"

A glint of irritation shows in his eyes, but he quickly covers it by smiling back at me. Perfect smile. Perfect teeth. Perfect lips. Perfection. Just like me, and everyone I've met in Hollywood. Amazing what veneers and caps can do, and who knows what else they did when I forked over thousands of dollars a few months back.

Everyone said it was essential. Get the look. If you want to make it big, you have to have the smile. If you are going to survive in Hollywood, you'll have to dye your hair. And get extensions. And wear the designer clothes.

When I look in the mirror, I barely recognize myself. The coppery highlights that I got from my dad are gone. So is my shaggy bob. I'm blonde, almost white blonde. And it's long and wavy and honestly makes me look like a movie star.

Then there are my lips. Collagen injections. My lips are plump and luscious-looking. They make my whole face look more seductive and older, romantic and, well, beautiful. But still, I wish I hadn't done it. Whatever. It's okay. Lips are fine. But that's as far as I'm going. No Botox to make me look younger. No face lifts or chin reductions or any of that other crap.

I never told my parents that I got my lips done. They were worried enough about my hair and the extensions. And the no carb diet I've been on for six months.

Tanned, Toned and Totally Faking It

Anyway, when my mom mentioned one time that my lips looked a bit different, I told her that I'd been trying out a new lipstick. Which is true. I had put new lipstick on that morning.

Sometimes my mom doesn't need the entire truth.

And as long as I don't get Cheryl too angry at me, my mom will never know.

I stand up and reach out my hand, saying, "It was good to meet you. And I will be in touch regarding the details. Plus, I'll see you in a couple weeks for the actual photo shoot. And all that."

I try to sound professional.

The man manages a smile. "It is always a pleasure, Miss Rivers." He shakes my hand and escorts me through the building, back into the hot, Southern California sunshine.

As he holds the glass door open, I catch a glimpse of myself in the reflection. Tall. Blonde. Long legs in a nice jean skirt. Tight American Eagle T-shirt with LOVE printed on the front. High heels. Big hoop earrings.

I look like a model.

Or a Grammy-nominated singer.

****

How in the world did I get here? Wasn't it just yesterday I was a college girl in Canada, stressing about midterms and planning on running a marathon one day and scheming with Rachelle on how I would win Matt back? I was normal and cute. I had my reddish-blonde hair and I liked playing basketball at night, strumming my guitar on our apartment balcony, and going swimming with Rach on Friday nights. I dated now and then.

And then it happened, so fast that my head is still spinning.

My sister convinced me to enter a campus talent show. "It'll be good," Rachelle had said. "The prize money is $300 and we could use it to go on a road trip after finals. Besides, Matt will see you. He'll be there and you'll be all hot and gorgeous on the stage, and he'll know what a fool he was to dump you."

So I entered. I took my guitar, showed up, and played a song I'd written years earlier. "Love Song." And Charles Nash was in the audience—the CEO of MusicStudios Inc. One of the wealthiest music moguls in the business, I found out later. He hadn't come to check out talent, which is kind of obvious. I mean, it was the University of Calgary, not NYU or Stanford or anywhere prestigious.

He had come to Calgary to attend a meeting with the Board of Directors of an oil company he had shares in. He just happened to be staying at a hotel near campus. And after his meetings he decided to walk around and stretch his legs a little.

He ended up in the Rozsa Centre auditorium just as I was taking the stage.

The rest is a blur. I didn't win the $300. That prize went to some band where they made their own instruments out of aluminum foil and old soda cans. Which is cool and all, but that doesn't matter, because Charles Nash found me in the crowd and offered me a recording contract. He said he had a gut feeling that I'd be marketable.

Rachelle, the loyal little sister that she is, stood beside me, clutching my arm in excitement, nodding her head and agreeing to everything.

That was it. He told me to find a manager, or he could supply one if I preferred. Cheryl, our roommate, who just happened to be graduating with her degree in business offered for only 15% of my earnings, and that seemed reasonable. Oh, plus she told her mother who in turn told mine that I would need a familiar face with me to make sure I don't get, like, homesick or turn to drugs and promiscuity. So my mom said she would feel better about it if I had someone from home with me and, well, I can't argue with my mother.

Besides, Rach and I got on fairly well with Cheryl the year we lived with her. You know. More or less.

I should have let Charles Nash assign me a manager.

Tanned, Toned and Totally Faking It

Nobody could be worse than Cheryl.

But that is beside the point.

Anyway, the next thing I know, Rachelle is registering for her next semester of classes and I am gone, flying out to sunny Los Angeles and never dreaming that life would become so different.

Six months ago.

Now I have an album out and am working on my second. My single *Break Up* is the number one hit for the fifth week in a row. And I have money. And the perfect life.

Right?

Except that I still cry myself to sleep most nights.

But that's normal.

Anyone is bound to have a bit of regret.

It's completely normal.

Chapter Two

I don't see my limo anywhere on the street.

I sigh. I really do have the perfect life. All that stuff I thought a moment ago? Clearly I was mistaken. Regret? What is there to regret? I play guitar for a living, and I get to send money home to my family and contribute and all that.

Plus I get to show Matt that I'm over him. That I have new, hot friends and I've completely forgotten about him. And every time he sees me in a magazine he'll realize what he is missing, and I'll be like 'Matt who?'

See? Perfect life.

I smile at my reflection in the glass window of *Celebrity Magazine* then look around again.

Where in the world is Cheryl?

She planned to go shopping, I think, while I had my meeting with the magazine. So she took the limo. I mean, it makes sense. Why should the car just sit here outside the building while I'm not using it? But still. She had promised to be back by noon. And it's almost one.

Tanned, Toned and Totally Faking It

And I still have to pee. So badly!

I should have mentioned it on our way out of the building. Although, to be honest, if I'd said anything, that guy probably would have started going on about how I need to get an iron bladder implant or something.

I peer through the glass door, into the lobby. Is that guy still there? Cause if not, I could go back in and find the bathroom without fear of him quizzing me in his condescending manner. I shift from one tiger-print heel to the other and pull open the door, suddenly decisive. It shouldn't matter if he's there. I don't need to hide from him. I'm Mikayla Rivers!

I step inside and look around. The room, although bright and spacious, is gloomy compared with outside. I blink a couple times and allow my eyes to adjust.

"Miss Rivers, did you forget something?" The receptionist has a phone to her ear and is typing away on her computer while still managing to send me a friendly wave. Impressive.

"Um, do you have a washroom I could use? I mean, a toilet?" I always forget that it's not called a washroom down here. The first time I asked to use the washroom, after I arrived in LA, I was at a restaurant and the waiter ended up leading me to the dish-washing area of the kitchen, sending me looks of confusion along the way. That was embarrassing.

The receptionist says something into the phone and puts it down. "I'm sorry, I didn't catch that?"

"May I use your toilet?"

I glance outside again, checking to see if my limo has returned for me.

The receptionist motions with one hand down the hall. "Yes, of course." I thank her and walk down the hall.

"Oh, and if my manager comes in, can you let her know I'll be right out?" I add, turning back to the receptionist. I don't want Cheryl to drive off if I'm not waiting there. Like that time two weeks ago when I shot some scenes for my cameo in *Law and Order: Los Angeles*. Cheryl got tired of waiting, and I had to take a cab home.

The receptionist nods, gives me a thumbs up, and I continue down the hall. Finally I spot the sign for the ladies room, and I push the door open. A young woman about my age is standing in front of the mirror, adjusting a gorgeous black and white shirt. Her hair is long and black and glossy, the kind of hair I've always secretly envied. She has a card around her neck on a long string that says INTERN.

I nod at her in an attempt to be friendly and make a bee-line for the nearest stall. I am closing the door and bolting it when I hear, "You're Mikayla Rivers, oh my god!"

I sit down on the toilet seat, but the desire to pee has vanished. I've never been the type to go to the bathroom with my girlfriends and carry on a conversation while I do my business. Some people manage that. I'm not one of them.

Relax, I tell myself. Pretend you're alone.

The girl continues, "Like, all my friends said that when I got hired here as an intern, I'd totally meet all kinds of celebrities. And this is only my first week and I've already met Jessica Alba, Gwen Stefani, and now you. This is, like, way too awesome."

I close my eyes, and try to think of the ocean.

"So, Mikayla, can I get a picture with you? I totally keep my camera on me at all times, just in case, you know?"

I try to concentrate on peeing, but I don't want to be rude. "Yeah, um, sure, we can get a picture together when I get out. Uh, that would be fine."

Crap. This means she's not going to leave until I'm done in here. And I better hurry up or she'll think I'm doing number two in here. She'll probably text her friends about it the second I walk out of here.

I sigh and stand up, pulling up my jeans and flushing the toilet. I guess I can hold it until I get back to the privacy of my hotel. I step out of the stall and wash my hands in the beautiful marble sink. When I turn on the hand dryer, the intern's chatter is drowned out. Then she whips out a digital camera and snaps a couple pictures with her right hand, while the two of us squish together and grin into the lens.

After the pictures, the girl steps in front of me, blocking me from exiting, and puts her hands on her hips. "So, have you ever considered playing at, like, a smaller, indie club or something? I know you're not really an indie singer, but it could be totally awesome for some of your fans to see you in a smaller venue, you know? There are, like, some rad hangouts in Echo Park and Koreatown that would literally flip out if you were to perform there one night with the standard, like, ten dollar cover."

I step back (she's in my personal space) and think about it. That would be kind of fun, actually, like what Matt and I went to back in the day. I used to play guitar at random things like that with friends back home, and it was always a blast.

"That would be cool." I twirl my hair around my finger as I contemplate it. "I don't know all the details about my schedule, like when I'm free and stuff, but that would be kind of fun."

The girl's face lights up. "Yeah? You mean it? Cause I know a bunch of us would love to hear you unplugged, you know? You're kind of like our idol."

"I'll talk to my manager about it, but that would be fun," I say again.

The intern beams at me. "Awesome."

I step around her, say goodbye, and head back outside.

Still no sign of Cheryl. No worries. It's a beautiful day. I'll walk back to the hotel. It can't be too far, and maybe Kurt will go easy on me tonight for my workout.

I'll be sure and tell him that I walked fast and broke into a sweat.

I walk down the street, swinging my arms and reminding myself how lucky I am to be here. How many girls would kill to make it big in Hollywood? To have random people in the bathroom idolize me? To be invited to the parties that I am invited to?

Exactly.

Anyone would be jealous of my life.

I'm not lonely. Rachelle is coming to visit me if she can get time off school, and then I go on tour; and after tour I get to go home for Christmas.

A shrill voice cuts into my thoughts. "Mom, look! It's her, I mean, it's really her!" I sneak a glance to my right in the direction of the voice and see a skinny girl of about twelve dragging her mother toward me, waving and calling my name. She is wearing a T-shirt with "Love is so last year!" written on it.

I hadn't realized that they'd made up T-shirts with my lyrics. I make a mental note to talk to Cheryl about it, and then plaster a smile on my face. I'll sign her shirt or whatever she wants signed, and then I'll flag down a cab.

Walking is overrated anyway.

And I really have to pee.

Suddenly more voices join in.

"It's her! Oh my god!"

"Mikayla Rivers! Over here!"

"Can I have your autograph?"

"I need a picture with her!"

"Do you think she'll sign my chest in blood?"

I am going to kill Cheryl. It's not like this is the first time she's stood me up and made me find my own way around LA. No more borrowing the car. Ever.

I force a smile and look at the swarming people around me. "Hi everyone. Look, I'm kind of in a hurry today but I'll sign autographs and do pictures for a few minutes. Five minutes. No more. Okay? So just, you know, please don't push or whatever. And I'll do my best to get to everyone."

Flash bulbs are going off and I see spots when I blink. The crowd is getting larger and I realize that this is futile. I can't sign autographs for everyone. I need to get going.

I try to push my way out of the crowd, but more people are pushing in. Everyone is yelling and shoving scraps of paper in my face and trying to take pictures with me on their iPhones.

The heat is getting to me and I feel a little faint.

Plus I still have to pee.

I have a sudden vision of me, urinating in the middle of the sidewalk, in front of all these people. I'll be all embarrassed, and it'll be all over the newsstands. My manager and hairstylist and everyone I know will be mortified and suddenly Depends and all these other adult diaper agencies want me to represent them and I'll never be able to go out in public again, and Matt will see it in a checkout line magazine and he'll think –

"Move! Get out of my way!" The voice is familiar, nasally yet commanding. It is the most beautiful sound on the planet. People are moving aside and backing off. I never thought I would be as happy to see Cheryl as I am right now.

Cheryl is smiling, showing off her nose job and boob job and who knows what else she's had done. She loves the fame. And she loves the random occasions when her picture gets put in a magazine beside me.

"Alright, alright. Mikayla needs to leave now. Busy schedule. If you want to buy autographed photos of Mikayla, visit mikaylarivers.com, all one word. Everything you need in the new online store."

Amazing. Cheryl manages to drag me from the grasping hands of the crowd, push me into the limo, and get marketing in at the same time.

The second the door of the limo whispers shut, I glare at Cheryl. "Where were you? I could have died out there!"

Cheryl holds out her right hand, displaying her French manicured nails. "Look, Micky. I was getting my nails done. I couldn't just leave. Besides, it's not a big deal. Tomorrow your picture will be in the paper and on the celebrity blogs. People will check out the new online store. No harm done."

She pats her ample chest in a satisfied way. Touching her implants has become a nervous twitch.

It's a little disturbing, to be honest. I should mention it to her sometime.

I lean back in my seat, reveling in the air conditioning. "Fine," I say tightly. I am not ready to forgive Cheryl. Maybe after I get to a toilet.

Cheryl looks at me from the corner of her eye. "What's this I hear about you giving Francisco attitude at your meeting?"

Francisco. Right. That was his name. Why did I think it was Biblical?

He called Cheryl and tattled on me? I'm twenty years old, and yet Francisco calls up my manager to complain?

"I didn't give him attitude," I say stiffly. "I simply disagreed with him on a professional level." I refused to get breast implants. That shouldn't be such a huge deal, seriously.

"Whatever." Cheryl taps her nails on her knee. "I smoothed it over with him. You'll wear the halter top and a blonde wig in a pixie cut with pink streaks. And they have permission to use as much airbrushing as they want." She glances at me. "Happy?"

I shrug and look out the window at the passing streets. Sunset Boulevard, a street sign says. Home of the rich and famous. Blonde, skinny women are everywhere, gossiping and carrying designer handbags and wearing super-high stilettos. Tanned, buff men are talking on cell phones, smiling their million-dollar smiles.

When did my life get so out of control? I feel like I'm not even me anymore.

Whatever. I push those questions away.

This is what every girl my age would have wanted. It's the chance to play my guitar and get paid for it. It's perfect.

Right?

Chapter Three

It's about three in the morning. I am lying in my bed, listening to Cheryl snoring across the room where she passed out after stumbling in a few minutes ago. I wish she would go back to her suite. And I wish I were back in Calgary. In my mind, I'm lying on the couch listening to Josh Groban on the radio and Matt is lying beside me.

Matt.

He is a physical pain in my chest whenever I think of his name. Or his smile. Or the way his blonde hair falls in his eyes when he bends over his guitar, plucking out a new tune by Heather Blush or Plain White T's or occasionally an original song that he came up with on the spot.

Matt.

I still don't know what happened. We were perfect. We were best friends for our first year of university. We met on the first day of orientation. After the tour of the university, our group leaders initiated a freshman ultimate Frisbee game. I was attempting to sneak off. Matt was, too. He wanted to check out the local bands playing in the Den that night. We bumped into each other as we were skulking behind a bush and, well, everything just clicked.

Matt and Micky. We were inseparable. Rachelle called us 'creepily twin-like.' We liked the same bands. We listened to the same music and watched the same TV shows. We laughed at the same jokes. We lived in the same Res Hall on campus and had three classes together each day.

When we started dating, it felt natural. Like it was meant to be.

But then everything changed. Summer came and I moved home to Okotoks. Matt got a summer job up north as a laborer in the oil sands.

At first we talked on the phone, sometimes three or four times a day. But then after a month, I would call and he wouldn't pick up. And he wouldn't return my calls.

I was hurt and confused.

I stopped calling. I put his pictures under my bed and swore that I wouldn't talk to him again until he explained himself.

I tried to rationalize it. Maybe phone service was shoddy up there. Maybe he broke his cell phone or dropped it in the urinal or something so he couldn't use it.

But alone at night, the thought would emerge like an evil demon. Maybe he just stopped loving me.

September. Classes started again. I was excited to have Matt come back. All our miscommunication through the summer would be over. It wouldn't matter.

I was sitting in Introduction to Biology, and I heard him. His voice. I spun in my chair and saw him, tanned and lean. The same Matt with the darling shaggy hair, but the voice that I loved more than anything wasn't talking to me. Matt had his arm around a tiny blonde girl's neck, his other hand on her waist.

She was gorgeous; petite, with a huge smile and a curvy figure, although she probably weighed no more than a hundred pounds.

As I watched them, Matt pulled her down into the seat next to him. Then he saw me.

I'll never forget his expression. It was a mixture of remorse and guilt and pity and then he looked away. When he glanced back, he had a mask on—unreadable. He nodded his head at me once.

And that was it.

I got up and walked out. I transferred into the Tuesday biology class and deleted his number. When I told Rachelle about it, we burned his pictures in a wastepaper basket.

Gone.

Ash.

And with the flames, a little piece of my heart died.

A tear trickles down my face and lands on my pillow. Okay. Calm down. Matt doesn't matter. I am Mikayla Rivers. I am an international singing sensation. I have a Barbie doll created in my honor.

Yet, deep down, I am still that girl to whom Matt gave a flickering look of disdain.

If I were all that great, wouldn't Matt be crawling and groveling at my feet? Wouldn't he be begging to have me back?

I don't know anymore. I have no idea who I am. My life is spinning, and I can't get my feet to touch ground.

I grab my cell phone from the night stand and feel my way through the dark hotel room to the massive en suite bathroom.

I close the door and flick on the light. The brightness burns my eyes. I close them tight, count to ten, and open them slowly.

There. Not quite as blinding.

The bathroom has beautiful gilded mirrors. A Jacuzzi. Lush rugs on the tile floor, and massive, downy towels hanging in a row.

I sit on the toilet and my forced self-control shatters. My shoulders shake, and I can't stop the tears.

Matt.

What was it? Why did he dump me? Was he afraid of

commitment? Because we could have slowed things down! Was it me? Is there something wrong with me? I mean, since Matt I've gone on plenty of dates. I've gone out with models and actors.

And yet Matt dumped me, without even having the decency to talk about it. He just drifted off.

I look at my phone. There's an unread text.

I open it up and smile through the tears. **Can i run away and live with u? Cant study for 1 more exam. New roomies are slobs and it makes me wish even cheryl were back here. Miss u! xoxox Rach.**

I love Rachelle. She is the best sister ever.

I hit reply and text her back. **Wish I was there. Miss you so bad. Come visit! I'll pay *wink* How r things at UofC?**

As I wait for her to reply, I start to fill the tub up with water. A nice bubble bath in the Jacuzzi will take the stress away.

My phone buzzes. **Not bad. Saw matt today. Dirty scum. Totally asked all about u. Said u looked amazing in People magazine. What a slime. So glad u r over him.**

My heart stops. Matt asked about me. He thought I looked good. I can't help it. I'm thrilled.

I hate myself sometimes.

Stop it. Matt is done. You're done with him. He is a pathetic excuse of a human being and…

I miss him so bad.

I stare blankly at the screen of my phone.

Empty. I feel empty.

I don't know what to think anymore.

Don't worry. I type quickly to my sister. **So over him. Whatever. Gotta go to bed. Love u. Xox.** I hit send and then crawl into the Jacuzzi. It's the truth. I am over him.

Aren't I?

Chapter Four

I have no idea what time I got to bed after my bubble bath, but the next thing I know, sunshine is streaming in the window and my personal trainer, Kurt, is leaning over me, poking me with something that looks suspiciously like a yoga block.

I would much rather go running for a good hour, but Kurt is adamant that we have to do cardio and a blended mix of yoga, Pilates, and some other twisting thing that always makes me pop.

I stumble out of bed and collapse on the floor in a heap. This is too early. My head is spinning and jumbled and I cannot manage a coherent statement. The carpet is cold and prickly.

Kurt pokes me. "Mikayla, hon, wake up."

I moan and roll over, smacking into one of the legs of the bed. It digs uncomfortably into my spine. "Go away. It's too early."

"Mikayla, it's already eleven. You need to wake up. It's a glorious morning." He pulls the curtains open and lets the sunshine stream in.

I try pulling down a blanket from the bed to cover my face.

"I want to die," I moan pitifully. Maybe if I sound pathetic enough, he'll leave me alone.

Kurt pokes me again.

"Ow!" I exclaim in indignation.

Kurt shakes me. "Hon, you need to wake up. We have a strenuous workout planned, after which Cheryl has arranged for Jill from hair and makeup to come by. Remember, you are performing at the UCLA campus tonight with all those other groups. Seven sharp. Remember? The benefit concert for underprivileged Americans? You're going to be singing *Break Up*. There's no time for you to lay around."

The concert. Right. I had forgotten about that.

Kurt looks at me thoughtfully. "You're homesick again, aren't you? Hon, your sister is coming out in a couple months. That's not too far away."

I nod. I don't want him to think I'm still having issues with homesickness. I mean, I'm not a dumb little teenager. I'm a mature adult, and I don't need to have my sister or my mother with me to be happy.

I roll onto my stomach and ease myself into a kneeling position. Kurt grabs my shoulder and helps me up. He's dressed in his workout outfit—bright blue spandex, with a black headband around his forehead and black knee socks. If I didn't love him so much I'd definitely mock him about his daily fashion choices. But he's my best friend in Hollywood, so I limit my teasing.

"Rachelle ran into Matt," I say, faking nonchalance and sinking down onto the bed.

Kurt raises his eyebrow in surprise. Kurt and I often share our boy troubles with each other. He's always good for 'girl talk,' as he calls it. "What did she say?"

"Well, I didn't get too many details, but she ran into him and he asked about me, and," I hesitate before I continue. "And he thought I looked really pretty in that *People* article last month."

I nervously play with the silver ring on my right hand. "What do you think? Good? Bad? What if I see him again? Do

I pretend like everything's cool?"

Kurt comes and sits on the bed beside me. "Darling, you don't need a boy like him. You'll find someone way better. What you need to do is ignore him. Like, Matt who? If you see him again, treat him the way he treated you. He can't dump you and then expect you to take him back when you're a big, fabulous, hottie pop star." He snaps his fingers defiantly.

Kurt's right. I know he is. But I don't know if I'll ever find someone like Matt again. He was so cool, so sure of himself, yet sensitive and loving. He always made me laugh and knew what to say to turn a brutal day into something fun.

I know what you're thinking. Girls don't deserve to be treated that way. It's just… I've always secretly hoped that Matt would apologize and we could go back to the way we were.

Matt made me hate myself after that. I questioned everything because of his betrayal. I know that he was a tool and a swamp creature and an immature jerk. But somewhere inside my still-aching heart, I wish we could go back to the way things were before.

Kurt gives me a hug and says, "You know what, sweetie? We'll hold off on the yoga today. Why don't we go for a run instead?"

Suddenly I feel energized. I can handle running.

We leave the hotel and flag down a taxi. We head for Santa Monica beach to run in the sand.

The sun is shining and it is already warm out, with a deliciously cool breeze coming from the ocean as we get out of the taxi. We lace up our running shoes and begin jogging, the sand shifting below each step. We run in companionable silence while Kelly Clarkson blares in my earphones.

The best way to forget your problems is to change your attitude. Attitude is everything. I will be positive. Here we go:

1. I am over Matt. I will never think about him again. Guaranteed. It's done. History. In fact, I'll write it on a

sticky note when we get back to the hotel and put it on my mirror.
2. I like having blonde hair.
3. I will be friendly and kind to Cheryl. I will no longer take strands of her hair from her brush and attempt voodoo with Kurt when she leaves the hotel. Cheryl is my friend.
4. I like yoga. I will be tranquil and meditate and become full of serenity. Everyone will know by looking at me that I am peaceful. Like Mother Theresa or—

Dang it!

I feel my foot turn and I sprawl on the sand, granules getting into my bra and mouth. I spit and sputter as Kurt reaches down in concern. "Micky, you okay?" He helps me to my feet.

"Yes," I say, feeling grit between my teeth. I move my ankle gingerly and, while a little sore, it feels fine.

Kurt grins at me and brushes sand off my stomach. "Cheryl will be ticked. Nobody saw you fall. No photographers around to plaster you on the next magazine cover."

We start jogging again, this time a bit slower. I watch the ground in front of me. Lame hole I didn't even see.

When we get back to the hotel a few hours later, Cheryl is pacing our hotel room, complaining to Jill, the hair and makeup artist, about how undependable I am.

"She always does whatever she wants, with no thought about how it inconveniences others. I had to track her down yesterday afternoon. She just up and left the magazine office and I had to drive the streets looking for her...."

She sees me standing in the doorway and trails off.

"Oh, hi! I was just talking about, uh, someone I know from a party." Cheryl doesn't look the least bit chagrined at being caught bad-mouthing me.

Remember, you like Cheryl. She is your friend.

Breathe.

I smile briefly, through clenched teeth. I jump in the shower to rinse off the sweat and sand and salty ocean spray. Ugh. I didn't even know it was *possible* for sand to be in some of the places I am finding sand.

I finally get clean and towel off and go back into the main room. Jill sits me down in front of the massive vanity mirror and begins to work her magic.

"I'm starving." I look at Cheryl in the mirror and open my eyes wide. Maybe if I look like I'm gaunt and pale, she'll take pity on me and order a decent-sized meal.

"Good, because you look like you need to lose weight." Cheryl applies some lipstick. She purses her lips and poses seductively. "The hungrier you are, the more calories you'll burn."

"Please?" I hate having to beg. "Kurt says I need to eat after I do strenuous cardio. It's the only way to replenish my, uh, endorphins."

I shoot a pleading look at Kurt who is sprawled across my bed, reading *Cosmo*.

"Of course, sweetie." Kurt says automatically.

Cheryl sighs. "Fine. You can have something for lunch. But no potato chips."

She walks to the phone and punches a button. "Yes, send up three Cobb salads to Mikayla Rivers' suite. Dressing on the side, low fat, and no olives." There is a pause and then Cheryl says loudly, "Mi-kay-la Ri-vers' room. Are you deaf?"

She rolls her eyes at me and hangs up the phone. "What a bunch of morons." She walks back to the mirror and continues examining herself. She frowns and pushes on the lines that appeared in her forehead. "What do you think? More Botox? I wasn't ID'd last night at the club, which probably means I'm looking older. Not a good thing."

Cheryl glares at me, as if I'm to blame for her looking her actual age. I shrug and try to hold still for Jill. Suddenly I remember something.

"Cheryl? I've been meaning to tell you. I was talking to an intern in the bathroom yesterday at *Celebrity Magazine* and she thought it would be cool for me to play a bit of music in the indie scene, like at night clubs and stuff. I wouldn't get paid much for it, maybe fifty bucks a gig, but it would be fun and good publicity, so I'd like to arrange something."

"What did you say? You want to play at night clubs? Are you insane? How will that help you gain credibility? Geez, you can be stupid sometimes."

I shake my head. "It would be fun. And it would be kind of a community service, you know? I could relate more to my fans and—"

Cheryl cuts me off. "Absolutely not. I am your manager. My job is to arrange everything. You can't plan your own career. God, Mikayla, you make me laugh." She turns back to the mirror.

Before I can retort, there is a knock on the door. It's room service with the salads. Cheryl hands me mine, and I stuff it in my mouth as fast as I can, amid Jill's grumblings that I am moving my head and not holding still. Cheryl doesn't mention the indie music venue again, and I don't bring it up. She's probably right; it probably is a dumb idea. Although I don't think it would have been the end of my career, like she implied.

Several hours later, I am dressed, presentable, and relatively full—make that not famished. I haven't been full in six months. Except for the time I was in Hong Kong promoting my new album; and when Cheryl left to go to a party, I called room service and ordered ribs, steak, lobster, and sushi. *That* was a happy night.

Cheryl, Kurt, and I go downstairs and climb into the waiting limo. It takes us without delay to the UCLA campus. We are early, so I tell Cheryl I want to explore a bit.

I pull a sweatshirt on over my tight tank top and promise Cheryl I'll be back in twenty minutes. I head off toward some promising looking buildings. What I love about traveling is seeing new things.

I like to explore.

I hurry away from where Kurt and Cheryl are arguing about if red or orange is the new black and duck into the first building

Tanned, Toned and Totally Faking It

I see. A few people are walking up the stairwell, but it is quiet everywhere. A sign says, 'Hugh and Hazel Darling Law Library.' That's a cute last name: Darling.

There is a huge painting on my left of a guy who looks intimidating. That must be Mr. Darling. He doesn't quite fit the name. He has a mustache and a proud expression on his face. I am about to step back and look at the painting from farther back, when a boy walks in the door beside me. I smack into him and my watch catches a strap on his backpack, jerking it to one side.

"I'm sorry," I say, fumbling with my other hand to get my watch untangled. This is so humiliating. I'm a super star, and here I am looking like some pathetic freshman.

The guy reaches over to help. He has big, strong-looking hands and his nails are clipped short. "No problem. My backpack is always catching on things. I need to get one without so many straps."

His voice is kind.

My arm comes free, and I smile at him. "Thanks."

He smiles back a little shyly. "My name is Jordan. I haven't seen you around the library before. Are you new to the faculty?"

He has a really nice smile. My eyes flicker up and down. He's tall, with dark hair and innocent brown eyes.

He doesn't recognize me? I can't remember the last time someone didn't recognize me. It's an odd feeling, and it catches me off guard. "Um, no," I say. "I mean, yes, I'm new, but not really." I trail off. Okay. Think, Micky. You are sounding like a fool.

"I'm not a student here. I'm here for the benefit concert tonight and was looking around."

There. That sounds better.

"Oh, is there a benefit concert tonight? I guess I don't stay too up-to-date on things happening around campus. I spend most of my time here, to be honest. I'm on scholarship and need to keep my grades up." He grins sheepishly. "Law school is too expensive for me to pay on my own."

I nod. That makes sense.

Jordan begins to turn away but then he looks back at me. "Do you live around here? I'd love to take you out to dinner sometime…"

He pauses, and I realize he's waiting for my name.

"Mikayla," I say hurriedly. "My name is Mikayla. I'm actually from Canada, but I'm here for a few months for, uh, for work."

"Mikayla." Jordan repeats my name. He has a nice voice. When he looks at me, there is so much warmth coming from his eyes.

"Uh, yeah, and dinner would be great!" I say, feeling a rush of excitement in my chest. His eyes are dragging me in. "I'll give you my cell number."

What am I doing? *You don't even know this guy!*

But I feel like I can trust him. Maybe it's because he's hanging out in the library with a massive backpack full of law books on a Friday night. Maybe it's what he said about being on scholarship. I haven't met anyone in LA who would dare to suggest they don't have money.

I can't seem to pull myself from his eyes.

He reaches into his jeans pocket and pulls out a battered cell phone. He flips it open and says, "Go ahead." I rattle off my digits, and he enters them carefully.

"So what do you do for work?" he asks, putting the phone back in his pocket.

I avoid eye contact. "I'm in the music industry."

"Yeah?" Jordan looks interested. "That's cool. I play a bit of guitar. Well, and the drums, but everyone can play the drums, right?"

No way! He looks too shy and quiet to be a drummer. The thought of this studious bookworm playing the drums makes me want to laugh, but I disguise it as a cough.

"That's awesome," I say genuinely. "I play guitar, too. We should totally jam sometime!"

Jordan looks down and then glances back up at me. He is so cute!

"That sounds good. Well, Mikayla, I'll give you a call then, in the next few days. But I should be going. I have a midterm on Monday."

With a half wave and a smile, Jordan turns and begins to walk up the stairs, taking them two at a time. I watch him go and vaguely realize that I have a ridiculous grin on my face.

Jordan.

My cell phone goes off in my pocket, and I pull it out. Cheryl. I hit ignore and hurry out of the library. *Alright, Cheryl, I'm coming.* I don't know why she's freaking out. I'm not on stage for another hour or two at least, because my number is about half way through the concert.

Whatever. I'm not going to let Cheryl spoil my mood when I just met the most adorable guy.

With his brown eyes lingering in my mind, I hurry off to the auditorium.

Chapter Five

The concert is packed. I peek out from the side of the stage. Royce Hall is full to capacity with people. My excitement levels are rising and I can't help but feel proud that I am helping to contribute to the end of poverty in America.

Not that this concert will totally end poverty.

I'm not stupid.

Only wouldn't it be great if it did? Because I know a lot of celebrities not coming who will be donating to the benefit. Elton John has already pledged a million dollars, and Jennifer Aniston promised to match donations dollar for dollar with those received from the people in attendance. And there are a lot of big names here. Faith Hill is the opening number, and I'm pretty sure Ricky Martin is doing some sort of duet with Jennifer Lopez right before I go out. And I know Rihanna and Katy Perry are coming, because I read about it on Perez Hilton's celebrity blog.

People are rushing everywhere, making sure one last time that the lights are working, that everything is going according to plan. Security guards are at every exit, watching everyone from behind dark glasses. I catch a glimpse of Marie Osmond down the hall, kissing people on the cheek and waving elegantly.

I'm the fourth song of the night. My drummer, Johnny, and bassist, Brian, are back in my dressing room, putting the finishing touches on their makeup.

I head back to my dressing room to see if I'm good to go. I walk behind the stage area and into a hallway, where all the impromptu dressing rooms are set up. I glance to my right as I pass an open door. Oh my gosh, it's Nick Lachey! I try to remember if I saw his name on the program they emailed out last week.

I've been in love with Nick Lachey since I was in junior high school. 98 Degrees was so popular and cool, and all the girls were in love with him. I've been secretly jealous of Vanessa Minnillo and Jessica Simpson ever since.

Not that I'm a crazy fan or anything.

I'm a professional. One singer to another, right?

Only I don't *feel* like I'm famous. I don't believe I'm in Nick's league, if truth be told.

I hesitate by the door. Half of me wants to go inside and introduce myself, the other half wants to leave. Besides, he probably has bodyguards, and they'll think I'm a psycho fan and will have me escorted out of the building.

"It's Mikayla, right?"

Nick is standing in front of me.

Oh. My. Gosh.

"Uh, yeah, Mikayla Rivers." To my astonishment, he holds out his hand and shakes my own.

"Nick," he says, smiling that famous smile.

"Uh, I definitely know who you are," I stammer, hating myself for being tongue tied. "I've been your hugest fan for, well, forever!" I sound like a bumbling school girl. Way to play it cool, Micky.

"Do you have a camera?" Nick asks, glancing at my hands.

"We could get a picture together. I'm a fan of yours too, by the way."

Did he really just say that? Nick Lachey is a fan of mine? Wait, what did he ask me? Oh yeah, camera. I shake my head no and say, "No, I don't have a camera on me, actually. But honestly, meeting you is enough! My sister is going to be so jealous!"

He laughs and steps back into his room. He grabs a camera off a stand in the corner. "Well, luckily I come prepared."

He puts his arm around me, leans in and snaps a picture at arm's length.

He smells good, like the Jack Black facial stuff that my dad uses. Not a strong scent, but clean and fresh. Nick glances at the photo, says that his manager will email it to me if I give him my email address. I scribble my email down on the scrap of paper he gives me. He hands it to a man behind him who nods and says hi to me.

Nick says, "It was good to meet you, Mikayla. Good luck on your song tonight." He goes back into the room and starts talking to the man with him, presumably his manager.

I turn and somehow get back to my dressing room. Unbelievable! Rachelle is going to freak when she finds out.

I actually met Nick Lachey, and he's as nice in person as I've always imagined.

I open the dressing room door. Cheryl is on the phone, lounging on the sofa in the corner while examining her manicure.

Johnny and Brian are finished getting their hair and makeup done and lean back in their chairs, chatting amicably. Johnny waves at me as I close the door, and they ask how long until we go up.

"Probably about thirty minutes," I say, looking at my watch.

They stand and say that they're going out for a quick smoke break, and they'll be back in five.

After Johnny and Brian leave, I glance at myself in the mirror. Tank top, jeans, the tiny, solitaire diamond necklace that

Tanned, Toned and Totally Faking It

Matt gave me for my birthday the year we were dating.

I pick up my guitar from its case and slide the leather band around my neck. I begin strumming it, playing a mindless melody.

Cheryl scowls at me from the sofa and covers the phone with her hand. "Do you mind?" she says. "I'm trying to talk to someone."

I roll my eyes at her and stop plucking at my guitar. I pull out my cell and decide to call Rachelle.

It rings twice before I hear her familiar voice.

"Micky! I'm so glad you called! I was going to call you, but I didn't know what time your concert was, and I didn't want to interrupt if you were in the middle of something."

Her voice soothes me as she babbles on for a minute.

"Kay, listen Rach," I finally say, cutting her off, but desperately wanting to tell her my news. "I have a couple super exciting things to tell you, okay?"

When I tell her about Nick Lachey, she shrieks and giggles just the way I knew she would. After she calms down, I take a deep breath.

"I met a boy," I say, speaking fast. "And not a famous boy, either. His name is Jordan, and I was exploring around the campus here before coming to get ready, and I met him. He's in law school and is super sweet. He didn't recognize me, which was totally weird. Most people his age know who I am. But anyway, he asked if he could take me out to dinner sometime, and I actually gave him my phone number, which is totally ridiculous, but he was so cute!"

I trail off and wait. This is the moment that she should be squealing and getting all excited. Rachelle is silent for a moment and then she says, "That's great! That's really great!"

Her voice is forced. Something is wrong.

"Uh, Rach?" I say, trying to sound nonchalant. "What's the matter? You sound a little worried or something."

Her voice still sounds strained, but she pretends that it

doesn't. "What? Micky, you crazy! Nothing's wrong. I was just like, uh, processing it. But no, that sounds super! I'm excited for you! You deserve this. Tell me what he looks like."

I describe Jordan to her, but now I am distracted. Rachelle is hiding something from me, and I am determined to find out what.

I'll phone Mom after the concert. She'll tell me. And if she doesn't know... I wrack my brain, trying to think of who I can get information from. Maybe Janie. She's been one of Rachelle's closest friends since kindergarten.

Cheryl gets off her phone. "Mikayla, you're on stage in ten minutes."

I tell Rachelle that I'll talk to her later and hang up.

I feel a quick wave of nausea and draw in a deep breath, forcing myself to think positive thoughts.

Maybe I'm weird, but I always get kind of sick before I go on stage. Or before Christmas. Or my birthday. I have a hyperactive body, my mom says. But once I'm on stage and doing my thing, I feel fine.

Oh God, please don't let me throw up!

I grab my guitar, checking once more that I don't have my underwear sticking out of my pants or that my bra straps aren't showing. I've always been anal about this. Which I know is dumb, because most performers have some kind of embarrassing moment on stage way worse than having a bra strap show. Hello, Fergie peed her pants. But who wants to join the ranks of humiliated performers?

We go out and make our way to the stage. I draw slow, calming breaths, and I hear the host of the evening (I've seen him on SNL, but I don't remember his name... Paul something, I think) making jokes and talking to the audience. He says my name, and the crowd cheers and hollers. I swallow once and walk out on stage.

The lights are blinding and I can't make out any faces in the audience. Just a sea of strangers, shrieking and clapping for me.

"And here is Mikayla Rivers with *Break Up!*" the man says, grinning at me.

I wave once, and look behind me. Johnny and Brian have come out unnoticed and so I say into the microphone, "Hi UCLA! Thanks for coming tonight. Give it up for my bassist and drummer, Johnny and Brian. They're the greatest!"

The crowd cheers again, and after letting them applaud the two guys for a second, I say, "We're doing *Break Up*, a song I wrote, and one of my favorites."

I nod at Johnny and he taps out the beat. After three bars, Brian and I start strumming. The music is familiar and I relax into it. I start singing and before I know it, the screaming crowd is on their feet, applauding and hollering, and we're done.

I wave and smile. When the host comes back out, I stride across the stage back to the hallway.

People shout out things as I pass and a few of them hand me pieces of paper. I scribble my name and try to be gracious in receiving compliments.

I once read an article that said you can tell a lot about a person by how they accept a compliment. I took the test and learned that I was a 'Bashful Denier'—shy and timid, don't like receiving compliments. I've been making an effort to be more of a 'Positive yet Humble Accepter.' I accomplish this by a) smiling, b) thanking without bragging, and c) complimenting in return.

That last one is the most difficult. It's hard to think of return compliments, especially when they come from strangers I see for only a brief second. Like when someone tells me I have a fab singing voice, what do I say back? That they have cute shoes?

Anyway, it's a work in progress.

Most of those crowding around me have name tags on, identifying themselves as sound guys, producers, light directors, managers. I barely glance at each face as I scribble my name on whatever they hold out for me. A few people pat me on the back as they go by.

"Mikayla, great job!"

"You were awesome! Such a catchy song!"

"Thanks for the song, girl! You're a natural performer." Oh, that one came from Rihanna herself. I beam at her, feeling in awe that someone as talented as Rihanna thinks I'm a natural.

I finish scrawling my name on a couple more papers, and then Johnny, Brian, Cheryl, Kurt, and I go back into the dressing room. I am super pumped up, the way I always am after a performance. I can't stop jumping around. We put on some music and Kurt and I dance along with it, goofing off with awkward dance moves.

Johnny and Brian linger a few minutes before grabbing their things, tell me they'll see me tomorrow afternoon at the recording studio and peace out.

"Let's go to dinner!" I am thinking hungrily of a double cheeseburger from McDonalds. I know they are off limits, but I still sometimes have dreams about them.

Cheryl agrees, and Kurt grabs his man-purse. We head outside to the limo. I sign autographs for a few fans who are waiting for me, and then we speed away into the warm, autumn California night.

Chapter Six

It's been two days and Jordan hasn't called yet. Despite going to the Malibu beach with Kurt on Saturday, and then Sunday shopping with him and Cheryl in Santee Alley, the hours dragged. I checked my phone every few minutes.

I am lying in bed on Monday morning, and that's all I can think about. That, and how bumpy the hotel ceiling is. As far as hotels go, this is one of the nicer ones, which is good since I'll be here for a few months. We're in the middle of getting my new album made. I've already recorded a couple songs for it, and now am practicing and whatnot with the guys to get the other songs at a recordable stage.

I love this new album. I liked my first one too, and it's been nominated for a bunch of Grammys and all that. It has been topping the charts, and I hear myself on the radio almost every time I turn it on. I've been compared to a "female Justin Beiber," a "less provocative Britney Spears," and a "sweetheart like Taylor Swift."

At this time last year I would never have imagined this. I

considered it an accomplishment if I was showered and on time for class on Monday morning.

Will he call? I am mentally practicing what to say when he does. Should I play it cool and be all like "Jordan who? Oh yeah, I vaguely remember you?" But it was only two days ago, and I don't want him to think I'm a player.

Maybe I could be laid-back and yet still act excited. Like, "Jordan, of course! How's it going?" That seems pretty casual, like we're friends. But what if it gives him the wrong idea? What if he thinks that I am only interested in being friends?

I need to let him know I am interested in him, without being a crazy, clingy girl. That is probably what made Matt freak out, and I definitely don't want to repeat *that* scenario. But I also want Jordan to know I'm into him!

My phone rings. I sit bolt upright. It's him! I just know it! I grab my cell from my nightstand and look at the caller ID.

It's my mom.

Which is fine. I've been trying to get hold of her since Friday, when Rachelle wouldn't tell me what's going on.

I push the accept button. "Hi Mom."

"Hi honey!" Her voice sounds a little tinny on my cell, and I feel a wave of longing to be home. I miss her so bad sometimes. "Sorry I didn't return your message sooner."

I can just picture her smiling face. She has some wrinkles around her eyes, but she has almost the same color of hair as I do (well, my natural dark blonde color, but without the coppery highlights that I got from my dad), and her eyes are just a little brighter blue. But other than that, she could be my older sister.

"No problem." I blink back the tears that come at the sound of her voice. "I was calling cause when I was talking to Rachelle on Friday night, she sounded kind of preoccupied. I told her about a new guy I am possibly going on a date with, and she seemed all distracted and forced and stuff. Do you know what's up?"

"Rachelle?" I can tell immediately from her voice that she has no idea.

"Yeah." Before she gets worried, I add, "Although, when I think about it, it was probably a bad phone connection. Don't worry about it."

We chat for a few minutes and then hang up. I lie back in bed, still holding my cell phone.

I scroll through my contact list until I come to Janie Kells.

It rings three times. A groggy voice answers, "Hello?" I must have woken her up. Eight in the morning is early for a university student.

"Hi Janie," I say, hoping she can solve the mystery. "It's Mikayla Rivers, you know, Rachelle's sister?"

There is silence and then Janie speaks, her voice a lot louder. "Oh my gosh, you're Mikayla Rivers! You actually are Mikayla?"

I raise an eyebrow and say slowly, "Yeah. It's just Micky. You've known me all your life."

Janie says, "Well, yes, but you've never phoned me as Mikayla Rivers before. You've always just been Micky."

"Right. Anyway, I'm still Micky, and right now I've got a question for you. I was talking to Rachelle the other day, and she was hiding something from me. I was talking about a new guy I'm interested in, and she got all awkward and artificial and everything she said sounded forced. Do you know what that's all about?"

"No, I have no idea. I haven't talked to Rach in a few months. You probably didn't know, but I transferred to the University of Lethbridge, so I'm not even at U of C anymore."

"Oh." This is disappointing. Janie was my last hope.

"I'm so sorry, Mikayla Rivers. I can try to call Rachelle or something, maybe, to see what's going on."

"It's just Micky!" I feel frustrated.

"Of course. Micky-kayla Rivers."

There is an uncomfortable pause. The silence stretches for a few seconds. "So, uh, Janie, how do you like U of L?"

"It's good, athough Lethbridge is a little boring sometimes. No cool music groups come down here for concerts. I always have to travel back to Calgary for them."

"Right. Well, look, next time I come to Alberta, I'll see if I can get you backstage passes or something. Would that be cool?"

She squeals so loudly that I have to move the phone away from my ear. "Oh my goodness, thank you, Mikayla Rivers!"

"Micky! I have to go, Janie, but I'll be sure and let you know about the tickets."

This is getting me nowhere. I'll just have to bring Jordan up when I talk to Rachelle next and pin her down if she gets shifty about him.

I roll over in bed. I have a few minutes before Kurt comes in for our workout. I snuggle down into the plush pillow and close my eyes.

My phone buzzes again, and I groan. It's probably my mom. She must have forgotten to tell me about someone she met in the grocery store who said something positive about me.

I reach for my phone and stare at the screen. It's a 424 number, which means it's someone in the Los Angeles area.

Jordan! I think then push the thought away. More likely it's someone thanking me for helping out at the benefits concert.

I clear my throat once to make sure that my voice won't crack or anything embarrassing and say, "Hello?"

"Hi, may I speak to Mikayla?" It's him. I recognize his voice! A little shy, yet sure of himself at the same time.

"Speaking." I try to keep my voice from getting too excited. Fail, Micky, fail. I totally sound eager.

"Hi Mikayla, this is Jordan Baker. We met on Friday at the law library on UCLA campus?" His voice is a little questioning, and that makes me smile. He is so cute!

"Yeah, of course, yes!" I stumble over my words. "How's it going?"

I can hear in his voice that he's pleased. "I'm good, thanks. So I was calling to see if you're free for dinner tonight. Or tomorrow, if that works better for you."

"Yeah, sure. I'd love to go out to dinner with you. Uh, both nights work for me, so why don't we say tonight?" My cheeks actually hurt, my smile is so wide.

"Awesome. If you give me the address of where you're staying, I'll come pick you up."

No! I can just see it—little innocent Jordan walking to the hotel and the photographers who lie in wait flash their cameras, and the tabloids go out of control printing up stories about my newest boyfriend, and –

I need to tell him who I am before he has to deal with the piranha-like paparazzi.

"Uh, yeah, why don't I meet you, actually? Just because I'm going to be over by campus anyway, so I can meet you somewhere." I cross my fingers and whisper a prayer to karma or God or whoever is listening out there to please just get him to agree.

"Sure," he says readily, and I breathe a sigh of relief. "I live in the Hilgard apartment complex on campus. The address is 870 Hilgard Avenue, and it's right near the medical buildings, if you're familiar at all with UCLA."

I jot down his address and tell him I'll meet him there around six.

He hangs up and I lie back in bed, staring in wonder at my phone.

He called! He actually called! And I have a date!

There is a knock on the door. I climb out of bed, throwing my robe on, and open the door. It's Kurt, standing there wearing bright pink leggings and a baggy white T-shirt. It's his yoga outfit, but nothing is going to dampen my mood this morning. Not even yoga.

I beam at him. "Guess who has a date tonight?" I say, holding the door for him so he can enter.

He glides past me and asks with interest, "Who with?"

"His name is Jordan," I say, keeping my tone neutral. "I met him on campus Friday, right before the concert. And he's totally cute. Law student. And the best part is, he didn't recognize me. He thinks I'm a normal girl!"

Kurt laughs and gives me a high five. "Way to go!" I get dressed in my yoga clothes while Kurt grills me for more information. I tell him everything I know. Soon we are dancing around the room, giggling. The feeling is electric.

Suddenly Kurt stops jumping. "Micky, love, you're trying to get me distracted from yoga. Jordan or no Jordan, get over here and get into Warrior One." He puts a CD into the music player on the desk and soft yoga music starts tinkling through the speakers.

I pull my arms up above my head and stand as tall as I can, stretching one leg out behind me. Kurt nods approvingly and mimics my position. Once we are both stretching, Kurt says, "You know, girl, I am glad you've found someone nice. You deserve it."

I do deserve it, don't I? Tonight is going to be incredible!

Chapter Seven

The afternoon with my band goes quickly. We are practicing a catchy new song about a girl who gets revenge on her dirty, cheating boyfriend by trashing his apartment and spreading rumors on Facebook.

Dirty, cheating Matt.

As soon as four o'clock comes, I take the guitar off my neck and stretch. Trying to be casual, like I'm not trying to rush out of there, I saunter over to my guitar case and say, "Well, I guess I'll be calling it a day."

Johnny is watching me. He is thirty-one and has been in the music business forever. He's played in Vegas and had random gigs with a ton of super famous people. He did some contract work on Holly Madison's Vegas show, what's it called? *Peepshow*? And he has millions of hilarious stories about the times he worked with Tom Jones and some of those Elvis impersonators. But until now, he's never been a permanent part of a successful group.

"Where you going tonight? Hot date?" His dark eyes meet

mine and he brushes back a lock of his black hair.

"What?" My cheeks start to burn. "Why would you assume that?"

Johnny laughs. "Cause you are usually the last one to get out of here. You stay behind and practice and write songs and fool around with the studio equipment. I've never seen you be eager to get out of here. Come on, *Princesa*, fess up!" He always calls me that. I think it means 'princess' in Spanish; it makes me feel warm when he says it, like I'm fragile and sweet.

I look at Brian, making my face look as innocent as I can. "What the heck, Bri, stand up for me!" Brian is more serious than Johnny. He and his girlfriend had twins a few months ago, and I think being a daddy has softened him up a bit.

Not this time though. "Not a chance, Mick. You're going on a date. Either that or you have secret plans to, I dunno, rob a bank, or go to a strip club. You're doing something secretive."

He winks at me while Johnny chimes in, saying "But hey, Micky, if you're going to a strip club, bring us with you!"

I stamp my foot in frustration. They make me feel like I am fifteen years old.

"Did you really just stamp your foot?" Johnny asks.

"Yeah, I thought that only happened in Shirley Temple movies," Brian adds. "I've never seen someone do that before."

They clearly love my discomfort. I raise my head defiantly and say with as much dignity as I can muster, "Yes, I am going on a date. Happy?"

Johnny hits me on the arm gently. "Sure we're happy. As long as it's not with that femmy model you went out with a few months back. Remember how the paparazzi caught you making out at that awards show and the pictures looked like you were kissing a chick?"

I glare at him. "Nigel was *not* a chick! He just had long hair! Plus I wasn't making out with him. He kissed me on the cheek.

That's all!" Okay, so Nigel had curly, black hair down past his shoulders. And he was slender. But he definitely looked like a guy!

"Chill, Micky. You know that we're overprotective of our favorite superstar. Besides, we won't pry." Brian winks at me benignly.

"Course we won't!" Johnny adds. "We'll read about it tomorrow in *Us Weekly.*"

"Hilarious, guys. Simply hilarious."

Johnny throws his arm around my neck. "We can't let you go, though. Not until you tell us who he is." He has the slightest accent, and it makes him seem like a dangerous gangster you'd see on CSI-New York. Johnny's parents are from Mexico, but he was born and raised in LA.

I try to duck out from under his arm. "If you see Cheryl, tell her I'll call her later."

Brian shakes his head. "You owe us if we have to pass on messages to her." He folds his arms over his stocky body and smirks.

"Fine, I'll tell you. His name is Jordan and he's a student at UCLA. That's all I'm saying. Happy?"

Johnny releases me. "Little *Princesa*, that's all we needed." He swats me on my bum, the way they always do in football movies.

Brian chuckles and bends down, placing his bass gently into its case. "That wasn't so hard, was it?"

"Can I go now?" I try to frown at them, but the corners of my mouth lift up and I start to giggle. They are so pesky!

"If you promise to keep your hands to yourself." Brian shoots a smile in Johnny's direction. "And if you make it home by your curfew."

"I'm out of here." I dash to the door and tug it open. "See you guys."

"Give us the dirty details tomorrow," Johnny calls after me. "Unless they get too dirty, in which case, bring photos."

Brian hoots with laughter and I slam the door shut, blocking out their final catcalls.

As I step outside into the bright sunshine, I breathe a sigh of relief. Okay. Now that I'm free of my ridiculing band mates, I need to get back to the hotel, get ready, and try to find a solution to my problem. It's what I've been struggling with all day. How can I look super cute and sexy and gorgeous, and yet still manage to hide myself enough that people don't notice me and take pictures and the whole screaming-fan-trying-to-rip-my-shirt-off-so-they-can-see-me-topless thing. Trust me. It's something to be concerned about.

I flag down a taxi and climb in, just as some people notice me. I wave, smiling at them, and the cab speeds off, taking me back to my hotel.

I make it back to my suite without incident and thankfully find myself alone. Cheryl is off somewhere, probably seeing how she can market my fingernail clippings or dirty laundry or something. Kurt is gone, too. I wouldn't have minded Kurt being here. He always knows what I should wear to make myself look incredible. He's been in the industry for years, planning the workout regimes for Cheryl Crow and Jenna Fischer and many others; he's bound to have some ideas on going incognito.

Hmm, where to begin? I open my wardrobe. Jeans are a must. I pull out my favorite pair of skinny jeans with the rip in the knee (the rip was accidental, but I think it makes them look cooler), and pull them on.

Now I survey my tops. Something pretty, but something I can blend in with. Black, maybe? Something black or grey, nothing bright and colorful. I stare at them, feeling mounting frustration.

I own like bazillions of clothes. How is it possible that I have nothing to wear? It's not even logical!

The black shrug makes me look fat. The blouse is frumpy. The cool Abercrombie shirt is, well, Abercrombie. I don't want Jordan to think that I'm stuck up. I suddenly have a brain wave.

Wait! What about my new shirt? The one my mom sent to me for my birthday. It isn't for another two months or so, but my mom was afraid that the mail service would be crappy, so she sent it super early. Like three months early.

I rifle through the carrier bags on the floor of the wardrobe and pull it out. It's perfect. It is dark green, a gorgeous, deep color that goes with my blonde hair. It has puffy-ish sleeves and goes tight in the mid-section. There's a cool-looking tie around the middle that is so long it hangs down by my knees.

I pull it on and hazard a look in the mirror. It is stunning.

I grab my hugest pair of sunglasses and brush my hair, letting it cascade over my shoulders and down my back. I study my reflection and decide to leave it as it is. I can always bring an elastic to tie it up if it starts to bother me.

I pull on my favorite black slippers. They have a cute little heel, and look so dainty and yet funky at the same time. The toe goes to a point and there is even a rad zigzag design along the side in silver and black thread.

I look myself up and down in the full length mirror. I still look like me, but hopefully I'll blend in enough that nobody will freak out.

It's five thirty. I have just enough time to flag a cab and get there. I poke my head out and see my new bodyguard standing in the hall, chatting on his cell phone. I feel a little weird having a bodyguard, but after that thing two months ago, when the guy came into the hotel lobby and threatened to blow himself up if they didn't tell him my room number, my mom has been a little freaked out. Luckily, the police came and it turned out the kid was wearing duct tape and hot dogs taped to his chest and only wanted to invite me out to the movies with him or something.

Since then, I've had a bodyguard. He stays in the room next door to me, in between my suite and Cheryl's but I don't remember his name. Cheryl fires the old and hires a new one every week or so, whenever she wants to feel powerful. The good thing about having them change so often, is I am usually able to sneak away, or at least get a few minutes by myself to think about stuff without fear of interruptions. Like this afternoon coming home from the studio.

Sometimes I need to be alone.

My bodyguard is still talking on his phone, his back to me. If I hang the Do Not Disturb sign on my door and manage to sneak away without him seeing me, he'll never know I am gone. He probably just came out into the hall to check on me and should disappear back into his room soon. I know he's here to protect me and help me out when I need him. He's not like a prison guard or anything. But the less anyone knows about where I go, the freer I feel. Plus, he might tell Cheryl, and I need to wait and see how my first date goes before I say anything to her.

I take a deep breath and slowly shut my hotel room door behind me. It barely makes a sound.

He's blocking the way to the elevator, but I see a sign for a staircase at the far end of the hall in the opposite direction. I walk fast, the carpet muffling the sounds of my feet. I glance over my shoulder, but my bodyguard hasn't looked around.

I head down the stairs and finally stagger out into the massive, elaborately decorated lobby. A huge chandelier hangs in the center, overtop an incredible golden fountain. I feel like a princess walking into a castle whenever I enter the lobby. There's a crowd of people outside, with flashbulbs going off.

Kim Kardashian walks into the hotel, posing and smiling and blowing kisses. She flaunts her gorgeous figure and finger waves at the people nearest her. This is a bad time for me to leave the hotel, with everyone and their dog clumped outside.

Near the elevator is a door with 'Laundry' written on an elegant plaque. That's it! I'll sneak out the back!

I head to the door. Everyone's attention is still focused on Kim, who is talking to the concierge while looking effortlessly hot and sexy. I am impressed. I never seem to look forever stunning, especially when photographers are around.

I push the laundry door open and step inside. It is an immense room, with overhanging bags full of bedding and loud machines clattering. Three dark-haired girls and a woman who could pass for their grandmother are chattering in Spanish by a long table where they are folding sheets. I duck behind a laundry cart. I need a door. Where is the door?

I don't see anything. I am ridiculously uneasy and keep jumping at the slightest noises. Finally I see it. At the far end of the room there is a little red EXIT sign. Okay. How am I going to get all the way across the room without being noticed by anyone?

Have I ever mentioned that I have an insane fear of getting in trouble?

Even when I went through my rebellious stage, I never wanted to shoplift or, you know, moon someone.

And now here I am, skulking in a laundry room, terrified that someone will look up and say, "You can't be in here."

I glance at my watch. I only have twenty minutes to get there. I have to go! Right now. Taking a deep breath, I stand straight and tall and walk confidently across the room. The Spanish girls look up and then go back to their gossip without giving me a second glance.

Really? They don't care? I open the EXIT door, feeling a little lame at how panicky I got for no reason.

I am in an alley behind the hotel. I walk as quickly as my little heels will allow and stop on the street. The crowd is still bunched around the main doors of the hotel.

I flag down a taxi and give the driver the address.

"It's by UCLA," I tell him helpfully.

He nods and speeds off. I hunker down into the seat and try not to worry about everything.

Chapter Eight

With two minutes to spare, the cab pulls up in front of the residence hall. I pay the man and climb out, realizing that Jordan didn't give me his apartment number. I am rooting around in my purse to get my cell phone to call him, when I see him. He's striding out the front doors, that lovely half smile on his face.

He's more beautiful than I remembered. He looks humble and sweet, and yet I can tell he's intellectual. And if he's going to be a lawyer, he clearly can't be too timid.

"Mikayla, hi!" he says, reaching out and giving me a hug. It's a brief, friendly hug, but it sets off butterflies in my stomach.

"Hey, Jordan!" I say, looking him over. He is wearing jeans and a dark grey and blue plaid button-up shirt. He looks so professional and, well, he looks hot! I haven't felt this way about a boy since Matt. Don't get me wrong. I'm over Matt. So over him. But even though I've gone out with lots of boys, none of them have given me that feeling deep in my heart.

Jordan steps to the side and put his hands in his pockets.

"Wow, you look incredible." His eyes are shining with genuine admiration, and I can't help but melt. I know that sounds cliché, but it's true. There is no other word to describe it. It feels like warm, melty chocolate on a hot summer day.

No boy has looked at me this way since Matt. I mean, ever since I became famous, boys look at me and tell me I am hot and gorgeous and whatever. But I know they don't mean me. They mean the famous me. They want to date a celebrity. They want to get their picture in the papers. They want to get into my pants and have another conquest.

But Jordan is looking at me and seeing me. He has no idea that I'm famous. Or rich. And I like that. Suddenly, I don't want to tell him. I don't want him to look at me differently, not yet at least. I need him to like me, the real me, without any of the frills and baggage that being Mikayla Rivers brings. My guilt-prone conscience is telling me that this is deceitful, and that I need to tell him the truth. But the selfish part of me pushes it away. No. I'll tell him later.

"So where are we going?" I glance around, half afraid that a camera will be sticking out at us from a bush.

Jordan hesitates. "Well, I don't have a car. And I can't afford anything really, uh, fancy or anything, so I thought maybe we could get some pizza and ice cream and then go bowling?"

He's nervous, I realize, and seeing that endears him to me. I open my mouth to say something, but all I can think of is pizza.

Mmm. Warm, gooey, cheesy pizza. Oh my gosh, I would kill to have some pizza right now. I haven't had pizza in so long, not since I was forced onto this horrific no carb diet.

I casually wipe my mouth, hoping Jordan doesn't see me salivating. "That would be absolutely perfect!" Jordan visibly relaxes at my words.

We walk down Hilgard Avenue until we get to Le Conte and turn onto it. It is a lovely street, lined with sprawling trees and everything is green and lush.

"So why law school? Why LA?" I ask him, after we get through the required how are you's.

He replies, "I grew up in a small town in Idaho, and my dad was a small-time defense lawyer. I've always wanted to be a lawyer just like him."

"That's cool." I am impressed. I changed my mind so many times when I was a kid about what I wanted to be when I grow up. "So if you're from Idaho, how'd you end up in LA?"

"My dad died when I was ten and when the bank was through, we were left with nothing. So my mom packed us up and we moved out here to live out her dream of being an actress. Nothing happened, so she started cleaning for people. She wanted me to go to college, and I saved for it from when I was twelve years old. Summer jobs cutting grass and helping out with my mom's cleaning business.

"Then I was offered a half scholarship from UCLA for my undergrad. I needed to live at home and it would be stupid to pass up on that money. Anyway, long story short, I was offered a full scholarship when I got accepted to law school, and so things are finally turning out pretty good."

He stops talking and looks over at me again. His brown eyes search mine. "So enough about me. Tell me about yourself. Last name? Where you grew up? What hobbies you have?"

We pass a few small shops as we walk, and up ahead I see a little hole-in-the-wall pizza parlor.

"My last name is Rivers, and I grew up in Okotoks, Alberta, also a small town. It's right outside Calgary, which is a pretty massive city, and I always wished I had grown up there instead of Okotoks. Just seemed cooler, you know?"

"I know the feeling. When I was a little kid I couldn't wait to leave that place in Idaho. I used to stare at the globe that my dad had in his office and dream of the day that I could go see those other places. New York. LA. China. India. Brazil." His eyes take on a bit of a faraway look. Melancholy.

I feel uncomfortable as I gaze at his face. It's like I've

seen into his soul without permission. "Okay, if you could go anywhere in the world, right now, where would it be?" I ask brightly.

"Machu Picchu."

"Macha whatta?" I repeat, baffled. Is that in China?

"Machu Picchu," Jordan repeats, winking at me. "It's in South America, an old Inca village that escaped discovery by the Spaniards when they colonized the Americas. Very historic. You have to walk up an old Inca trail to get there. My dad used to tell me about it."

"Wow. So are there still Incas there?"

"No. The city was abandoned hundreds of years ago, but since the Spanish never found it, they couldn't destroy their religious and cultural icons. Historians love it."

We are at the door to the pizza place. Thoughts of ancient Inca tribes disappear as we walk in the door. There is a sort of magic about it, and Jordan seems to unwind as we enter. The atmosphere is laid back and chill. It smells amazing.

"It doesn't look like much," Jordan says, "but it *is* the best pizza in LA."

"Truthfully, I haven't had pizza in about six months. It's going to taste incredible to me no matter what!" A waitress comes up, dressed in a bright red jumper and leads us to a corner booth. We slide in, and she hands us the menu.

"So," Jordan catches my eye, "you choose. We can either get a massive pizza to share, or if you would prefer an individual pan pizza we can do that, too."

I lick my lips and stare at the menu. There are so many options! Chicken alfredo. Meat lovers with extra pepperoni. Vegetarian. Bacon, ricotta, spinach, and mushrooms. Buffalo chicken. Over thirty different choices on toppings alone. Not to mention that I can make it stuffed crust, thin crust, regular crust. Oh man! My stomach whines plaintively.

Jordan is watching me salivate over the menu. I can't decide! "Alright, Jordan, there is something you should know about me.

I am really, really, extremely bad at making decisions. I'm talking bad. So if you are hungry, you should order something massive for both of us, because otherwise I will be here for hours, trying to decide."

He laughs. "Fair enough. Does pepperoni with extra cheese work for you? That's my favorite."

"Definitely. I definitely would be okay with that!"

He places our order and leans back, surveying me with interest. "So, Mikayla, you said you are here for a few months with work. What do you do?"

Crap.

I had been hoping that question wouldn't come up.

"Well," I say, hedging around the question, "I was going to the University of Calgary, just finished up my second year, but I decided I needed some, uh, life experience before I continued. So I got a job and came out here for a bit."

He nods. "What were you taking at university?"

Phew. Solid ground.

"I was majoring in General Studies, actually. Took a lot of music classes. I wanted to become an elementary school music teacher one day. At least I did when I signed up for classes. But then I took a sports medicine class and suddenly I wanted to be a physiotherapist. And then I wanted to be an astronaut and work for NASA after I took an astronomy class. It was kind of a work in progress, but I really enjoyed my different classes."

I laugh awkwardly, hoping that Jordan won't think I'm a flighty loser. My dad always told me I needed to buckle down and stop drifting from one major to another. But it was hard. I had no clue what I wanted to do forever.

Jordan takes a big swallow of Pepsi. "It's hard for kids right out of high school to figure it all out. I'm lucky that I always knew what I wanted to do." He sounds sincere, like he genuinely understands my dilemma.

I sip my orange soda and smile, relaxing my shoulders. We talk about classes and the best and the worst professors we've had. We talk about our families, and I find it really easy being with him.

Like Matt was.

Stop it. Don't think about Matt!

The pizza comes, a huge pizza, the size of two normal large pizzas, and we dig in. As I sink my teeth into my slice, I close my eyes and let out a low moan of pleasure.

Humiliated, I open my eyes and see Jordan watching me with twinkling eyes. "You really haven't had pizza in a while, huh? Don't worry, there's plenty."

We focus on eating. I finish my slice and eagerly dig into a second. The cheese is melty and the pepperoni is perfectly crisp. The crust isn't too soft or too crispy nor too puffy. There's just the right amount of sauce.

"So if you love pizza, how come you haven't had it in so long?" Jordan asks lightly over my third piece.

I take a bite so that I can think while I chew. I swallow and say flippantly, "Um, well, you know the pressure to be thin in Hollywood, right?" I hope he'll change the subject, but he doesn't. He puts down the slice he's holding and looks at me with concern in his eyes.

"Mikayla, I don't want to sound preachy, but don't get sucked into that. I saw what it did to my mom. I know you said you're in the music industry, but don't try to become famous. Don't sell yourself and starve yourself and pay money to make yourself plastic and fake. You're too nice a girl to get caught up in that."

He says 'famous' like it is a dirty word. Of course, I would be on a date with a perfect guy who happens to be the one person in Hollywood who thinks that being a celebrity is something shameful, as if it was the same as being a prostitute or a porn star or a tax collector.

I never thought I would be ashamed of being a well-known singer.

I quickly take another bite and then say, "Don't worry. I'm

not trying to be famous."

Which is true. I already am famous. I don't have to try anymore.

He nods, satisfied and then talks about movies and music. He loves *Star Wars* and *Lord of the Rings*. Plus he's an oldies and jazz kind of guy. He likes Elvis and Queen, the Beatles and Johnny Cash. We talk about old music, and he confesses that he doesn't pay much attention to the current music chart toppers.

The waitress approaches, offering refills on our drinks. I look at the table again, terrified that she will recognize me. I shouldn't have agreed to go out in public.

I think briefly of my photo shoot scheduled for next week, when I will appear on a magazine cover in a halter top, a blonde and pink wig, and with inserts to make my boobs look bigger.

I need religion, I decide. I need religion and a God who will listen to me and answer my pitiful prayers. Because Jordan is going to freak out when he finds out who I am.

"I find that music has sort of lost its magic in recent years," Jordan says, sipping his Pepsi as the waitress walks away. "Every song is about breaking up or hooking up and has the same beat and melody as every other song out there. It's a little monotonous. Like who's that one chick, you know the crazy one with the wigs and the outrageous costumes? She's such a huge figure, and yet her music? Meh." He makes a dismissive gesture with his hand.

"Um, Lady Gaga?" I ask, trying to figure out which crazy chick he's referring to.

"Isn't that the name of the new orangutan down at the zoo?" Jordan asks. A monkey? He thinks that Lady Gaga is a monkey? And what is his problem with today's music? As a current music chart topper, I feel slightly wounded by his words. Sure, my songs aren't revolutionary, but they're fun and nice and a good way to vent about an ex-boyfriend.

"I disagree about the music," I say. "If a musician wants to make money, they have to conform to what society wants. Right now, society likes the same contemporary beats and melodies."

What would Johnny do without my band? Or Brian? Both of them were struggling artists when Charles Nash signed them. They had families and mortgages and were trying to save for their kids to go to college. Now they can afford cars that don't break down on the side of the freeway. They can go on family vacations to Disneyland. There is nothing wrong with earning money this way.

"It's not like musicians rob banks and beat up the homeless," I continue. "Making music is no different than being a doctor or a lawyer or, or anything else. A job is a job."

Jordan grins. "Sorry, Mikayla. I didn't mean to get you riled up. I forgot that you work with these people." He waves for the bill. "So, before I forget, you never did tell me what exactly you do within the music industry. Do you play, or are you more administrative, behind the scenes, or are you in recording, or what?"

"Uh, sort of all of the above," I say, avoiding eye contact by pretending to be fascinated with the lady at the table beside ours.

She has bright pink hair, all spiky and jagged, and vivid red nails like talons. Thick eye makeup gives her a slightly animalistic appearance, like a raccoon. Jordan looks at her and winks at me. I make a silent vow to never go out in public dressed in something freakish. Cheryl loves wearing clashing orange and pink so that people stop and stare. She tries to get me to "push the boundaries" of fashion and "make a statement" like Madonna did. But I can't. I really don't want to look like this woman. Or Madonna.

I just want to look like me.

After Jordan pays the bill, we go bowling. The bowling alley is fairly empty, which is what you'd expect for a Monday night.

Jordan kills me every round. The first three times I'm up, I only succeed in landing gutter balls. Jordan comes and stands behind me and puts his hand over mine on the ball. He moves his arm with mine and demonstrates how to hold and roll it to make it go straight. This time when I toss it, it rolls all the way to the end and knocks over three pins.

I jump up and down in excitement, and Jordan laughs at my jubilation.

The rest of the time is a blast. We are joking and laughing, and it feels like I have known him for years. After an hour, we're done bowling. Jordan has early class tomorrow, so we decide to call it a night. I take my shoes off and carry them back to the rental booth. The girl is chewing gum and looks bored. She takes my shoes, looks up at me, and her face glints in recognition.

No! I whisper a silent prayer to my newfound deity; please don't let her freak out or anything.

The girl says loudly, "You're Mikayla Rivers, aren't you? Can I get your autograph?" Jordan is still on the bench, untying his left shoe. Deciding that it will be safe to give her my autograph as long as I am super fast, I nod my head and reach out my hand. She pushes a notebook in front of me. I scribble, "All the best, Mikayla."

She takes it back as Jordan approaches the desk. I quickly hand her my shoes and walk toward the door, muttering "Goodbye" as I dash away. Jordan hurries after me. I glance over my shoulder and see the girl talking on her cell phone. She waves and watches us leave the building.

Phew. That was a close call.

"Hey, I'll flag down a cab and take you home," Jordan says gallantly, holding out his hand.

"Uh, don't worry about it. We can take the cab back to your place first and then you can get some sleep before class tomorrow, and that'll work out perfectly."

Jordan hesitates. "Okay, if that's what you want, but you can never tell my mom that I didn't take you home on our first date."

I like the way he said first date, like it won't be our only date.

I laugh lightly. "Deal." I hold out my hand for him to shake, sealing our pact.

"You're an awesome girl, Mikayla," he says after a brief

pause. "You're a lot of fun, and I had a great time. Would you be up for another date on Friday?"

His eyes are a little guarded, as if he's afraid I'll say no.

"Of course I would." I am pleased. "I had a great time, too. Call me later and we'll set something up for Friday night, then."

A cab pulls to the curb, and we climb in. Jordan puts his arm casually across the back of the seat, and I feel the butterflies in my stomach awaken. As the cab pulls up in front of Hilgard apartments, Jordan pauses with one hand on the door. He looks over at me, and I can see indecision in his eyes.

Is he going to kiss me? I wonder. I usually don't go for kissing on a first date, but with Jordan I would make an exception. He leans in and I close my eyes, my hands almost shaking in anticipation.

His soft lips brush my cheek, and I open my eyes. His gorgeous eyes meet mine and he says, "I'll call you before Wednesday night." And with the promise of a future date ringing in my ears, he climbs out and lifts his hand in a small wave farewell.

I sink against the taxi seat.

I am in love. This is it. I am officially, one hundred percent in love.

The cabbie is eyeing me in the rearview mirror. "Hey, ain't you that singer girl?" he asks in a raspy drawl.

I nod.

"My daughter is your hugest fan."

"That's sweet," I say, feeling uncomfortable with the compliment. "You'll have to tell her that I said hi."

"Yeah," the cabbie continues, changing lanes swiftly, "she wants to be a singer one day. I'm pretty sure you're her idol. She wants to be you one day."

That touches me. I'm an inspiration to a little girl. I reach into my purse and root around for a second. I can only find a crumpled dollar bill, so I take it out, asking his daughter's name.

"Sindi. S-I-N-D-I," rasps the cabbie. "My ex had issues.

Loved making a name different." He rolls his eyes in the rearview mirror and grins at me, expecting me to commiserate with him about the foolishness of women. I bob my head once and write, "Dear Sindi, Good luck reaching your dreams! xox Mikayla." I hand it to him over the seat.

He glances down at it. "This is good, Sindi'll love this. Thanks!"

The rest of the cab ride home is a blur. The sweet compliment from a little girl. Jordan. How perfect and charming and funny and nice and… I am in love. Even if I wanted to, I can't stop thinking about Jordan, and I don't even mind when I climb out of the cab in front of the hotel and a million flashbulbs go off in my face. Nothing can spoil my mood tonight.

Chapter Nine

I open my eyes. My mind is blurry. What day is this? Wednesday? I think it's Wednesday. Because yesterday was Tuesday, the day after my date.

My fingers feel rough as I rub my eyes. They are always calloused, since I play guitar every morning with the guys. Yesterday I stayed behind in the studio and started writing a new song.

I stretch my arms, yawning. Today is definitely Wednesday. And so Jordan has to call today. Right? He said he would call by Wednesday. Or did he say he'd call before Wednesday? Because if he said 'before' then he's already late, which means he may not call at all.

I sigh. I feel antsy yet drained of energy, like I want to get up and run ten miles, but the thought of it makes me exhausted. Will he call today? My nagging brain won't let up. This is it. Moment of truth or something like that. It's got to be today.

I hear the shower running. I have no clue who it is. Maybe Cheryl? Although why she's not using the shower in her suite,

I don't know. Maybe it's Kurt. He lives with his Aunt Eileen in Malibu and is always trying to escape from her and her cats. She's a crazy cat-woman, and her house kind of smells funky, but not like urine or feces or anything. Just like… cats.

I met her one time, right after I met Kurt six months ago. She's a small, wiry woman, with tight curls and a wide, Julia Roberts mouth that never stops moving. She had cats on the furniture, cats on the window sill, cats on the kitchen table and counters. I sat down on the sofa and when I stood up my bum was coated in fur.

Aunt Eileen raised Kurt since he was a teenager and his parents died in a car crash. If rent wasn't so expensive in Malibu, he would have moved out by now. Most of his friends live in Malibu, and he doesn't want to leave that area.

One of my secret fears is that I will never get married and become a cat-woman myself. Ever since I met Eileen, I've had nightmares about it. There I am, wrinkly and old, sitting in a rocking chair and stroking a cat in my lap. Other cats loll around me, and I look up and say in a hoarse voice, "You know, I used to be famous." And then I laugh this weird witch laugh. It's the most disturbing dream.

I shudder and leap out of bed. I have to avoid that fate. I can never get more than one cat. Or dog, for that matter. And if I don't get married, I'll just, I don't know, adopt a bunch of babies so I'm never alone and creepy like that. But then I might become the crazy-baby woman, like Angelina Jolie twenty years from now, only with a baby from every country in the world.

I strip off my pajamas and throw on a pair of jeans and am just fastening my bra when a complete stranger walks out of my bathroom, wrapped in a towel. I shriek and duck behind the wardrobe door, looking around frantically for my phone. Where is my cell phone? Who is he and why was he in my shower? And how the heck did he get into my suite? So much for hotel security.

Tanned, Toned and Totally Faking It

"Oh, hi, Mikayla. I didn't know you were awake," the guy says from across the room.

Who *is* he? Why is he talking to me normally like we're friends?

"Why are you in my room?" I ask, trying to make my voice harsh and tough.

"Cheryl was in the shower in her room, and I have to get to rehearsal in half an hour."

Right. So he's another of Cheryl's one-night stands. I am furious but try to hide it. How dare Cheryl send her random lovers into my room when I am asleep (asleep!) and let them shower. How *dare* she! Oh, she's going to hear it.

"Look, I don't know you. You're in my room. And by the way, Cheryl doesn't have the authority to let people into my room. Get out or I'm calling the cops."

"Oh, I'm sure you've heard of me," the guy says. "I'm Percy Bryant."

Percy Bryant? The name doesn't even come close to ringing a bell. "And why should I know you?"

"I'm an actor," Percy says, adjusting his towel around his waist. "I've been on Broadway for years, and now I am breaking into the Hollywood scene. I know all there is to know about making it big in this industry. I can get you auditions with the top directors, if you want. It's all about connections, you know. I might be willing to do you a favor and introduce you to Steven Spielberg."

Serious? He thinks he's at Steven Spielberg's level? The absurdity of it makes me want to laugh, but I restrain myself. I open my mouth, trying to think of a response to that, when I hear a click and the door opens. I peek around the wardrobe door and breathe a sigh of relief. Kurt is standing there, wearing a plaid fedora and skater jeans.

"Morning, love," he says, closing the door behind him. Then he stops in his tracks as he spies muscular Percy wrapped only in a towel. He looks over at me and sees I'm wearing only a

69

bra. "Whoa, Micky, am I interrupting something?" He gives me a knowing look.

"No! We just met. He's one of Cheryl's, uh, friends, and I didn't invite him in."

Understanding dawns on his face and Kurt turns to Percy. "If you're Cheryl's friend, what are you doing in here?"

Percy leans against the bathroom door, as if this is an afternoon barbeque. "As I was telling Mikayla, I'm an actor, definitely the hottest new actor in the Hollywood scene today." He raises his left eyebrow into an arch and adjusts the towel again, tightening it around his waist.

His blatant arrogance must rub Kurt the wrong way, because he says in disbelief, "You mean it? You actually think you're the next big thing? Honey, I have never seen you before."

Percy chuckles like Kurt is a silly little boy. "Well, let's just say that I can't go anywhere without being mobbed. That's more than you two can say, that's for sure."

Kurt takes off his fedora and plays with it, hitting it lightly against his thigh. "Look, towel-boy, you are a pathetic wannabe who is not 'breaking into' the Hollywood scene. You probably have a one liner in a lame Adam Sandler movie and you're trying to sleep your way to getting the roles you want, but you will fail. Mikayla is a Grammy-nominated singer. She has made millions. She gets paid to party. She has turned down more movie roles than you will ever be offered. Now, get out of this room immediately, or we are phoning the police. Right, Mikayla?"

Kurt glances at me, and I nod. Percy still stands there, one eyebrow raised, his eyes flickering up and down Kurt and then at me. He glances down at my chest (crap, I forgot I'm still wearing a bra with jeans) and smirks. "Fine. We'll see who's laughing when I'm named *People's* Hottest Bachelor."

Right. Because he will beat out that *Glee* kid and Zac Efron. Honestly. This guy has more unwarranted pride than Cheryl.

I point, sternly, at the door. Kurt comes over and stands confidently beside me, arms folded. Percy cracks his knuckles and walks out into the hall. I run to the door and close it with a bang. Oh, I could kill Cheryl.

Kurt frowns at the door. "Wow, Micky, what a tool! I would have loved to punch that smug face of his. I don't condone violence, you know, but for this guy I'd be willing."

The thought of Kurt punching out muscular Mr. Universe Percy makes me smile, but then a buzzing noise interrupts my thoughts. My cell phone! It's lying on the floor beside my bed. I lunge across the room and grab it.

Jordan!

"Hello?" I say, breathlessly.

"Mikayla, hi, it's Jordan." He sounds so sweet and normal.

"Jordan, hi! How are you?" Kurt glances over at me in interest when he hears the name. I widen my eyes and nod excitedly at him as Jordan says, "I'm good, thanks. You sound out of breath. Did I catch you at a bad time?"

Ha! If only he knew that his call was the only thing keeping me from running over to Cheryl's room and firing her on the spot.

"No, I just had a bit of a surprise. I woke up and there was a random dude in my shower. My, uh, friend, let her boyfriend into my room because she was using her shower and they both had to get to work. And she didn't exactly tell me. I woke up and kind of freaked out a bit. I mean, I'd never met him and suddenly there is this stranger in my shower. Believe me, I was scarred for life! I'm going to need a whole lot of therapy after this."

Jordan laughs. "Some friend."

I join him. It is a little funny. "Seriously. I think our friendship is over."

"Well, I'm sorry you had a traumatic morning."

Just hearing his voice makes me happier. "No, it's all good, no worries. Your phone call made my day though. What's up?"

Jordan hesitates. "Look, I was hoping you'd be up for a date on Friday like we'd talked about. We could grab some dinner and go to a dance club. You mentioned that you like dancing, so I thought that would be kind of fun."

That would be fun. Except for the whole I-want-to-stay-inside-so-nobody-recognizes-me thing.

"Dinner sounds great," I say, and Kurt gives me a thumbs up from my bed where he's sitting cross legged, reading *People* on my laptop. "But instead of going out, why don't we order in Chinese food and then, um, we could stay at your place and have a *Lord of the Rings* marathon? I doubt there is anyone in Hollywood, other than you and maybe Orlando Bloom, who would actually consider that fun and not a horrendous form of torture. What do you say?"

I cross my fingers. Come on, Jordan, say yes!

"I bet even Orlando Bloom would think it's a form of torture," Jordan says, laughing.

"You up for it?" I ask again, just to make sure that we have a deal before I agree to come over. Kurt gets up from the bed and walks into the bathroom, closing the door behind him.

"Sure." Jordan's tone is almost grateful, as if he really hadn't wanted to go dancing. "I'm definitely okay with that. Awesome!"

"Great! See you Friday."

I grab a cute Abercrombie T-shirt out of my wardrobe. I pull it on and collapse onto the bed. I can't stop smiling.

He wants to take me out again! A real date with a boy I want to be with!

I run to the bathroom door, knock on it and hear a slightly muffled "What's up?" from Kurt.

"He asked me out again! Another date!"

"I figured as much. Doing what?"

"His place to watch a movie. It's going to be awesome!"

Kurt chuckles. "Funny how your version of awesome is my version of utter boredom. I'm going to jump in the shower. I found cat hair on my arm. Be out in a bit."

A door slamming outside makes me jump. I hear the lock on my door click, and it bursts open.

"Who the hell do you think you are?" Cheryl snaps, stomping over and smacking me on the leg. She must have talked to Percy.

"What? You're mad at *me*? You sent a random stranger into my hotel room while I was sleeping!"

How can she possibly be upset with me? I think Cheryl is honest-to-goodness insane. She should be put away in an institution. Or become BFF's with a Real Housewife from that reality show, because I really think they would click. Why do I put up with her?

Cheryl glowers at me. "Thanks to you, Percy got offended and will never call again."

"Okay, Cheryl, first of all, you've got something wrong with you if you think a guy named Percy is a keeper. I mean, the only thing that was possibly keeper-ish about him were his rippling pectorals. They are so full of steroids and silicon, I doubt they'll ever go away. Not even a nuclear holocaust could get rid of those things."

The corners of her mouth turn up like she's trying to fight a smile. Or maybe her facial features have stopped being controlled by her brain and she is twitching randomly.

"And, number two? He thought he was the biggest name in Hollywood!"

"Okay," she concedes, smirking. "So he was a little lame. But still, you should have treated him better. I liked him."

"Alright," I say. "Maybe I shouldn't have gone all diva on his hiney. But you should have told me before you send him into my room. That seriously freaked me out!"

Cheryl nods. "I'm sorry, too. I didn't think. Friends?"

I don't think "friends" really describes me and Cheryl, but I say, "Friends."

She nods her plastic face. "Oh, and I got a call about the new *Star Trek* movie. They're auditioning soon and said you'll be at the top of their list if you're interested."

Star Trek? Wow! Matt and I were the hugest Trekkies. I'll have to think about it. Jordan is helping me heal, but when I think about Matt it's like this gaping wound in my soul.

Acting in *Star Trek* might be like pouring salt into my wounds.

"What do you think?" I ask.

Cheryl sits down on the leather sofa in the corner, pulling off her high heels and curling up into a ball. "I think money. Theaters will be packed with insane Trekkies and sci-fi nerds."

"True, but I want to focus more on my music, I think. I mean, I've already had guest roles on *NCIS* and *Law and Order*. Plus I'm slated to be the lead in that new romantic comedy with Zac Efron right after I'm back from my tour." I flop down on my bed. "I don't know if I want to commit to a *Star Trek* movie right now."

Cheryl scowls. "It doesn't just have to be about your music, you know. Any publicity will help your music in the long run. You need to say yes."

I sigh. "I'll think about it and get back to you, all right?" There. That's the best I can do to appease her.

Cheryl adjusts her right breast. "Fine. Also, speaking of your music, I received an email about your tour. You are sold out in every arena, so they are hoping to get you a couple extra nights in a few of the largest cities. That way we can probably rake in an extra ten or twenty million. Sound good?"

"Yeah, that should be fine." I dread going on tour. I have band practice. I do the occasional gig (private parties and stuff) in LA. After promoting my first CD all over the globe, I am content to stay right here for now, where life seems normal.

"Good," Cheryl says. "Now, I purposefully left your calendar empty this morning so we can go down to the Santa Monica pier and do yoga on the boardwalk. It will be a great photo op and should get us some nice publicity. Be sure and make a comment about how yoga leads to world peace, or something flowery like that. Okay? Also, don't forget you have a photo shoot next week for *Celebrity Magazine.*"

"Thanks. I have to pass on the yoga this morning though.

I'm not feeling up to it, so I think Kurt and I will go for a little walk. And just so you know, I have plans for Friday night, so don't schedule anything for me."

Cheryl's eyes narrow. "What plans?"

"Just some plans. And I'm not changing them. So don't try."

She shrugs and gets up from the sofa. "Whatever. I don't really care."

Yeah, right. Cheryl micromanages my entire life, always trying to squeeze an extra dollar out of me. Of course she cares about what I'm doing. Cheryl rolls her eyes and flounces out, slamming the door behind her.

I hear the water turn off. Kurt will be out in a minute. I put on a pair of sneakers. On our walk, I'll tell Kurt about my phone call with Jordan. He'll analyze every detail of what Jordan said, and how long he paused, and it'll be great.

Chapter Ten

Friday I return to the hotel after practicing with my band. Kurt is sitting on my bed, trying on a pair of high heels. Oh Kurt. At least it's not as bad as the time I found him trying on my bathing suit, a pink, polka-dot one piece that he stretched completely out of proportion.

"Hey man," I say, throwing my purse on the desk.

"Micky, kisses!" Kurt blows a kiss at me that I snatch and place on my cheek. I love air kisses.

"How do I look?" Kurt stands up in my neon green stilettos. He twirls for me and I throw a pillow at him.

"You better not bust those," I warn. "They're my favorite pair."

Kurt totters to the other end of the room and looks out the window at the street below. "So remind me again what you and the boy toy are doing tonight?"

"Delivery Chinese and *Lord of the Rings*. I was so worried before our first date, especially since I knew we'd be in public. This time I'm just excited."

"Mmm, that's right. That will be fab for you." Kurt makes his way gingerly back. He sinks down onto the bed and takes my shoes off. He looks at them contemplatively. "I wish we had the same size foot."

I snort. "If I had the same size foot as a man, I think I'd shoot myself." I pick up one of the stilettos and eye it in trepidation. He didn't stretch it too badly. It should still fit.

Quickly, before Kurt can try on another pair of shoes, I jump at him. "Help me do my hair?" Kurt's eyes light up. I knew that would do the trick.

"Of course!" He abandons his fetish for waltzing around in my shoes and comes over to my dressing mirror. He touches my head and wrinkles his nose.

"Mikayla, you have to shower. Baby powder in your hair can only take you so far."

"Only if you promise to leave my shoes alone."

Kurt reaches for my eyeliner. "No shoes. Pinky promise."

Once I am clean and relatively dry, Kurt turns the hair dryer full force on my matted hair while struggling to run a brush through it. I do my makeup as he plays with my hair. Lip gloss. A bit of mascara. A tiny bit of foundation to hide the dark circles under my eyes and that's it. The good thing about having a thousand dollar skin-care regime is that my complexion has never been better.

Kurt keeps jerking my head around and soon my head is aching from all the pulling, prodding and pinning. Thirty minutes later, he steps back.

"Ta-da!"

He has arranged my hair so it's curly and bundled up on my head. He must have used about ninety million bobby pins, so no going through metal detectors tonight. But it works. It looks sophisticated yet casual.

"Now pair this with jeans and your new BCBG Mazaxria shirt and you'll look perfect," he orders, going over to my wardrobe and taking out the top. It is a gorgeous shirt, grey but all filmy and slinky and fashionable. He tosses it on my bed. I grab my pair of jeans with the torn knees. I add my zebra striped heels that thankfully Kurt has not yet tried on.

I survey myself in the mirror. I'm tanned from running outside so much, and I look toned and muscular from Kurt's boot camp workouts.

Kurt says, "You totally look the part of a hot, single girl! Excellent."

I thank him and say goodbye. I tell my bodyguard that I am going out with friends and would prefer to be alone. He nods. I take the elevator to the main floor and check out the lobby doors. It doesn't look like anyone is waiting outside. I hesitate. Maybe I should sneak out the laundry room again, just to be safe. Still, everything is quiet. I think I'm okay. I exit the main front doors, and the doorman standing outside helps me get into a waiting car.

I stare out the window as the car speeds away into the dusk. I try to bite the nail on my ring finger, but I have acrylic nails on. I guess that's one way to overcome a bad habit—plasticize yourself.

The night life is yet to appear, but I see couples going out to dinner, climbing from their cars and heading into nice restaurants. Tonight will be fun, but I can't help thinking it would be nice to go out with Jordan sometime, somewhere expensive and full of people. And we will, because on our next date, I will tell him that I am a superstar.

Tonight, however, I am just going to chill with a cute boy and not worry about all my issues.

The cab pulls up in front of the Hilgard Apartments, and I step onto the pavement. Two college girls with backpacks slung over their shoulders go by giggling. I feel a pang of regret watching them. I miss Rachelle. The girls glance at me and do a double take.

"Excuse me?" One of the girls is looking at me. "You're Mikayla Rivers, aren't you?"

Tanned, Toned and Totally Faking It

"Yes," I say, stopping so they can catch up. Let's get this over with. I really hope Jordan doesn't happen to look down from his window and see me being accosted by a couple strangers. That would bring on a whole slew of uncomfortable questions.

"Could we get a picture with you?"

Why not? "Sure."

One of the girls pulls out a small digital camera. The three of us squeeze together with me in the middle and the girl reaches out her arm and snaps of picture of us.

"Thank you so much," they say, all gleeful and excited.

"No problem." I don't mind. I mean, it kind of comes with the territory. You get the paycheck, you get the fans.

"Why are you on campus?" one of the girls asks me eagerly.

"Uh, I have a friend who goes here."

"Wow, that's so cool! I wish we were friends with a pop star!"

"Well, it was good to meet you." I start to edge away from them.

They nod and wave and thank me again for the picture. They stand there, watching me as I enter the building. I dig through my purse until I find the scrap of paper with Jordan's apartment number.

I walk upstairs, hoping that nobody else will recognize me. Luckily no one is on the stairs. I take a deep breath and knock on the door.

It opens instantly and Jordan is standing there. "Hi Mikayla!"

"Hi!" I say, as he reaches out and gives me a big hug. Be still, my soul!

"Come on in."

His apartment is a little one, student style. A large, puffy couch is squeezed into the living room. It's your typical masculine apartment, except there aren't any half-naked pictures of women.

That was one thing that bothered me about Matt. He had the latest Playboy Playmates and Victoria's Secret Angels covering his walls. I kind of look like that now, so it's not an insecurity thing about my own body. I just don't like having a boy I date having mental images of other naked women. Guys that look at porn aren't attractive to me.

The decorations in Jordan's apartment are minimal. A framed autographed Colorado Avalanche jersey hangs above the TV. A StarCraft 2 poster with some creepy alien thing on it is taped to a door. But that's it.

"You're an Avalanche fan?" I motion to the jersey.

Jordan smiles that sweet smile. "Yeah, they're my team. My dad was from Colorado, and I still have a lot of family living there. I'm a huge Avalanche fan. I'm impressed you recognized their jersey."

"Well, what can I say? I'm Canadian. Go Flames Go, and all that."

"The Calgary Flames?" he asks. "But they suck! They go on a two-game winning streak and then fail for another five."

I raise one eyebrow. "Excuse me? They make the playoffs almost every year. And they have Iginla, one of the top paid players in the NHL. I think someone needs to watch a bit more hockey."

"Okay, truce. I won't bad mouth your team." He gives me a mischievous smile. "Well, I won't bad mouth them until we watch a game together. Then I will tell you exactly how I feel. I'll have to check when the Avalanche plays the Flames."

I roll my eyes but feel another little shiver go through my body. He's such a sweetheart! And he wants to watch hockey with me! Matt had liked football, but wasn't into hockey.

Stop thinking about Matt, I tell myself.

"The Chinese came about three minutes before you got here," Jordan says. "I put it in the oven so it wouldn't get cold. If you want, we can load our plates and start watching *Lord of the Rings*. I even have the extended editions."

And that's it. We eat. And eat. It's delicious. As we eat we talk—about everything, about nothing. It's light and fun. Jordan has a twisted sense of humor, innocent and sweet yet hysterically funny.

He's telling me about one of his eccentric law professors. This prof throws books at students if they aren't paying attention, and he gets distracted from the lecture at the drop of the hat. Although the story isn't that funny on its own, the way Jordan tells it makes me laugh and laugh.

I take another bite of food. Delicious. I love shrimp fried rice. The entire time we eat we can't shut up. Conversation just flows naturally between us.

I groan and lean back. "I think I'm having a heart attack," I moan, holding my stomach.

Jordan shovels another bite into his mouth. "Let's put the rest in the fridge. Later, we can warm it up and have a midnight snack."

We heave ourselves up from the sofa and put the remaining food in the fridge. We stagger back into the living room and collapse on the couch. Jordan has the DVD set up. He hits play and suddenly the *Lord of the Rings* theme music fills the room.

The TV is small. The sound system isn't the greatest. It's the best night of my life.

Jordan puts his arm around me and we kind of lean into each other, putting our feet up on a stack of law textbooks in front of the couch. He grabs a folded blanket from the floor to spread over us.

We get through the first *Lord of the Rings* movie and our second helpings of Chinese food, warmed up in the microware. We are half way through the third movie before we fall asleep. Jordan holds me tighter and groggily punches the TV off. We snuggle in, and that's all I remember.

Peace. Warmth. And a feeling of completeness. I haven't been this happy in… too long.

*****

I open my eyes and look around at the unfamiliar room. Where am I? TV, law books, Avalanche jersey. Right. Jordan. He's not on the couch with me, but the blanket is tucked in around me and a pillow has materialized under my head.

I smell something delicious. My stomach grumbles. How can I possibly be hungry? I ate more last night than I eat in a week.

Is that pancakes? But first, I need a bathroom. I walk into the bedroom and see the bathroom attached to it. I rush in and relieve my bladder.

I flush the toilet, wash my hands, and stare at myself in the mirror. My makeup is smudged, mascara clumped around my eyes. At least my hair looks decent. Kurt did such a good job with the hair spray and bobby pins that it's never coming out. I lean over the sink and, using a bit of hand soap, wash my face and get rid of the caked on makeup. Feeling much more refreshed, I go back into the living room.

"Micky, you up?" Jordan calls from the kitchen.

"Yeah." In the kitchen, Jordan is flipping pancakes in a small frying pan on the stove top. He leans over and kisses me on the cheek.

"Wow, you look beautiful!" Jordan says, doing a double take.

I beam at him. There's nothing like a compliment first thing in the morning to start your day off perfectly. And a kiss on the cheek. Although I really wouldn't mind a kiss on the lips. You know, eventually. "Thanks! You look pretty good yourself!"

His eyes are a little squinty from sleep deprivation, but he looks so darn cute I can hardly stand it. He has some faint freckles across his nose that I hadn't noticed before. Dark-haired guys usually don't have freckles; it makes him look all the more adorable.

"How'd you sleep?" He takes the two pancakes from the pan and tosses them onto a plate. There are eight or nine pancakes waiting there, warm and steaming.

"Thanks for letting me stay over. Although I don't think I left you much choice when I passed out on your couch."

"Hey, you can stay over any time. Besides, it's not your fault you passed out. I'm pretty sure I crashed too." He hands me an empty plate. "I hope you like pancakes."

"Are you kidding? I don't think I could call myself Canadian if I didn't adore pancakes doused in maple syrup. Mmm, with half melted butter all over them. I think that is what heaven is going to taste like. Fluffy pancakes with syrup and butter, all gooey and delicious."

Jordan flips a pancake and shakes his head. "No way. Heaven is going to be Chinese food and *Lord of the Rings*." He looks over his shoulder and winks at me.

"That too," I agree. "Anything I can help with?"

"Nope, not a thing. This was the last batch, so now we're ready." Jordan turns to face me and makes a grand, sweeping motion toward the plate. "There's no maple syrup, I'm afraid, at least not genuine Canadian maple syrup, but I've got some Aunt Jemima's and jam."

I choose the Aunt Jemima's. We pile pancakes and butter and syrup and go to the living room. Jordan doesn't have a table; we eat off our laps like we did last night with the Chinese.

My cell phone in my purse is going off. I ignore it and keep eating.

"So how do you get virgin wool?" Jordan asks me.

"What?" I ask. And did he just say virgin? Like virgin as in… virgin?

"How do you get virgin wool?" Jordan repeats, popping a bite of pancake into his mouth.

I shrug. "From sheep?" I hope I don't look stupid next to this intelligent law student.

Jordan grins. "From ugly sheep. Get it? Virgin wool, ugly sheep?"

"Okay, that's funny. But, you don't want to start a lame joke contest with me, Mister! I'll kick your trash."

"Bring it," Jordan says, eyeing my last pancake now that his are gone.

I cut it in half, dropping one half onto his plate. "Why can't Jimmy ride a bike?"

"Why?"

"Because Jimmy's a fish!" I crow.

Jordan says, "Okay, what's big, green, and fuzzy and if it falls out of a tree, it'll kill you?"

I think for a second and shrug. "A monster?"

"No! A pool table."

"Yeah? What's fluffy and looks like a cloud?"

Jordan waits expectantly.

"A sheep with no legs!" I say.

After we run out of lame jokes (and yes, it goes on for longer than you would think), we spend the rest of the day together. It's a gorgeous day out, and we go for a walk around campus. I see a few people look over at me, but since I'm wearing huge sun glasses and one of Jordan's UCLA sweatshirts, I blend in pretty well.

Jordan shows me where his different classes are. He takes me to the music building and we linger in the hallways, listening to the trumpets and flutes and other instruments being practiced in the small cubby rooms. I tell him about the music theory classes that I used to take and we tap our feet to the music and chill, listening to the mixed medley of songs. And then we end up at the law library. We walk inside and Jordan takes my hand.

"This is where we met," I say, looking at him. He reaches over and takes off my sunglasses and leans in. He kisses me softly on the lips. And then we kiss a bit harder, and my head is spinning, and I feel like I might just explode I am so happy.

"I know," he says, pulling back.

I put my sunglasses back on as we go out into the sunshine. We walk closer, and Jordan puts his arm around my shoulders, pulling me in to him.

Chapter Eleven

The night clerk at the front desk looks up at the sound of my footsteps on the marble floor. "Miss Rivers." He tilts his head and smiles at me.

"Hi." I wave slightly. I push the up button at the elevator, mentally reliving everything that happened tonight. After we kissed, we went back to Jordan's apartment and watched the last half of a Flames game. (Unfortunately, the Flames lost to San Jose, much to Jordan's delight.) Finally, at around eleven, I told him I had to go home and he called me a cab. And here I am.

Bing. The elevator door opens and I step in, punching my floor. I lean against the side of the elevator and yawn. As the elevator rises, I take out my phone and check for messages.

I have one text, from Cheryl. **Where the hell r u? We leave for NY at 8. U better be ready or else.**

New York? Oh yeah! I'd forgotten all about that. How in the world do I forget about New York? We've been planning it for months. I'm going to be signing CDs at the Sam Ash music store in Times Square, and Cheryl has arranged for me to go on

The Late Show with David Letterman. It's going to be awesome!

I'll have to make up some excuse with Jordan. Maybe I'll tell him that I'm sick. Or that my boss is making me work late for a couple days.

I better go with that one. At least it's partially true.

The elevator comes to a stop and the doors open. I make a beeline for my room, insert my key card and push the door open.

No sign of Cheryl. She's probably out clubbing. I kick off my shoes, latch the deadbolt to keep Cheryl out until morning, undo the top button on my jeans, and collapse into bed. My eyes close instantly, and with memories of Jordan's kiss, I fall asleep.

*****

My room is still dark, but there's incessant banging on my door.

"Mikayla Rivers, open this door *now!*"

I roll over. Everything is stiff. My jeans have somehow managed to twist themselves around, making it impossible to move.

"Mikayla Rivers, if you don't wake up right this instant and let me in, I'm going to break your door down."

I roll to the edge of the bed and uncomfortably stand. "Coming," I croak, staggering toward the door.

I pull it open. "It's about bloody time," she snaps, shoving by me into the room. "We leave in less than an hour for the airport."

"Going where?" I manage to ask.

Cheryl glares at me. "New. York. We. Leave. In. Forty. Five. Minutes." Every word is drenched in poison.

Right. New York. How could I have forgotten again?

"Of course, right." I walk past Cheryl into the bathroom, and grab my toothbrush. After brushing my teeth, I splash water on my face. Feeling somewhat refreshed, I return to the main room, adjusting my jeans as I go so they no longer cut into my flesh.

"How long are we gone for?" I reach under my bed and pull out a travel-sized suitcase. It's a Gucci bag, and I spent more on it than I like to admit. But Cheryl had told me it is essential for a pop star to have nice luggage, so I bought a whole set.

"Two days. We have to be back by Tuesday night as I have a hair appointment that I refuse to miss."

"Other than *David Letterman* and the CD signing, I don't need formal clothes at all, right?"

Cheryl snorts, which I take to be an affirmative.

I hear voices in the hallway and my door opens. Kurt is standing there, talking to someone on his cell phone. "But of course, love, I wouldn't miss it for the world. We're just gone for a couple days." He mouths the word "Hi!" at me and then hangs up.

"I left my suitcase with the bellhop," he says, motioning somewhere out into the hall.

"Are you coming, too?" I feel a little more excited now.

Kurt starts rummaging through my wardrobe. "Clearly. Why else am I awake at this ungodly hour? Besides, it's New York. I could never pass up a chance to go to the city that never sleeps."

Cheryl coughs. "You've got ten minutes left, Mikayla. Hurry up."

"You haven't packed yet?" Kurt looks incredulous.

I fold a pair of underwear and a strapless bra and place them gently in my bag. "Not exactly."

"Let me help you." Kurt shoves me out of the way and starts dropping things into my suitcase.

"Swim suit, yoga pants, T-shirt, Chloe jeans, D&G shirt, DKNY shirt, Burberry jacket, Alexander McQueen skirt, strapless high heels, Chanel flats." Every now and then Kurt makes a noise of excitement when he sees something he likes.

After three minutes, he closes and zips the suitcase. "Done. Now hurry and shower and get dressed."

This must be the fastest shower I've taken in my entire life. I'm in and out in two minutes flat. I towel off and go back into the main room.

"You have exactly three minutes." Cheryl is standing by the door, tapping her six inch Alexander McQueen heel impatiently.

I put on my comfiest Lululemon sweatpants and an American Eagle long-sleeved shirt. I throw my hair into a wet ponytail and cover it all up with an LA Lakers cap. "Ready!"

Traffic is fairly light since it's early, and we get to LAX in record time. We climb out of the limo and cameras go off.

I wave and they all start talking at once.

"Mikayla, where are you heading?"

"Where did you get your shoes?"

"Mikayla without makeup! Doug, try to get a close-up. Our readers will *love* this."

"Are you an LA Lakers fan now?"

"Is it true that you are dating Chord Overstreet?"

"Do you fly commercial or private?"

I stop and pose with Kurt for just a second and allow them to take a pile of photos. Cheryl and my bodyguard stand beside us. Cheryl is thrusting out her chest and beaming at the paparazzi, blowing kisses, and winking at the men.

"We're heading to New York for a couple days to go on Letterman and do some CD promotion," she announces. "And, of course, we're flying private."

We give them another two seconds and then Kurt and I grab our luggage and enter the airport. Cheryl enters behind us and says, "This way." She leads off, swinging her hips and chatting with the bodyguard.

We go through a tunnel and then out a door into an open hanger. There are some small planes lined up and people rushing around, loading things into them and wiping the windows off.

Cheryl marches up to the nearest employee. "I need the Charles Nash plane."

"Right this way, Miss." The employee sets off, beckoning us

to follow, all the way to a gleaming, silver plane near the massive roller-door. The steps have been lowered and Cheryl hurries up, her shoes clicking.

Kurt, my bodyguard, and I follow, leaving our luggage at the bottom for someone to load up. Inside, the furnishings are pale peach and tan, with billowing curtains over the windows, reclining chairs, an elegant table bolted to the floor. Tinkling music filters through the cabin and a beaming flight attendant wearing a slinky black uniform welcomes me.

I sit down beside Kurt, who is pouring himself a glass of champagne. Cheryl also has something in a cup. The bodyguard is talking to the flight attendant about an omelet.

"It's about time we get to use the private jet," Cheryl says in my direction. "I can't imagine how horrid it would be fly commercial right now."

"Isn't this supposed to be bad for the planet though?" I am curious. "You know, global warming and damaging the environment?"

Kurt laughs. "Honey, everything is bad for the environment."

Cheryl nods. "You're just too naive, Mikayla."

It's rare for Kurt and Cheryl to agree on anything.

"Excuse me." We turn toward the cockpit and see a muscular man with tanned skin and a gleaming white smile. "I'm your pilot for the trip, Josh Graham. If you need anything, feel free to ask Emma, our flight attendant. We should have you at La Guardia in just over five hours. Enjoy the flight." He steps into the cockpit, closing the door behind him.

I hear the engines whine, and someone outside closes the passenger door. I watch out the window in excitement.

I'm going to meet David Letterman!

Chapter Twelve

I grasp the seat cushion and bite my lip as the limousine eases around another corner, barely missing crowds of pedestrians jammed along the sidewalk. Cheryl is talking on her cell phone, my bodyguard is chatting with the driver, and Kurt is leaning on my shoulder, fast asleep.

New York is insane. As soon as we passed the toll booth leaving the airport, traffic became crazy. We are bumper to bumper in a sea of yellow cabs, Mercedes, Bentleys, and BMWs. Buildings loom above me and I feel a little claustrophobic.

Our driver narrowly misses a street sign.

It's about two o'clock in the afternoon and there are thousands of people crowding the sidewalks. Men and women dressed in black suits stride into glass-paneled buildings. Guys in sweatshirts wave knockoff designer purses, sunglasses, and wallets at passing tourists while shiftily watching for cops. We pass the bronze, or it might be gold, bull standing at the front of the street and drive down Wall Street. Everything is posh, exciting, busy.

Tanned, Toned and Totally Faking It

I peer out the window, trying to take it all in. That song by Alicia Keys and Jay-Z replays in my head. New York. The place where dreams are made.

Within a few minutes we enter Times Square. Billboards everywhere, neon lights flashing, a couple policemen riding by on two docile horses. I don't even notice that the limo has stopped until I see that Cheryl has the door open and is climbing out, still chattering away on her cell, complaining about how difficult it was to find a limo driver who spoke English.

"Kurt. Kurt, wake up!" I nudge Kurt a couple times and he jerks up, eyes bleary.

"Where are we?"

"We're at our hotel," I tell him, and he looks around, blinking several times. He wipes at the corner of his mouth.

"Eeew, did you drool on me?" I swat him.

Kurt ignores my protest. "Let's get unpacked and check out the city."

We get out of the limo. The smell hits me first. It's a mixture of sewage, Chinese food, exhaust, sweat, and... something. I've never smelled anything like it. I follow Kurt and the others into the hotel, the Marriott Marquis. It's a very modern-looking building. The lobby is spacious and open, with a grey, marble floor. The entire left side has a long row of customer service desks. The center is open, and I can see up into the upper levels. Glass elevators are zooming up and down efficiently and silently.

While Cheryl checks us in, Kurt and I remain in the center with the bodyguard.

"Mom, look! It's Mikayla Rivers!"

A harried-looking woman with frizzy red hair is being dragged toward me by two teenage girls. The bodyguard stands at attention, ready to intervene, but the girls are harmless.

"Can we get a picture with you?" They have the sweetest British accents.

"Sure." I step towards them. Kurt volunteers to be the

photographer. I squish in next to the three of them, and he snaps a photo.

"So what brings you to New York?" I am attempting to be friendly, welcoming them to North America.

"Business trip with their father," the mother says. "He's in meetings all day."

"Cool."

The mother looks at her watch. "Girls, we need to go catch the lorry if we're going to make it out to Ellis Island before dinner."

We wave goodbye, and they head out.

After we get settled into our rooms, Cheryl says, "Chuck and I are going to the Statue of Liberty. I don't care what you guys do, as long as you're well rested for *Letterman* tomorrow." And she and Chuck, the bodyguard, leave together.

"I didn't know they were sleeping together." Kurt watches them retreat down the hall with mild interest.

"Cheryl sleeps with everyone," I respond.

Kurt and I head back down the elevator. As soon as we step out the main lobby doors, people begin screaming my name. Cameras go off, momentarily blinding me. Everyone is shouting and clawing. I have no idea how so many people could have appeared in just seconds. I've been mobbed in LA and Hong Kong and Paris and Frankfurt, but it is nothing like this. I guess the sheer number of tourists in New York amplifies the craziness.

"Can I please have a lock of your hair?"

"Just one picture? Please, let me get one picture with you!"

"When's your birthday, and do you like apple pie?"

"Oh my god, it's her! Can I have your autograph?"

"How does the current political situation in Canada affect your career?"

I scribble my name on everything in front of me.

"Um, my birthday is in January," I respond to the questions. "Yes, I love apple pie, but my favorite is actually blueberry."

Tanned, Toned and Totally Faking It

I bite my lip and keep writing. Concentrate. Name after name. I begin shortening it to just my initials. MR. Over and over. I grab the next paper, but it's not paper. I feel cloth. I do a double take. Ew, somebody handed me a thong to sign.

"Um, I think this is enough," I say, dropping the thong on the ground and wiping my hands on my pants. "This isn't going to work."

People are swarming in closer, their hands waving, eyes bright and excited, grasping and groping for even a little piece of me.

I eye Kurt in panic. "What do we do?"

"Let's run!" He grabs me by the hand, and we hurry back into the hotel lobby where the trusty hotel security stands guard, keeping the unwanted tourists and paparazzi at bay.

"I'm not going back out there." I'm breathing hard, as if I had just run a marathon.

Kurt shakes his head. "That was madness. Utter madness. Just like Cheryl to take your bodyguard the one moment we actually need him for crowd control." He squeezes my hand. "Let's go back to the room, shall we?"

I shoot one longing look back outside. I've always wanted to see St. Paul's Cathedral and Central Park. But I guess I'll have to make do with pictures from Google. We go back upstairs.

"Was Cheryl always this way?" Kurt asks as we head down the long hallway to my room.

I push a lock of hair behind my ear and loop my arm through Kurt's. "Kind of. She's always been controlling, even back when we were in grade school. When she got teased, it made her feel better to be a jerk to someone else."

"Why was she picked on?" Kurt inquires.

"She was a bit chubby. Not overweight, but she had some baby fat, you know?"

Kurt looks aghast. "She was fat? No!"

I insert my key card into the slot and push open the door.

Kurt kicks off his shoes and sits cross-legged on the floor.

"She's always so critical of people's weight. She told me yesterday that my butt is looking big."

"I think that's *why* she's critical." I sit on a hard chair near the TV. "And why she cares so much about money, you know. It's like she couldn't control her life before, but now she has money and connections. She got liposuction our first week in LA, and then the implants. She doesn't want to be that chubby kid from Canada anymore."

Kurt shifts his legs so they are on top of the opposite knee, in some kind of yoga pose. "Was she ugly before?"

I take out my cell phone and open a new game of solitaire. "No, not ugly. She's always had a pretty face. In fact, I think she looked prettier then than she does now."

Kurt closes his eyes and breathes in and out rhythmically. "She is fairly gorgeous now, to be fair, even though she's transformed herself into another Hollywood clone." He shifts his legs a little higher along his thigh. "But you know, you can put lipstick on a pig, but it's still a pig."

I giggle. "That's mean, Kurt."

He grins wickedly. "But true. Hell, she said my butt looked big. Cheryl deserves what she gets."

I put down my phone. "Want to go find the pool?"

"Sure." Kurt unwinds his legs and stands gracefully. "Let me grab my swimsuit."

Five minutes later we're changed, me into a black one-piece, and Kurt into a brilliant green Speedo. We have towels draped around our necks and flip-flops on our feet. We set off down the hall, following the smell of chlorine until we get to the pool. A couple of kids are playing on the waterslide, the only people around.

"Hot tub first?" I suggest.

"Definitely."

Kurt drops his towel and steps into the hot tub.

"Hey, Kurt?"

He sinks into the steaming water. "Yeah?"

"Your butt isn't fat."

"Micky, darling, that's why I love you." He reaches into the water and splashes it toward me. "Now get in here, girl. Hot tubbing is miserable if you're alone."

I climb in beside him, thinking how lucky I am to have a loyal friend like Kurt. The jets tickle my legs. My skin turns bright red as I immerse my top half.

Dang, the water's hot.

The rest of the evening passes quickly, laughing and gossiping with Kurt at the pool, then ordering a Thai tofu dish from a restaurant we found in the phonebook. We eat while watching reruns on TV.

New York is an awesome city.

Even though I've only seen it from the hotel window.

Chapter Thirteen

Cheryl is playing with her hair and examining her fingernails while talking a mile-a-minute to the sound guy. She's complaining about the sunburn she got yesterday on the ferry to the Statue of Liberty and bragging about the celebrities who are her BFF's.

"And so I told Drew that we'll have to get together for lunch sometime and she, like, totally agreed with me." Cheryl shrugs. "No big deal though, and I'm not even that thrilled about it. It's not like she's George Clooney or anything."

The sound guy looks over at me and raises an eyebrow. I suppress a smile.

The music stops as David Letterman's voice resonates through the room. "She's been nominated for Grammy's. Her first movie is coming out next year. She's broken more hearts than Justin Bieber. She may even have broken Justin Bieber's heart. Please give it up for—Mikayla Rivers!"

The sound guy reaches out and pats my arm. "Mikayla, you go out in three-two-one. And walk."

This is it. I swallow and feel my heart race wildly as I step out from behind the curtain, just as we practiced a few hours earlier. I cross the stage. The noise is deafening. Clapping, hoots and catcalls from the audience. Someone shouts, "Please go to prom with me!"

For a moment I am blinded by the lights, and then I see David Letterman standing up from behind a desk to my left.

I walk over, concentrating so I don't trip in my heels. I manage to blow a kiss to the crowd.

David reaches out with both hands as I approach and lightly grabs my right hand. "Mikayla Rivers, ladies and gentlemen." He kisses my hand. "How are you?"

"I'm good." I can barely hear him over the applause. "Thank you for having me."

I stand awkwardly, not sure when I should sit on the white sofa. David adjusts his glasses and motions for me to sit. He takes a seat as well and waits for the noise to die down.

I sit carefully, holding my vintage black skirt down. I don't want to flash the audience.

"I always thought the backdrop of your set was a real window." I blurt it out, not intending to be funny, but the audience roars with laughter.

David smiles. "Of course it's real." He winks at me. "Although, just for the record, if it were real, it would be awfully hard to look this brilliant and twinkly outside when it's four in the afternoon."

I blush and shake my head. I want to say something witty and clever to redeem myself, but nothing comes to mind. "Yet another thing I've learned since coming to Hollywood," I say lamely.

David leans forward, and I hazard a glance toward the audience. I can't make out any faces, just a sea of blackness and the occasional glint of light off someone's glasses.

"So what else have you learned since arriving?"

I lick my lips and squeeze my hands together to hide my

nerves. "Well, I've learned that I honestly cannot have a life anymore. It's crazy, but yesterday after we arrived here, my friend and I tried to go walking through Times Square, but we were literally mobbed. I had wanted, you know, to go to the cool places you always hear about, like, uh, Greenwich Village and the Empire State Building, but seriously I couldn't. We ended up going back to my room where we watched *Friends* reruns so we at least felt like we were experiencing New York on some level."

The audience laughs again. I am sweating profusely. I hope nobody notices.

"It's better anyway," David deadpans. "You probably would not survive being in New York, a little thing like you. See, traffic signals here are more guidelines than actual rules."

"I learned that in my ride from the airport to the hotel, actually." I wrinkle my nose. "I think my limo hit about twenty people, dodged five traffic lights and went the wrong way down a one-way. It's probably best that I had to be sequestered in my hotel!"

"In this case, I would agree with you," sniggers David. "So if you were stuck in your room, you missed seeing the Naked Cowboy."

"Uh, I haven't heard anything about a naked cowboy," I stammer. "Don't you have laws about nudity here?"

Dave chuckles. "I love the pure ones." The audience roars with laughter and David continues, "The Naked Cowboy is a fixture in New York. You'll have to check him out sometime."

"I don't actually watch porn or anything, so I probably, uh, won't."

David holds up a snapshot of a guy with a cowboy hat, wearing tighty-whitey underwear and holding a guitar. "This is the Naked Cowboy. Honestly, I wouldn't recommend porn to one so young." He winks at the audience and they applaud.

I have no idea what we're even talking about anymore.

Dave sees my confusion and says kindly, "Enough about

this. Let's back track for a moment. Now tell me, do you never get to go anywhere you want since becoming a celebrity?" His face shows mock concern.

My mind flashes back to when I managed to sneak away and hang out with Jordan. I miss him. But, of course, nobody is supposed to know about that.

"Uh, well, no, not really. Not unless I go sneaky like a spy." I somehow manage to splutter out a reply. This is a slightly better topic than a nude cowboy.

"Sneaky like a spy," David echoes. I nod and he continues, "Even then you're not unseen, you know. Look what I was sent in the mail yesterday." He motions to a TV screen just down from where I am sitting.

Terror grips me. What if someone saw me and Jordan on campus? What if I wasn't as sneaky as I thought? What if this gets back to Jordan and he freaks out because I lied to him? What if –

The picture flashes up on the screen and I instantly relax. It's a photo of an old woman wearing baggy sweatpants, a yellow sweater and carrying a garbage bag full of old soda cans. She has wrinkled skin, matted grey hair and is missing about four teeth.

"Mikayla Rivers, undercover," David announces.

I laugh and clap my hands together. The audience laughs as well and I allow myself a sigh of relief. My secret is still safe.

Although, I'll probably tell Jordan the truth the next time I see him.

Or next week.

Soon, anyway.

"Tell us how Hollywood is different from Canada."

I sit back slightly. "So many ways, really. I haven't met a single person in LA who's eaten moose meat. In fact, even me saying I've eaten moose meat will probably get PETA to picket outside. Then there is the temperature difference. Right now LA is still sunshine and heat. At home it's snowing. Not going to lie, I don't miss the cold."

"So Canada, then, is a lot like Sarah Palin's Alaska, is that correct?"

The audience boos, and I laugh. "I'm not entirely sure how to answer that without offending Canadians everywhere," I admit.

David stirs his coffee cup with a pencil thoughtfully. "Perhaps you're right. Let's not answer that. Moving on. What would you be doing right now if you were not a singer? Britney Spears recently said that if she wasn't a pop star, she'd be a lawyer. What about you?"

I bite my lip slightly. "I don't know, to be honest. Probably still in school, taking a million different classes and trying to figure it all out. No clue."

David chuckles. "Good thing you can sing, then, right? I always wished I could sing, or dance or act. Instead I ended up a talk show host. Life is funny sometimes."

The audience applauds and cheers while David grins at the camera. "That's all the time we have right now, folks, so let's give it up again for Mikayla Rivers. Thank you, Mikayla. And coming up after the break, we'll have two of the *Twilight* actors stop in, but I'm not telling which two. You'll have to stay tuned to find out."

The red light on the camera goes blank and David turns to me. "You were magnificent, Mikayla. And if your singing career ever dies out, I think you could kill it in comedy. Thanks for playing along with the Naked Cowboy thing."

I'm not entirely sure if he's making fun of me. We both stand. He shakes my hand and escorts me to the edge of the stage while some musicians entertain the crowd. "When you're in New York again, please give me a shout. We'd love to get you back on here." David looks like he genuinely means it.

"Thank you so much," I shake his hand and exit the stage. Cheryl is waiting for me.

It's about five o'clock now, local time. Which means it's two in LA. Jordan is just getting out of class. I could be riding in a cab to his apartment right now.

It's okay. Tomorrow night I'll be back in LA. I can see him then.

Only one more day.

I never thought I could miss someone more than Matt.

"Mikayla, great job on the show! You were a rock star!"

"Your shoes look amazing!"

"Can I get your autograph for my niece?"

I smile at the people who are walking past me in the hallway, stopping to scrawl my name on a couple publicity photos that Cheryl magically procured. Then, bracing myself for the inevitable onslaught of fans, I step outside with Cheryl.

I heard an actress once describe being famous like being raped. And she got a lot of flak about it and had to issue an apology and everything. But, seriously, some days it's a pretty fitting description. In LA there are so many celebrities around that you can still function for the most part. But if you go somewhere different, suddenly people freak out.

Like Justin Bieber in Israel where he couldn't leave his hotel and walk where Jesus walked.

Fame is funny sometimes.

Not that I would change anything. I knew what I was getting into when I signed up for this job.

Although, truthfully, I only expected to play my guitar and earn a bit of money when Charles Nash made me the offer. I never expected it to take off so quickly and blow up into the huge thing that it is now. Or for Cheryl to take such an active role in planning out my day-to-day routine.

About three hundred autographs later, I make it to the waiting limo. My hand is killing me. I need to hire a helper monkey, someone who can sign things for me. Or maybe just buy a stamp with my name on it.

Cheryl is posing for pictures and passing her phone number to the cute men she sees, so I climb in without her. The cameras are still clicking madly, focusing on my tinted window in hopes that I show my face again. I wait for Cheryl, who is taking her time.

I reach into my Coach purse and pull out my cell phone.

Work is crazy. Cant wait to be done working late... sooo happy i get 2 see u soon!

Texting Jordan makes me feel more at peace.

His reply is almost instant. **Agreed! Tell your boss you quit if he tries to make you stay late again!** ☺

I had told him that I got called in to work Sunday and had to work late again today.

Cant quit... w/o a job i'd be deported and you'd never see meee again!

Haha, good call. I'll have to settle for seeing you Tuesday night. <3

A virtual heart. Adorable. I close my eyes and lean back against the seat. When Cheryl climbs in, the limo whispers its way into the honking bedlam of traffic, back to the serenity and quiet loneliness of the hotel.

Chapter Fourteen

I wake up early the next morning, rested and wide awake. Sounds of traffic float up to my eighth floor window. New York is humming and it's not yet six thirty.

Cheryl, Kurt, and Chuck the bodyguard went out last night to some club. I had contemplated going but decided against it. My mother would have a heart attack if she read a tabloid report of me going into clubs. She'd start to worry that I'd end up like all the other pop starlets who bounce in and out of rehab.

Besides, I had had enough attention for the day.

As soon as they left, I called room service and ordered the biggest, juiciest hamburger on the menu. I emailed Rachelle, talked to my mother on the phone, and watched the swarms of people outside my window, amazed at the sheer volume.

I watched four episodes of *The Simpsons* and drifted off to sleep around nine.

If I stare at the ceiling long enough, the bumpy texture seems to go in, not out. I am mesmerized by it, until loud noises outside peak my curiosity.

I crawl out of bed and peer out the curtain at the scene below. A bus lumbers by, crowded with people. Limos and yellow cabs race each other, weaving in and out of traffic. A police siren wails in the distance but nobody moves over.

A taxi cab lurches to a stop at the curb below me, brakes squealing. A distraught-looking business woman climbs out, tosses some cash into the front seat, and then taps off toward a gleaming building to my left.

New York is fascinating and terrifying. I step away from the window, feeling a little dizzy. Heights normally don't bother me, but it is different here with the concrete swarming with people and cars.

I have a few hours of freedom before Cheryl and Kurt wake up in the other rooms. What should I do? I check my phone. Maybe Rachelle has called. Or Jordan. Thinking of him makes me feel like a giggly schoolgirl.

I take it off its charger and flip it open. One unread message. I click on it and smile. It's from him, sent around midnight when I was fast asleep.

U wont believe it, but there is some chick on the Letterman show who looks just like you. dont know her name, but its kinda crazy. ☺

I gag and clap a hand over my mouth. Are you kidding me? He watched the Late Show? He never watches TV! He told me that a few days ago! Does this mean he knows? I have to call him. I have to make him see that I didn't mean to lie.

With trembling fingers I punch in his phone number.

Ring once.

I pace the room. Come on, Jordan, pick up!

Ring twice.

Where are you?

I mean, sure, it's six thirty in the morning, but Jordan's usually awake by now, studying.

Oh man, it's not six thirty. I forgot about the time difference.

I hang up the phone and go sit on the bed. My legs are too shaky to support my body weight at the moment. If it's six thirty here, it must be… what? Three thirty? Whatever it is, it's much too early for me to call him.

My phone vibrates. I look down and see that it's Jordan calling me back. I hesitate. Do I really want to face the truth right now?

But I just called him. I have to pick up.

I hit accept. "Hello?"

"Micky? It's Jordan." His voice is crackly and groggy. "You called. Is everything okay?"

"Uh, yeah, I, um, well I just checked my phone and saw your text." I pause. I need him to say the words first, to tell me that he knows everything now so that I don't have to.

His voice becomes more animated and awake. "Yeah, it was crazy. I was flipping through the channels to see what the final score was with the Avalanche game and I saw some chick on the Late Show. Didn't watch the whole thing, so I have no clue what her name is, but wow, she could have been your twin. She even talked like you."

He sounds amused, but not angry. Or suspicious. Does he still not know?

I should tell him. I should come clean right now and confess that she *is* me and that's why we look alike. And the chips can fall where they may and all that. I'm sure he won't hate me for being a secret celebrity. Right?

But I remember all the times he mocked the famous. The bitterness in his voice when he talked about his mother. His disdain for people who chase that elusive Hollywood rainbow.

If I tell him, everything will change. And I cannot allow that to happen. Not when I finally have a real relationship for the first time since Matt.

Plus, I especially can't tell him over the phone. When I tell him, it has to be face to face, so he can see that I was not trying to lie to him, that it just – just happened.

"Wow. That's crazy." I sound fake. He's going to hear my tone and know something's up, but I plough ahead mindlessly.

"I've heard a theory that everyone in the world has a twin. Like, somewhere in China there could be a guy who looks just like you or maybe not China because then he would look Chinese and you definitely don't look Chinese, but maybe he's in Europe or something." I'm babbling.

Jordan chuckles. "I've never heard this theory, but it's hilarious that you had to call me at three in the morning to tell me. Here I thought it was some huge emergency when I saw you calling."

I force a laugh. "Yeah, oops. I just, uh, was awake and saw your text and called you before I remembered that it was too early. Ha. Ha."

"You're awake? Did you only leave work now?" Jordan sounds concerned.

"No, well, a few hours ago. I just, uh, happened to be awake and forgot how early it is."

"Can't sleep?" Jordan's tone is softer now. Like he cares about me.

"I miss you," I say. "I'm glad that I'm nearly done with my bizarre schedule so I can hang out with you again."

"Me too." He yawns.

"I'll let you go back to sleep." I don't want to hang up the phone, but I feel brutal keeping him awake when he has homework and deadlines.

"I hope you're getting overtime for having to work this weekend."

"Yeah, they're paying me pretty good for it."

"Good. Alright, well, go back to sleep, sweetie, and I'll see you tomorrow."

Sweetie. He called me sweetie. "Okay, bye." I hang up and lean back against the wall. That was terrifying and has drained all my energy.

I can't believe he saw me on *Letterman*.

Thank goodness he accepted my explanation.

I have a strange urge to cross myself like they do in the

occasional movie, but decide against it. I'm not Catholic and I don't want to subject myself to eternal damnation if I do it wrong.

And with that, I flop back into bed.

*****

"Micky, hon. Micky. Wake up!"

I open my eyes and focus. Kurt is standing above me, a towel wrapped around his head turban-style. He is sporting a bright pink, beaded T-shirt.

"What do you want?" I croak, shutting my eyes tightly. "What time is it?"

I feel the bed shift as he settles in beside me. "It's almost nine, girl. Why are you so wasted? You didn't even come clubbing with us last night."

"How was it?"

"Fab-u-lous. We went to a couple different spots. At one point, I am sure I saw Paris Hilton getting into a cab. Great drinks, the music was hopping. And Cheryl didn't drive me completely crazy. Although," Kurt leans in toward me, "I'm pretty sure the guy she brought back here is Arthur, not Martha, if you know what I mean. He was checking me out before Cheryl latched on to him."

I giggle. "No way!"

"Way!" Kurt leans against me. "How was your night? Did you watch yourself on *Letterman*?"

"No! But you'll never guess who did?" Before Kurt can guess, I spill it. "Jordan."

Kurt looks horrified. "No," he breathes. "So the secret is out? Is he pissed? What happened?"

I shake my head. "It's bizarre, but I don't think he actually knows it was me. He texted me. Here look." I grab my cell off the pillow and hand it to Kurt. He opens the text and reads it, his brow furrowed.

"He thinks there's a celebrity who looks exactly like you, but isn't you? And here I thought this boy was smart." His face shows utter bewilderment.

"Yeah!" I let my breath out slowly between my teeth. "I called him this morning and he totally thinks that. He didn't watch much of the show, but saw the girl, well, me, while flipping through channels. He didn't even bother to find out her name or anything."

Kurt sighs and kisses the top of my matted hair. "Somebody up there loves you, girl."

"I know," I add fervently.

"So are you going to tell him when you get home? Or hold off on it a bit longer?"

I shrug. "I dunno. Maybe. I mean, I will tell him, but it has to be the right timing, you know?"

Kurt squeezes my arm. "Of course, you're right. Besides, it's no big deal. Everyone lies. Some people lie to hide things, some people lie to make themselves look good, and others for the hell of it, but everyone lies."

His words sting, as if my guilt-prone conscience is poking at me. "Not *everyone* lies," I say, frowning. I don't want to think of myself as a liar. Really, I'm simply hiding the truth for a moment until the opportunity presents itself.

Kurt laughs shortly. "Trust me, everyone lies. Look at Cheryl. Basically every word that comes out of her mouth is a lie."

I think I might throw up. Not in a million years do I want to be compared to Cheryl.

Kurt sees my expression. "Don't worry so much, Micky. It's not the end of the world. Didn't Lord Byron say that a lie is only the truth in masquerade?"

Masquerade. The word is soothing, as sudden images of people wearing fancy ball gowns and feathered masks appear in my head. That's a bit nicer way to put it, but I still feel miserable. "I hate lying. And I'm going to come clean. The next time I see

Jordan, I'll tell him exactly what happened."

The words sound good to my ears but can't quite erase the hollow feeling in the pit of my stomach.

Kurt frowns. "Seriously, girl, you worry too much."

"But I want to be a good person. And I want Jordan to love me." I sound pitiful.

"You are a good person. And Jordan does love you." Kurt's tone is final. "Look, we're in New York. This is no place for such a heavy discussion. Change topic?"

I nod, but my mind refuses to let go.

Kurt's tone becomes cajoling. "You have to get up so we can do some yoga and get ready. The CD signing is from noon to four. We only have a couple hours."

I pull myself out of bed. Two yoga mats are already spread out on the floor. Kurt plugs his iPod into a set of speakers and yoga music fills the silence.

"Do you need to get changed?" Kurt surveys my torn plaid pajamas in distaste.

I step onto my purple mat. "Nope. I'm comfy in this."

"Good thing I love you, girl, because your taste in clothes is definitely lacking." Kurt kneels down on his pink mat and goes into the folded position, Child's Pose.

"I base my fashion sense on what feels good," I say, grunting slightly as I feel my shoulders stretch.

"You can't judge fashion by what feels good." Kurt moves into Downward Dog and I remember why I dislike yoga. Blood rushes to my head and my arms shake.

Kurt continues, "Nudity feels good for some people, but you don't see naked people running the country."

I burst out laughing and my weakling arms give way. I collapse onto the mat. "I like fashion, you know I do. But when I am alone with you, why do I care how I look?"

"Get back into Downward Dog." Kurt waits until I heave myself back into position and then replies, "It is *always* fashion time."

An hour later, Kurt calls it a day, and I roll off my mat. "I want to die," I moan.

"Jordan's calling on your cell."

I leap up, looking for my phone. "Where is it?"

Kurt chortles. "That got you moving. Now go shower, girlfriend."

I pull my shirt up and over my head and chuck it at Kurt, disappearing into the bathroom before the shirt connects. Just as I close the door, I hear Kurt splutter and know that my aim was true.

Kurt's awesome.

Time to get ready for a CD signing.

Chapter Fifteen

I got back from New York two hours ago and somehow managed to sneak away from Cheryl. She was in the process of firing Chuck, so it wasn't too difficult. I am now sitting on the couch at Jordan's apartment, eating one of the chocolate cupcakes that we just took out of the oven.

Some people claim that men can't cook, but Jordan makes the most amazing cupcakes. And he understands that sometimes triple chocolate is not quite enough and you need that extra layer of chocolate chips on top of the thick, fudgy icing.

He's amazing. And perfect. Except I don't really know how to answer his question right now.

I try to hide my panic by taking a huge bite of cupcake and some gooey icing gets onto my cheek.

Jordan laughs. "You goof!" He hands me a napkin from the counter.

He sits down beside me and stretches his legs out on top of mine. "So, what do you say?"

I had hoped that if I didn't reply, he'd forget about it.

I swallow and wipe my face with the napkin. I run my tongue over my teeth so that when I open my mouth to talk I won't have nasty-looking icing on them. I clear my throat.

"Well, yeah, I mean, we totally could go, but um…" I trail off, hoping some inspiration will pop into my head. "It's just that I really wanted to go to, uh, the art gallery."

Art gallery? Where did that come from?

"An art gallery?" Jordan sounds confused.

"Yeah, I love art," I say then stop. What if he asks me what artists I like? Because I don't think I know a single artist. Maybe Goya? Or maybe that is a type of food. Um, Dali? Was he an artist? Or that guy who went crazy and cut off his ear—Picasso, right? He was an artist, for sure. Only I don't know if he was a painter or sculptor.

Maybe I should tone down my love of art. "What I mean is that I want to *begin* to like art. I've never really liked art at all, but think I need to get more, well, cultured."

"More cultured?" Jordan stares at me in bewilderment. I kind of understand why he's confused. I like watching old reruns in sweatpants, and eating popcorn and pizza on the floor while playing Rook. I'm not exactly the most cultured person on the planet.

Suddenly understanding dawns on his face. "You're nervous about meeting my friends, aren't you?" His eyes search my face.

"No, not at all," I begin and then trail off. I sigh. "Okay, fine. You're right. I am kind of nervous about meeting your friends."

Jordan puts his arm around me and pulls me in tight. I snuggle up into his neck and try to figure out a plan. Don't get me wrong. I have nothing against parties in a random dorm room. And I really don't mind meeting new people. Back when I was at the University of Calgary, I loved doing that.

But, I know what's going to happen here. We walk in, Jordan says, 'This is my girlfriend, Mikayla.' And every person there recognizes me as *the* Mikayla, and I get mobbed, and Jordan goes ballistic and realizes that I have been lying outright to him.

I keep trying to tell him the truth, but the opportunity never arises. And this morning I definitely couldn't say anything. Telling him something this huge over the phone? That would have been the worst.

"Look, Micky, you don't need to worry," Jordan says. "My friends will love you. But honestly, if you're feeling that self-conscious, we don't have to go. We can stay here."

Why does he have to be so perfect and thoughtful and loving? "Honestly, it's fine. I need to get over my fears, right? And it'll be fun. Really."

Jordan grins. "Awesome. Well, let's run down to In-N-Out and grab a burger before we head over. I think it'll be games and snacks and maybe we'll break into a dance party if Chris brings his CDs. You'll like that, won't you?"

I force an enthusiastic smile. I get up from the couch. Maybe if I stall and say that I need to, uh, use the bathroom and then I'll splash water on my shirt and we'll need to wait for it to dry, and then order three burgers or something and take forever to eat them, then maybe it will be too late to actually go to this party.

"I need to go to the bathroom," I say, kissing Jordan on the cheek as I walk past. Okay. I'll figure this out. I'm sure I can figure out a way to get people not to notice me.

I wonder if I could buy a wig? And wear sunglasses? And change my name?

I stay in the bathroom for three minutes. I flush the empty toilet and wash my hands, generously splashing myself with water.

I come back out and see Jordan standing by the front door. He's holding my sweatshirt; he looks at me and winks. "You ready?"

"Look! I splashed myself somehow." I try to look pitiful. "Can we wait a few minutes for my shirt to dry?"

"Why don't you wear something of mine? I've got a few

extra sweatshirts that might fit you."

He goes to his bedroom and returns with a baggy, green sweatshirt that looks insanely comfortable. I slip it over my head. It's big, for sure, but it doesn't look too bad.

"Great, all set?"

I look around in panic. There's got to be something else I can do!

"Uh, do you have a baseball cap I can borrow? I'm having a bad hair day, and I think it would be best to cover it up."

Jordan goes back into his bedroom and returns with a Chicago Bears cap. I put it on and tuck my hair into it.

"So, just for fun, can we pretend like we have accents tonight?" I shoot Jordan what I hope is a winsome smile. If he goes for the fake accent game, I'm sure I can convince him to call me Shelby or Marsha or Emily or something. I've always liked the name Emily.

"Accents?" Jordan raises his right eyebrow.

"Yeah," I say. "It'll be a fun game. I have to talk in an accent and pretend to be from a foreign country. Like Russia or something. An exchange student."

Jordan frowns. "You *are* from a foreign country. Canada's foreign."

Okay. I have to sell it to him. He has to see how important it is to me to have an accent and fake foreign name. I open my eyes and say, "But sweetie, I get nervous meeting new people; and if I can pretend like I'm someone else then I won't be as, like, scared or whatever."

Jordan thinks about it for a second. "If it means that much to you, then go ahead and fake an accent. Where are you from?"

"I am from Russia. Vere are you from?" I say, in my pathetic Russian accent.

Jordan stares at me, and we burst out laughing. "Well, Olga, if you manage to get through the night without anyone beating you up, I'll buy you a candy bar."

I wrinkle my nose at him. "Ve vill see. Olga likes candy bars,

Tanned, Toned and Totally Faking It

by the vay. Hence, she vill vin."

Jordan reaches for my hand and we go into the hallway. While he locks his door, I sneak a look at my watch. It's only five o'clock. I'll have to drag out the In-N-Out burger experience by about four hours if I want to miss the party. And the problem with fast food is, well, it's fast.

Maybe I should tell Jordan my secret while we're eating. He can't dislike celebrities that much, can he? He's made disparaging comments about famous people in general, but he knows me. And if I come clean, I'll only have lied to him for two weeks.

We cut across campus toward the nearest burger joint. We approach a little newsstand and I follow his gaze toward the newsstand. He stares at the magazines and shakes his head.

"Famous people. They sell their souls for five minutes of fame."

Maybe I won't tell him that I gave up on getting my university degree to become famous.

"Wanting to be an actress destroyed my mother. She had such high hopes and got nowhere. And how many who *do* make it get through their careers without destroying their families or turning to drugs? Why do kids idolize these people?"

His words sting. I'm not on drugs, but the disdain in his voice hurts. I try to keep my tone light. "Not all celebrities or movie stars are bad."

Jordan squeezes my hand. "I know," he says. "But fame tends to ruin people."

"What happened to your mom? I thought you said she's a cleaning woman."

Jordan runs his free hand through his hair, a gesture that I absolutely adore. "My mom is an alcoholic," he says. "She came out here, you know, after my dad died. She wanted to reach her dream of being a famous actress. She used to say that one day she'd be like Audrey Hepburn. She auditioned and auditioned without any luck. We ran out of money and she still auditioned. She got rejected from everything."

His voice begins to grow bitter. "And then someone told her she had a good shot at one particular role. She tried out, and the casting director stayed overnight at our apartment a lot, and my mom was finally happy. He told her that she had potential. Then he disappeared. Later she found out that someone else got the part. That was the final straw. My mom started drinking.

"Sometimes she'd be passed out when I got home from school. She didn't work. She maxed out her credit cards. At one point, we were homeless. That's when she got work as a housekeeper, so we could move back into an apartment."

I reach out and pull Jordan into my arms. The pain in his voice cuts me. "I'm so sorry." The words feel inadequate.

Jordan lets me embrace him. After a minute he says, "I'm sorry. I always forget you work in the music industry. These are your coworkers I'm trash talking."

It's actually me he's trash talking, but I let it go. Now is not the time to tell him that I was offered a role in the new Sandra Bullock movie as her rebellious teenage daughter. He might think I had to sleep my way to the top; which is entirely not the case, if you're wondering.

We make small talk the rest of the evening, laughing and talking about random things. The cumbersome topic of Hollywood still weighs on my mind, but neither of us mention it.

Finally, after eating more burgers than I thought possible, along with a massive helping of fries and a soda, we head back to campus.

I don't know what I'm expecting at his friend's party. Jordan is a sweet guy, who doesn't drink, do drugs or know the first thing about pop culture. But I couldn't see there being any more like him at UCLA. I am sure the party will be a beer-fest with hot, scantily clad women and sweaty football players. There will be loud music playing; and everyone talking loudly and acting stupid as they get wasted.

Jordan knocks on a dorm room door. There is some laughter coming from inside and I hold my breath. This is it. Moment of truth. A guy about my height with glasses and short brown hair opens the door.

"Jordan!" he says. "Come on in, man."

I keep my head down, barely able to see anything from underneath the visor of the ball cap.

As we take our shoes off, I glance at the guy who opened the door. He looks like that scientist actor from Big Bang Theory. Nerdy, but nice. He looks at me and says, "Jordan, you brought your girlfriend?"

Jordan nods and puts his hand on my back. "This is Olga," he says, smirking slightly.

I had forgotten that I have to fake a Russian accent. The guy reaches out and firmly shakes my hand. "I'm Chris."

"So, are you een law school vith Jordan too?" I ask.

Chris makes an exaggerated shocked face and staggers back a step. "Me? Law school? No way! I'm a micro-biologist. In fact, the only other person in law school besides Jordan is Hannah. The rest of us are in the more socially-acceptable field of science." He sneaks a sideways glance at Jordan, and I laugh. He seems like a nice guy.

Chris motions for us to follow him into the living room. People are sprawled around on the couch and floor, scribbling away on little pieces of paper. "Come on in. We're in the middle of Scattergories, but if you guys want to join us, we can start again."

A few look up and acknowledge us briefly. One guy nods his head; a girl gives a little wave and then keeps writing on her paper. But otherwise, everyone is immersed in their game. And even better, nobody is screaming for me to sign their buttocks.

I can handle board games and small talk. The group looks more academic than what I had pictured. There are only two girls. One is slightly overweight with brilliant blue eyes and curly blonde hair. The other is tiny and looks like a cute little mouse with her small face, spiky short brown hair, and freckles on her nose. Neither seems to be the type who spends hours each day surfing the net, looking at celebrity photos. And as for the guys, they also seem studious and good and oblivious to the Hollywood scene. Like Jordan.

Jordan and I sit down on the carpet and lean against the wall. Jordan grabs a sheet of paper and a pencil. "We'll be on the same team, okay, Olga?"

I smack him lightly on the arm and murmur, "It's okay. I'm not that nervous anymore. I can be Mikayla."

Jordan shakes his head. "No way! You're my Russian girlfriend. I want you to speak in accented English all night." He pokes me in the side and I squirm.

"Fine. You vant me to be Russian? I can be Russian. Just vait and see, Mister."

The crowd finishes their round. "Everyone, this is Jordan's girlfriend, Olga," Chris says politely.

"Hello," I say in my made-up accent, half waving at them all.

The blue-eyed girl pulls her knee up to her chest and rests her chin on it. "You probably get this all the time, but you look just like that singer who was on *Regis and Kelly* a few days ago."

I feel my mouth go dry. "Um, uh, vat, uh, vat girl?" This is bad.

She glances at the guy next to her. "Do you remember her name? It was Michelle something, I think. You'd think I'd remember her name! Her songs are on the radio all the time!"

The guy shrugs. "Yeah, you do kind of look like her, but it was the *Letterman* show because I saw it, too."

Jordan puts his arm around me and squeezes slightly. "I asked her that same question yesterday. I thought she looked a lot like that girl, but there you are. Genetics are funny, aren't they?"

One of the guys sprawled on the couch looks up in interest. "In the lab a week ago I found two mice almost genetically identical and yet were from two different litters of the same parents. They were basically identical twins but a year apart in age."

The girl with the spiky hair looks bored. "If I wanted a biology lesson, I'd have taken biology." She must be the other lawyer that Chris mentioned when we first come in.

A few people laugh and the girl says, "I'm Hannah, Olga. It's good to meet you. Where are you from?" She speaks in a painfully slow voice, like she thinks I don't speak English. Which is kind of nice of her, because I'm sure Olga struggles with the language. You know, theoretically.

"Vell, I am from Russia, but I live here now for school," I say choppily. Jordan sniggers beside me, but I ignore him.

Suddenly the girl says something in what I think is Russian. She actually speaks Russian? Why didn't Jordan warn me that one of his friends speaks my language? Well, Olga's language.

I look at Jordan in panic. What do I say? I don't speak Russian!

Hannah stops and gazes expectantly at me. I smile blankly. "Da. Very good. You speak vell." I'm fairly confident that *da* is a Russian word. I'm pretty sure I heard Matt Damon say it at some point in the Bourne movies.

Hannah seems pleased. "I haven't used my Russian in so long. But that's awesome that I still remember it. Do you want to practice with me?"

I gulp and say, "Um, no, I tink I need to practice my English, no speak Russian."

She nods. "That's so true. So where are you from in Russia?"

What the crap? Will the questions never end? The only Russian city I know of is Moscow. "Zee capital," I say awkwardly.

"Ah, you're from Moscow. I've always wanted to go to Moscow."

I smile awkwardly at Hannah. She looks like she's about to say something else, when one of the boys interrupts. "New game?"

Everyone nods in agreement and soon we are playing a lively game called Cranium, where people have to act out things and hum songs and make stuff out of clay and draw pictures with their eyes closed and all these other random activities. It's pretty fun. We are on teams; girls (plus Chris and Jordan) against boys. I soon lose myself in the game and stop worrying. Competition brings out the best in me.

It's our turn and I roll the dice. We move forward three spaces and land on the card where you have to act things out without speaking, or sing, or whatever the card tells you to do.

"You're up, Olga!" Jordan says. I reach forward and grab a card, reading it silently.

Hum the song Break Up *by singer Mikayla Rivers. Your team has to guess the name and artist.*

I ignore the inkling of worry in the pit of my stomach. I'll hum it carefully, adding a few wrong notes so that nobody will guess it's really me.

I start humming my song. The notes come easily and I love purposefully hitting wrong ones. It's kind of fun, fooling around with it. I see Hannah start tapping her foot to the beat and the other girl starts humming a couple notes along with me. Their faces twist in concentration as they try to guess the name.

"Shania Twain?" The blonde girl looks at Jordan and Chris and they shrug their shoulders.

"I have no idea," Jordan says. "I haven't listened to anything other than jazz and the Beatles in about ten years."

"No, it's not Shania. It's Taylor Swift," Hannah says. "Right? Taylor Swift and the name of the song is like Break My Heart or something like that."

The blonde shakes her head. "No way is it Taylor Swift. It's like Britney Spears, I think. Something about being innocent."

Wow. My songs sound nothing like Britney Spears' songs. Honestly. It's quite funny watching them.

"You're almost out of time." Buzz-cut boy is watching the little grains of sand moving down the hourglass. Another few seconds and he slams his hand down on the table. "You're out of time, suckers," he says gleefully.

Jordan jumps up and says, "I need some water." He conveniently heads to the kitchen as my team says, "Okay, Olga, who was it?"

I say quietly, "*Break Up* by Mikayla Rivers." I half expect someone to look at me and yell, "It's you!" but nobody does.

The girls groan and the blonde one says, "I knew that, too! I love Mikayla. She's like the best singer I've heard in so long. Man, I can't believe I didn't know that one!" She dramatically tosses her head to one side. "Especially because she's the one we were talking about a few minutes ago, the one you look like, Olga."

Hannah adds, "Totally! I totally should have known that."

Jordan sticks his head out of the kitchen. "Need some water, babe?" he asks me. I nod gratefully and return to my chair. I cannot believe my luck! If Jordan had stayed in the room even one moment longer—

I am sweating profusely from nerves.

We stay for another half an hour, and then Jordan looks at the clock on the wall. "Sorry, guys. I don't want to be all lame and ditch out early, but I have an exam tomorrow. I need to go home and study."

He gets to his feet. I jump up, too. I haven't been able to relax the entire evening. Plus it gives me a headache having to speak with a Russian accent.

Hannah yawns and stretches. She smacks Jordan lightly on the leg. "Hey, do you think Professor Hazelton will ask anything about those briefs we read last week?"

Jordan shakes his head. "I doubt it. I spoke to him after class last week and from what he said, it's going to be mainly theory this time. There might be a couple questions though; I'd look them over if I were you."

"That's what I was afraid of. I guess I better head home, too." She looks over at me and says something in Russian. It's short and I can only assume that she is saying goodbye. I grin awkwardly and wave. She doesn't say anything else, and I breathe a sigh of relief.

We say goodnight to everyone and leave the apartment. Jordan puts his arm around my shoulders. "That wasn't so bad, was it, Olga?"

I smile sweetly at him. "No, it wasn't bad at all. I was expecting something different. But you know what, you owe me a candy bar!"

I smirk at him and he laughs. "Honestly, Micky, you earned it. When Hannah was asking you all those questions about Russia and then when she actually spoke to you in Russian, I thought I would burst a lung trying not to laugh. But you played it well. Good job!"

We walk back to his apartment in companionable silence. The stars are shining above us, and campus is dark. It's romantic and crisp and cool. If I were to die right this instant, I would die happy.

Chapter Sixteen

Back from New York a week and standing in line at the grocery store, I am wearing massive sunglasses and waiting for the person ahead of me to unload her overloaded cart. I have a box of donuts that will hide in my purse until I see Jordan tonight, and celery, soy milk, and low-fat yogurt.

I am in between bodyguards at the moment, so it wasn't too difficult to sneak out.

I fidget in line, hoping that the woman will hurry up and get her things onto the conveyor belt, when something beside me catches my eye. "What did they do to me?" I breathe softly. I stare at the picture on the magazine. *Celebrity Magazine* October Edition, to be exact. I am staring at my own face, but I hardly recognize myself. Wow. I look gorgeous, like insane model hot. More like hott with two t's. Ridiculously good looking yet kind of channeling Katy Perry or Nicki Minaj with the colors I'm wearing.

I do not, however, look anything like myself.

Which, I reflect, might not be a bad thing since there is no danger that Jordan will see it and recognize me.

I pick up the copy and flip through it until I see the section on me.

In a candid interview, America's Canadian sweetheart opens up about love, fashion, and finding her dreams. As any fan of hers knows, most of her songs are about breaking up and hating love, but Mikayla, age 20, says that love is not something she despises. "I went through a bad breakup and of course that affects me. But I haven't given up on the idea of love. One day, definitely, I would like to get married, to have a family, to settle down. Until then, I'm just living life and trying not to get swept away."

Did I say that? I read the rest of the article and am a little overcome. I don't remember saying any of these things. I think I said "Yes" when they asked if I wanted to get married one day, and I'm fairly sure that when they inquired if I had ever gone through a break up, I told them that I had, but really? All I remember of the interview was me giving a lot of noncommittal answers while the reporter took notes on my clothing.

I take out my phone and punch in Cheryl's number.

"Hello?"

"Cher, it's me," I say, beginning to unload my small basket onto the conveyer belt with one hand. "So I'm at the store and I saw the *Celebrity Magazine* cover. They totally misquoted me, and I thought you'd want to know."

"Oh, right, I must have forgotten to tell you. They didn't like your interview answers, so they emailed us a questionnaire, and I filled it out for you."

I sigh. "Cheryl," I say in what I think is a patient voice. "Look, you have to start letting me actually say what I want to say and stop controlling everything so much. Like this line: 'I'm living life and trying not to get swept away'? What is that? What does that even mean?"

Cheryl laughs briefly and makes a snapping noise. She must be chewing gum and blowing bubbles. I can just picture her, and the image in my mind makes me angry. Cheryl has been nothing but trouble from day one, refusing to let me make decisions, molding me into whatever lame little creature she wanted, and threatening me that if I get rid of her, she will tell my mom about the collagen injections.

"Look, Mikayla, you should be thanking me for making you sound more poetic and intellectual. Your answers were fairly pathetic," Cheryl says, snapping her gum.

"But why didn't you just give me the questionnaire? I could have filled it out myself." I am upset. She had no right. Honestly, it's like she's trying to live vicariously through me.

"How many donuts do you have?" the cashier chirps, motioning at my box.

"Donuts?" Cheryl is still on the line. "You can't buy donuts."

I adjust my ever-tightening skinny jeans and try to tuck in my shirt. "Uh, I don't have any donuts." I hold up four fingers to the cashier.

I'm planning on going back on my diet soon. Maybe next week. And besides, not even Kurt has noticed that I've gained seven pounds.

The cashier winks at me and says, "All you girls dieting."

"Bye, Cheryl. Gotta go." Curses. Now Cheryl will search my purse when I get home and find the donuts and freak out.

Maybe I won't go home. I eye the milk and yogurt. I could put them in Jordan's fridge until I am ready to go back to the hotel and face Cheryl.

I thank the cashier, take my bags and leave the shop. A few people loitering on the sidewalk snap my picture as I walk to the bus stop, and I smile and wave. I sit down on the bus bench and wait.

I adore taking transit. It makes me feel so normal and average. Sometimes people recognize me, but usually I can sit in the seat and not worry about a thing.

After about five minutes the bus pulls up and I climb on board, showing the driver my monthly pass that I bought when Cheryl wasn't watching.

The bus is nearly empty and I have my choice of seats. I walk to the back, having to grab a pole for balance as the bus lurches and pulls out into traffic.

I sit down and look out the window, enjoying watching the world move past me.

Suddenly I hear a small noise. On the bench across the aisle is a little girl, about eight or nine years old, with tears streaming down her face. She has shoulder length, scraggly, dark brown hair and mournful black eyes. She's like a non-animated, depressed Dora the Explorer.

"Hi," I say quietly so I don't startle her.

The girl looks at me fearfully. Great. Now she probably thinks I'm a kidnapper.

I place my shopping bags on the seat and step across the aisle to sit beside her. "My name is Micky," I say in a calm voice. "What's your name?"

She sniffs and wipes her nose on her sleeve. "Eva."

"Hi, Eva." I smile at her. "What's wrong? Why are you sad?"

Eva rubs her eyes. "I was running away from home, but then I didn't want to anymore and now I'm lost and I'm hungry and I don't know how to get home." Fresh tears pour from her eyes and her scrawny little shoulders shake.

The poor little kid.

I stretch my arm across the aisle and root in my purse until I find the box of donuts. I lift it out and offer a donut to Eva. She takes one and whispers, "Thanks."

She takes a bite and then another and another. In about three seconds flat, the donut is gone. I eye the other three. I can always buy Jordan more donuts. I hand her another one and take one for myself.

Mmmm. That is a good donut. Soft on the inside, a crisp glaze on the outside. Delicious.

I finish mine just as Eva finishes her second. I offer her the last one and she takes it. She is no longer crying. Donuts really are miracle cures.

Tanned, Toned and Totally Faking It

How am I going to get the kid home? First I should get her off the bus. Then we phone her parents, if she knows the number, and I can call a taxi to come get us.

I pull the bell to signal that I want off at the next stop, and turn to Eva. "If you come with me, I will help you find your mommy and daddy. Just come off the bus with me, and we'll sit on the bus bench and figure it out. Okay?"

She nods her head and places her sticky hand in my own. I gather my shopping bags and purse in one arm, hold Eva's hand with the other, and as soon as the bus pulls over, we climb off.

"So, do you know what your phone number is?" I open my cell phone, my finger poised over the keys. Eva looks uncertain and begins to cry again.

I sigh. That won't work. I have to find out more about her. "Okay, that's fine. Tell me, Eva, why did you run away from home?"

Eva hangs her head and looks at her scuffed sneakers. "Mommy said that she doesn't have enough money for me and my brothers. So I ran away so Mommy can buy them food."

I am shocked. "Your mother told you that she doesn't have enough money to feed you?" I am outraged at this unknown woman.

Eva shakes her head. "No, she tell my grandma but I hear her on the phone. She think I was sleeping."

That poor mother. "Do you have a daddy?"

Eva shakes her head and keeps her eyes down. "My brothers have a daddy, but he left and they never see him. I don't think I have a daddy."

I call for a taxi. I give the street intersection, and the dispatcher says that a cab will be there in about twenty minutes.

"What we're going to do is go for a ride in a taxi to the police station. Because policemen are good and can help us find your home."

I take in her appearance. We are outside a Gap store and there are a bunch of other retail shops down the street.

I'm going to buy her some new clothes, I decide on a whim.

"Eva, when is your birthday?"

She lights up. "On January third. I'm going to be seven!"

Hmm. She's only six. Apparently I estimated her age wrong. I've always been bad with age, and now that I'm in Hollywood it's even harder. Nobody looks their age. Fifty year old women look as young and tanned and toned as twenty-year-olds.

"Well, guess what? We're going to pretend that today is your birthday and we'll go buy you some clothes and maybe some toys, too. Would you like that?"

She jumps up and starts pulling my hand. "A Barbie? Can I have a Barbie? Mommy said I could have a Barbie last year, but then she said that she couldn't, um, naford it."

Reaching out for her hand, we walk into GAP.

It's surprisingly easy to shop for little girls. I just told the clerk that I need six and seven-year-old girl clothes, and suddenly there are rows and rows of them. And they are cute and I love it! I grab a couple dresses that are adorable and that Eva loves (pink with big bows) and a plaid jumper. I pay for them and then we walk down the street to a toy store. As we enter, the bell on the door tinkles gently.

Eva lets go of my hand and runs to a far aisle that is emitting a faint pinkish glow; clearly the Barbie section. She stands in awe, staring at the shelves of dolls. Pilot Barbie. Teacher Barbie. Mikayla Rivers Barbie. Gymnast Barbie. Barbie who has her hair change color when she gets wet. Dozens of Barbies. A sudden memory of me and Rachelle flashes into my mind. We are sitting in our basement and playing Barbies until four in the morning, whispering and muffling our giggles in our hands so that our parents didn't hear us.

Little girls need dolls.

"Eva, you can pick any four that you want," I say, picking up a baby Barbie. Wow. They didn't have these cool different ones when I was a kid, that's for sure!

Eva looks like she has died and gone to heaven. She is

staring wide-eyed. She might need some help, I think. I reach over and pick up Surfer Barbie. "Do you want this one?" At her wordless nod, I put the doll under my arm.

"How about this one?" I point to Teacher Barbie. She comes with two student Barbies sitting in desks, and a blackboard. Eva nods and I grab it along with a Spanish-looking Barbie with some sparkles in her black hair.

And I choose Graduation Barbie, too, in hopes that it will inspire Eva to stay in school and graduate.

We pay for the dolls and go outside into the sunshine. Just as we head back to the bus bench, a taxi pulls up and I flag it down. We climb in.

"Where to, miss?" the driver asks in accented English.

I hesitate. "Um, do you know if there is a police station, or a hospital around here?"

The cabbie thinks for a second, his brown eyes meeting mine in the rearview mirror. "I think there is a hospital down the street."

"Okay," I say and the taxi drives off.

I reach into the toy bag and pull out Surfer Barbie. "Here, you can hold this. We'll take it out of its wrapping when we get you home, deal?"

Eva nods and sits quietly beside me, holding the doll in both her hands. "I love you, Micky," she says suddenly, looking up at me.

Wow. She actually remembered my name.

The cab pulls up in front of the hospital, and we climb out. I have the two grocery bags, a massive bag from Gap and the Barbie bag. And my purse. I grab Eva's hand and we walk through the hospital doors. The smell hits me first. Medicinal, sterile, that hospital-y smell that you would recognize anywhere. There is a waiting room with a little line up, so we go and get in line.

The waiting room is full of people. One man has a bloody bandage wrapped around his wrist. A lady is holding a screaming toddler with a nasty-looking rash. A girl whose face is decidedly green is leaning against her mother. And a sketchy man is sitting in the corner, glancing around at people and shaking his head over and over. I look away fast before we make eye-contact.

Just then I hear my name. "Mikayla Rivers!" A nurse is standing beside me, holding a clipboard and looking positively thrilled.

She says, "Oh my goodness! I'm a huge fan. I love your music. Especially since my husband left me for his secretary, I've been playing your songs almost non-stop. What are you doing here?"

I step out of line so that the people behind me can move forward, and motion with my head to Eva, still clutching her Surfer Barbie. "I found her on the bus. She's lost. She said she ran away from home yesterday and now she doesn't know how to get back. I gave her some food and bought her some toys and clothes while we were waiting for a cab, and I figured I'd bring her here. I don't know what to do with her."

The nurse's eyes get wide. She bends over and says, "Hi, sweetie. Why don't you come with us and we'll find your mother, okay?"

Eva and I follow the nurse down the hall. "I always knew you were a good girl," the nurse says, "but this confirms it. How many celebrities would stop for a lost kid? Honestly!"

The nurse leads us into a room marked 'Security' and a man wearing an LAPD uniform and sitting at a desk looks up. He is middle aged, has sandy hair and a friendly face. He looks at the nurse questioningly.

"We have a lost little girl," the nurse says, and then turns to me. I explain what happened and how I'm just new in LA and didn't know where a police station was, and a look of pure relief crosses the man's face.

"I was at the station this morning, and Eva's mother was there. Felt real sorry for the woman. She was going out of her mind with worry. She lives in Pico Rivera, which is a rougher part of town, and the woman was terrified that someone had hurt her little girl. Police were searching, but had no leads."

He picks up the phone and dials a number. "Patterson here. A woman just brought that missing girl, Eva Morales, into the hospital. She is not hurt, but the woman is from out of town and didn't know where else to take her."

He listens and says, "Yup. Yup. No, Eva ran away. She said that she ran and got scared and tried to go home but couldn't. The woman found her on the bus and helped her out."

He hangs up and turns to me. "We've got a squad car coming to take Eva to the station. Her mother is waiting there. You can go with her too, Miss –"

"Rivers. Mikayla Rivers," I say quickly.

The policeman's eyebrow raises. "Like the singer?"

I flush and say, "Yeah."

"Wow," the man says, looking at me a second time.

The nurse had left the office and now returns holding a tray with a little pudding and some sandwiches. "Are you hungry, Eva?"

Eva eyes the pudding happily and nods. The nurse gives her the pudding and Eva sits down to eat it.

As she finishes, there is a knock on the door and two policemen enter. One of them says, "Eva, we're going to take you to your mother."

The other one says, "I'm sure Eva's mother would be thrilled to meet the woman who found her daughter. You are more than welcome to come with us if you would like."

I nod and we go out to the waiting squad car. We climb in and they turn on the siren and flashing lights.

Cars move out of our way and we speed through red lights.

"Is it hard being a policeman?" I lean forward slightly. Eva reaches over and takes hold of my hand, as if she's afraid I'm going to disappear.

"Define hard." The cop in the passenger seat turns slightly and looks at me appraisingly. "Long hours, crappy pay, but I do feel like I'm making the world a bit better."

"Have you ever shot anyone?"

Both of them laugh shortly. "That's our most frequently asked question," the driver says, turning a corner, and neatly avoiding the topic. The car is going so fast that Eva squeals in delight as we all sway to the left.

I look over at Eva. "This is kind of a like a rollercoaster, isn't it?"

She giggles. "I never went on a rollercoaster, but I seen them on TV before." She is getting more and more animated.

"Look at all those cars, Eva," I point out the window. "They're moving for you so you can get home to your mommy faster."

Eva's eyes widen. "Whoa." She presses her little face against the window. "It's like I'm in a parade!"

"It's like you're a princess," I say.

It's only a short drive to the police station, no more than five or so minutes. We pull up in front of the building and climb out of the car. A short woman with dark circles under her eyes comes running down the sidewalk and embraces Eva. Eva clings to her and the woman starts whispering to her over and over again in Spanish.

"Mi bebe, mi bebe."

She turns to me and says brokenly, "You woman who find me *bebe?*"

I nod and smile. She hugs me. Her arms are small, like her, but she holds me tight and whispers something into my ear that I cannot understand, followed by the words, *"Gracias, muchas gracias."*

Our little procession goes into a small room with glass walls. The policeman who drove the car asks Eva's mother to fill in a form. They ask Eva to tell them what happened while they fill in another form. I sit there, listening to Eva tell how she left home and got lost, and then I found her and helped her and gave her food and a Barbie.

Tanned, Toned and Totally Faking It

Finally the paperwork is in order and we are free to go. Mrs. Morales gives me another hug and says more things in Spanish. Eva hugs me too and tells me that she loves me. The police shake my hand and then Eva, her mother, and I walk outside together. It is getting a little chilly, and feels like it might rain. Mrs. Morales turns to walk her daughter to the bus stop.

"Wait," I say. "Mrs. Morales, what do you do for a job?"

She looks down and says, "I was waitress, but they fire me for being sick. I have four children. I cannot find other job. My mother help little bit, but she not have a lot."

"Hey, I'd like to help you." I reach into my wallet. "Have you graduated from high school?"

She shakes her head no, eyes downcast.

"Okay, look, I'm going to pay for you to upgrade so you can get your diploma. Then I'll pay for some kind of administrative classes so you can become a secretary or something. Maybe some ESL classes to help you learn English better. I'll pay for it. And as long as you are going to school, I promise that I will give you a few thousand dollars a month. So you can buy food for your babies."

I know Cheryl will be angry, but I don't care. It's my money, not hers. She makes her fifteen percent and gets paid expenses. I can spend the rest of my money on what I want.

And I want to do this.

Mrs. Morales looks uncomprehending. "I don't understand. Why you do this?"

I shrug, not having the words to explain how I feel. "Because I have the money to help you, so I am going to." I reach into my purse and pull out my check book. "What's your name?"

"Maria Morales," she replies, eyes huge as she watches me.

Two thousand dollars should be enough to get her out of this current slump. I write the check and hand it to her.

She takes it with trembling fingers. *"Dios mio,"* she murmurs, staring at it in disbelief.

"If you give me your number, I will phone you next week.

I'll help you find some classes you can take, and hopefully within a few months you'll be able to get a better job, something more stable."

She writes her phone number on the slip of paper I hand her. She hugs me for the third time. "Thank you," she says softly.

I blink back tears.

A cab is driving down the street. I flag it down and tell Maria and Eva to climb in. "You've had a stressful day; you shouldn't have to worry about buses and transfers and all that."

Maria's eyes are shining as she thanks me again. I lean into the front door of the cab while Maria and Eva climb in the back. I hand the driver three fifties and tell him to take them home.

"Sure thing, missy." He winks at me and pockets the cash.

They drive off, Eva and Maria waving from the back window. For the first time in a long time, I feel really good about myself. I am making a difference.

I want to share this with Jordan, but I can't. He'll wonder how I got enough money to do it. And why I was riding the bus on a sunny afternoon instead of being at my supposed job.

I hate not telling him the truth. I promise that I will tell him everything this weekend. Or maybe next week.

Soon.

Ish.

Chapter Seventeen

My days are melding into one. I wake up at ten, exercise, shower, and then eat a lunch of shrubbery. Kurt claims it's a healthy detox salad diet, but it tastes disgusting. I would die of starvation, except that I'm cheating on my diet each night with Jordan.

After lunch I practice with Johnny and Brian, and at four I head over to Jordan's. And I spend the rest of the evening with him. I can't remember the last time I was this happy. When I am away from Jordan, all I can think about is him, and I count down the minutes until I see him again.

I am walking through the neighborhoods around campus. Jordan had a tutorial after his classes, so I still have time to kill.

There is a junior high school across the street. Kids are swarming around in the field, sitting in clumps on the grass, and there are some adults standing along the fence and sitting in lawn chairs. I can hear some tinny music playing faintly. A huge banner hanging on the fence says "Mt. Whitney Middle School Karaoke Fundraiser – Visitors Welcome."

Karaoke, huh? I see a makeshift stage set up with a microphone. It looks like fun!

I cross the street and duck under the rope fence. I sidle up to a woman near me and say, "What are the donations going to?"

She says in a perky voice, "It's for the underprivileged children who attend the school. There are about thirty or so kids who can't afford to go on the eighth grade camping trip, and so we are fundraising to pay their fees."

I reach into my purse and look into my wallet. I have a ten dollar bill.

To my left I see a folding table set up, with a huge box labeled "Donations" in the middle. I put my money in. As I do so, an announcement comes over the reedy microphone. "Next up is Sarah and Jenny, singing *Can't Forget You* by Mikayla Rivers."

There is a smattering of applause as two girls climb onto the stage. They look so sweet and innocent, and for a second I wish I were back at their age. And how cool that they're singing my song. I should say hi or something.

I'm still at the back, and I wonder if there is anything more I could do for the kids. I'll write them a bigger check, I decide. Actually give a decent donation. But what else? What would I have wanted Britney Spears to do if I were singing her karaoke at my junior high?

Suddenly I have an idea. Just as the music starts to play, I step forward and raise my hand. "Hi, hello."

People turn, and their faces brighten as they recognize me. "I know they're starting, but do you think I would be able to sing with them?" I ask the woman standing near the front who appears to be in charge.

She grins broadly. "I can't see that being a problem."

Sarah and Jenny are beaming and jumping up and down. All across the school yard kids are elbowing each other and enthusiasm is spreading.

Tanned, Toned and Totally Faking It

"It's her!"

"Wow, I think that's Mikayla Rivers!"

"That's not Shakira, is it?"

What? Do I look like a sexy Spanish model?

People are moving out of my way and waving and saying my name as I walk to the front. I climb onto the small stage beside the girls.

"Hi everyone, I'm Mikayla Rivers, for those who don't know me, and I hope you don't mind me interrupting. I was just walking by and thought I'd stop in." Kids are pushing their way to the front. I turn to Jenny and Sarah. "You guys ready?" They nod wordlessly.

"Great, let's kick it!"

The crackly music starts again, and I tap along. I step back so the girls are closest to the microphone and jam my hands into my pockets. I feel awkward without my guitar. I've never performed without it. But the kids in the audience are pumped and the two girls are glowing.

I sing along, the girls and their high-pitched voices trying to keep up to the music. Everyone is applauding and cheering.

We finish and everyone stands up and claps.

"That was so cool!" Jenny squeaks, her voice nervous as she smiles shyly at me.

Sarah bobs her head vigorously beside her, her hands jammed deep into her jean pockets. "You're our hero. That was the coolest thing, like ever!"

I give them each a hug. "You both were pretty awesome too," I say. "Thank you for letting me sing with you."

The girls and I step down. The woman in charge grabs my arm. "Miss Rivers, would you mind staying for a minute and doing a song for us? I know the kids would love it."

"I would actually like that," I say.

The woman speaks into the microphone. "If we can keep everyone's attention, Mikayla has agreed to sing a song for us."

Back on stage, I say, "I'm going to sing my newest song, not released yet. It's called *Hate. Love.* I hope you like it."

I tap my feet to find the rhythm and start singing. Nobody is singing along, since they don't know the words, but when I finish, I get a standing ovation.

"Um, everyone? I just want to let you know that I will match whatever donations you earn today. You guys deserve an awesome camping trip. Thanks for letting me stop in!"

People are cheering and clapping and hollering. The woman takes the microphone back from me. "You mean it? You'll match the donations?"

"Sure, how much do you think you have?"

"Probably a few hundred dollars."

"Look, I'm going to give you a thousand dollars, okay? And just make sure the kids have fun at this camping thing. Nobody should be left out because of money."

The woman announces, "Everyone, can we give Mikayla a huge round of applause to thank her?"

I thank them and wave goodbye, heading toward the fence. Kids mob me, so I stop and give hugs and write my name on a plethora of school binders and notebooks and the occasional textbook. I pose for cell phone pictures. When I finally get free and the kids are back under control of their teachers, I duck back under the fence.

That was fun. I feel like leaping and dancing.

I look at my watch. Almost five. I'm enjoying walking and who cares if I'm a little late. It's only about another half an hour to campus.

By the time I arrive at Jordan's door, I am sweating and my legs burn. California is so darn hilly.

I knock on Jordan's apartment door. He opens it, reaches to hug me and then pulls back. "Wow, Micky, you're awfully, uh, wet," he says.

I lunge for him. "Come on, hug me!" He dodges out of my way. "Come on, a little Micky-sweat won't kill you!"

I chase him into the living room and tackle him. We sprawl

onto the floor and I secure my arms around him tight. Yum, he smells good. All spicy and masculine. He shifts under my weight and wraps his arms around me, giving me a huge hug.

"Hi," I whisper. We lie there for a moment, enjoying each other's company. Man, I love this boy.

"Can we get up?" Jordan asks after a second. "I think I have a textbook digging into my spine."

I roll off him. "You wouldn't have that problem if you stopped leaving your books everywhere," I say in mock rebuke.

He sits up and pastes a semi-chagrined look on his face. "Yes, mother," he says. I swat him, and we get up. "So you want some dinner?" Jordan asks me.

"Sure." Papers and textbooks are everywhere. He clearly was in the process of studying. "You know what?" I motion to the area in front of his couch. "You're studying, so why don't I make us something and you can keep going?"

"Really?" Jordan looks surprised. "You wouldn't mind?"

"Course not! It's the least I can do."

"You know how to cook, right? This won't end with us eating cereal on the floor?"

He's mocking me. I'll show him! "Don't look so doubtful, mister. I can cook. I'm not completely handicapped, you know!"

"We'll see." Jordan kisses my forehead and returns to his books.

I head into the kitchen and open cupboards. There's got to be something in here I can make. Besides, I used to cook when I was in college. I'm a good cook.

Chapter Eighteen

I absolutely cannot cook.

It had started off well. I found some spaghetti noodles in the pantry. And some sauce. I figured that I could make pasta. So I boiled water and put in the spaghetti.

But the water boiled over and spilled everywhere. I tried to mop up the puddles without Jordan hearing, but then the stupid spaghetti burned. I added more water and thought that would take care of the problem. The sauce was spattering all over, so I turned it down. And while I fiddled over the sauce, the spaghetti turned into a disgusting, burnt, glutinous mass.

I stare at the lump of carbohydrates and poke at it gently with a steak knife. Okay. Don't freak out. Only it may not be fit for human consumption.

"Everything going okay?" Jordan calls from the other room. "You're awfully quiet."

"Uh, yeah, yeah, definitely, sure, it's great, I mean, yeah, I'm good," I stammer.

Please don't let him come in here, I pray to whatever deity

Tanned, Toned and Totally Faking It

is listening. Please let him go back to studying so I can air out the kitchen and throw all this crap out and then make a fantastic meal.

"Well, if you need me, I'm right here." He sounds amused.

I'll show him, I vow. I can make a meal. People cook all the time. My mom, for example, used to make dinner every single night. Steak, and potatoes, and roasted chickens, and pasta, and all sorts of food. And I can't remember a single time when she burnt it. Or when it didn't taste absolutely incredible. Even my dad used to cook amazing shrimp and pasta dishes, carefully using a knife to slice up the fresh garlic, and everything was delicious in the end.

Come on, genes, don't let me down. It's hereditary. My mom and dad can cook, so clearly it's in me.

I take the spaghetti and put it into the garbage. It falls in with a thwack. Yuck. I am so glad we didn't try to eat that. I wash the pot and dump the splattered sauce down the sink.

Okay. Refresh. Start over. There has to be something else in the cupboards. I peer into them. Cereal (yummy Lucky Charms, my favorite!) Bread. Peanut butter. A can of chili. Ramen noodles. More spaghetti, but I'm not going to go there again. I sigh. It's the pantry of a student. Which is not surprising given then Jordan is a student, but not what I want since I desperately want to cook a masterpiece.

I will not go out and admit defeat. I refuse.

I open the cupboard door again, hoping that by some miracle something awesome has just appeared.

Nothing.

Maybe I could order in. And then pretend I made it. As long as I don't actually *say* that I made it, it won't count as a lie. Jordan will just assume I did, and I won't bother to correct him. But I don't know what places nearby have a home-cooked feel to their food. I don't want to ask Jordan where his phone book is, because he'll want to know why. And there is the little problem of how they will deliver it. Since Jordan is right there, in the front room; unless I can somehow get him to leave the front room.

I bite my lip and try to think of something. Then I have a brainwave.

I punch in the number and wait. "Hello?" Kurt sounds breathless, like he had to run for the phone.

"Kurt, love, it's me. Um, look, I'm in a bit of a pinch and I need your help."

Without hesitation he says, "Sure, what's up?"

I love Kurt. I quickly fill him in.

"Sure, I can order something for you, darling. I take it you want some pasta?"

"Yeah, that's good, especially if Jordan smelled the pasta sauce cooking. I don't want him to get suspicious."

Kurt says that he'll be here in twenty minutes. He promises to phone two minutes before he knocks on the door so that I can get the rest of my plan into action.

See, it's a genius plan. I'm going to clog his toilet. And while he unclogs it, I'll go to the door and Kurt will hand me the food and I'll whisk it into the kitchen before Jordan comes out. Because as embarrassing as clogging a toilet in front of my boyfriend is, my pride will not allow me to confess that my cooking skills are non-existent.

I wait in the kitchen for fifteen minutes before going to the living room. "So dinner will be ready in a couple minutes," I say casually. "I'll use the bathroom and then we can eat."

In the bathroom I am bunching up toilet paper and tossing it into the toilet. When the basin is full, I flush.

Brutal. It went down, smoothly and easily.

What do I do? I can't flush again… Jordan will hear me flushing repeatedly.

Well, I guess I can flush again. It'll be my way of trying to fix the toilet, if he asks. I crumple the toilet paper and stuff it in. I search his cupboards. Where's a good tampon when you need one? He's got nothing. Unless you count this manky old user's manual for an electric razor that I find in the back corner under the sink. It's all shabby and dusty. I look at it thoughtfully. I doubt Jordan would ever miss it. In fact, I doubt it even belongs to Jordan. It has probably been in here for years.

I rip it up and stuff it into the toilet. Then, as a finishing touch, I pull the cardboard from inside the toilet paper roll and throw it in too. I cross my fingers and flush.

For a second it looks like I might have won. Water builds up and I let out an exuberant laugh. But then, right before my eyes, the toilet paper goes down. And so does the shaving manual. And the cardboard tube. All of it. Gone.

Stupid toilet. How come when I don't want to plug a toilet, it'll get clogged and stinky at the drop of the hat; and yet when I need to clog one up, it won't. Stupid clog-free toilet.

There is a knock on the door. "Micky, you okay?" Jordan sounds concerned. "Is the toilet clogged again? It overflows at least three times a week."

What? It is a highly-cloggable toilet and yet I can't get it to clog? Pathetic.

"Uh, yeah, I'm good," I call back, staring desperately into the toilet. It gurgles triumphantly, as if mocking me. I hear a faint knock from the main room. Someone is knocking on the front door.

Is it Kurt? But he was supposed to call first! He can't just knock on the door!

I bolt out of the bathroom and see Jordan opening the door. Kurt is standing there, holding two trays of pasta that smell amazing.

Jordan seems confused. "Yes?"

Kurt looks surprised. He wasn't expecting Jordan to open the door, but he plays it off well.

"Delivery for Rivers."

Jordan glances over his shoulder. "Micky, you order something? I thought we were having your fabulous cooking tonight?"

143

I want to kick him. I step forward and take the pasta. "Um, thank you," I say.

Kurt winks at me. "And your total is thirty-five dollars."

"Just put it on my tab." I could kill Kurt. This isn't going at all the way I envisioned.

Kurt nods.

"Thank you." I close the door and see Jordan smirking at me.

"Home cooking?" He attempts to give me a hug.

I pull away and walk into the kitchen with my head held high, refusing to grace him with a reply. Jordan follows me and wrinkles his nose at the smell. Curses. The kitchen still reeks of smoke. Who'd have thought that burnt spaghetti could be so rank?

I feel like crying. Stupid spaghetti. Stupid toilet that wouldn't clog. Stupid Kurt for not following the plan.

Jordan sees the expression on my face and touches my arm. "Micky, don't worry about it. I was just teasing you. You are such a perfect girl, it's a good thing you can't cook. You make me feel inadequate just being around you. I'm secretly glad to find something you're not good at."

I blink back tears. "Really?" I sniff.

He hugs me. "Sweetie, I love you. I don't care if you can cook or not. You've been freaking out in here, haven't you?"

I wipe my eyes. "Yeah. Kind of. I *thought* I could cook. I mean, I used to cook stuff all the time in college."

"Like what?" Jordan asks.

"Like hot chocolate. And microwave ramen," I say, flushing. I hesitate for a second. "Okay. So I have never cooked before in my life. I was on the meal plan, actually, the one where you pay for points on your ID card that lets you eat anywhere on campus. And my mom was such a good cook I never bothered to learn when I was at home."

"You may not cook, but you can order delicious food. That pasta smells amazing. What do you say? Can we eat?"

I look up and meet Jordan's eyes. They're dancing with amusement, but there is something else in there too.

"Sure, we can eat." Then something he said registers. "Wait. A minute ago, you, you said you loved me." He had. He had said it. My heart is pounding as I stare at him. Did he mean it?

Jordan smiles that crinkly smile I love and lowers his eyes a bit. Then he looks up at me and says, "Yup, I guess I did. I meant it, Micky. I love you."

I stare at him. He sounds legit.

He laughs at my expression. "Don't look so bowled over," he says blithely, reaching out and tucking a strand of flyaway hair behind my ear. "I didn't mean to freak you out by telling you that."

I shake my head. I want him to see what this means to me. "I love you too, Jordan. I honestly do."

He says simply, "Good." He kisses me gently on the lips, his mouth soft. My heart is racing and I kiss him back, feeling a warmth spread throughout my body.

He kisses me deeper and his hands wrap tightly around my back. I reach my arms up around his neck and then suddenly he's kissing my neck and we're all wrapped up in each other. And then –

Well, let me just say that… never mind. It's just perfect. That's all.

When we get up from the couch, our food is cold, but we don't care. We load up plates, eat and talk and laugh. Things are normal and fun. After we eat, we head back out to the living room. We stretch out on the couch, and Jordan flicks on the TV. *Two and a Half Men* is on, and we hunker down, curled up next to each other.

Jordan kisses the top of my head. "I've never told a girl that I love her before, by the way. I want you to know how special you are to me."

I don't think life could get any better.

Chapter Nineteen

I stare at Kurt in shock. He's wearing yellow spandex and a bright pink latex-looking top and red high-top shoes. But it's not his outfit that has me gaping.

"Five hundred sit-ups? Right now? Like all together? Without even like, stopping and watching TV?"

Are five hundred sit-ups in a row physically possible? Kurt never makes me do sit-ups. We do other ab workouts, like Pilates and stuff, but not straight sit-ups!

"Look, Micky, I didn't want to say anything, but I have noticed that you've put on a couple pounds in your waist. So we're going to up the workouts. We can't have you looking chubby."

Crap. He's noticed! I thought I hid it well. My clothes still fit. Sure, I have to lie on the bed to get my skinny jeans all the way up, but once they're on, they look fab.

"Am I fat?" I ask pitifully. Fat. Probably the worst word in the human language. Or at least the worst word in Hollywood.

Kurt hits me lightly on the arm. "You're not fat, Micky. You just need to do some butt-shaping exercises and tighten up your abs."

Cursed third helping of Chinese food last week. Stupid pasta last night.

Kurt grabs my hand and drags me into the center of the suite. "Now, we can either do them here, or we can go to the gym. Which do you prefer?"

If we're here, I can moan and complain. If we're in public, I'll have to smile and pretend like sit-ups are my favorite thing in the world. "Definitely here."

"Good." Kurt motions to the floor. "Lie down and put your legs up. We're going to begin with five hundred crunches. Bring your elbows all the way to your knees. Alternate."

I begin with one. Ouch. Oh the pain. I haven't done sit-ups since junior high gym class.

I grimace and look at Kurt. "We do count in increments of ten, right?"

Kurt mock glares at me. "No. We go up by one."

"Compromise with increments of five?" I ask hopefully.

"Not a chance." He effectively crushes my hopes and dreams.

Okay. I am going to die. There is no way I can do four hundred and ninety nine more sit-ups. Maybe if it was over the next, say, month or two. Then it might be a possibility.

But today? Right now?

I wonder if Kurt would believe me if I faked a heart attack. I sneak a glance at him. He is looking down at me sternly.

"You've only done one," he says.

I pull myself up and let my elbows touch my knees.

How can I have such weakling little abdominal muscles? Kurt and I do Pilates all the time!

I grunt and try for the third.

"I. Hate. You. Kurt." I struggle for air.

I pull myself up for sit-up number four. I hate gravity. This would be so much easier if I were in space, or on the moon.

Sit-up number five.

I can't do this. I literally cannot do this.

But I can't admit defeat. I am not a quitter.

I stare at the roof and try to muster up the strength for sit-up number six.

I need someone to interrupt us. That way I am not quitting because I am a wimpy weakling. I am quitting because someone needs me.

Alright, God. I say in my head, staring up at the ceiling and hoping that there is actually a deity of some kind staring back at me. Please make something interrupt this workout session. I can't do five hundred sit-ups. I just can't. So if you could make some kind of emergency, then I would appreciate it. Thank you very much.

I wait.

Nothing.

I heft myself into sit-up number six and use the momentum to propel myself into sit-up number seven.

My shoulder pops as I come back down.

Wow. For someone who exercises daily, I sure am out of shape.

My stomach muscles are quivering, and I don't know if I can continue.

Come on, God. Just a little earthquake. Or a fire downstairs in the café that makes the entire hotel evacuate. Not anything too major. I'm not asking for a lot.

Nothing.

Kurt is standing there, looking down on me. "I can wait all day, Micky." He would too.

I go for another sit-up. Number eight.

I am sweating and for some reason my neck hurts.

This has got to be the worst idea Kurt has ever had. Ever.

Just then there is a knock on the door. Kurt gives me a stern look. "You keep going. I'll see who it is."

I strain myself and using all the strength I have in me, I pull myself into sit-up nine. I can't believe I haven't gotten to ten yet. This is so pathetic.

I have to finish. I'm supposed to meet Jordan tonight. We're going swimming at the college pool. And then ordering pizza.

Yum.

I wipe away the drool that has appeared on my lips at the thought of pizza and heave myself into sit-up number ten.

Kurt is talking to the person at the door. They are laughing now.

Great. Here I am, miserable, and hearing the sound of Kurt laughing makes me grumpy on top of it. Why should I be suffering through these sit-ups while Kurt is free and roaming around my suite, talking to people and having fun?

I am insanely bitter.

As I pull myself into sit-up number eleven, I make out a couple of words from their conversation.

Anonymous stranger: "-yan Seacrest's radio show."

Kurt: "Yeah, I'm sure she'd love to, but I'll have to ask her. Is the interview right now?"

Anonymous stranger (now becoming my hero): "In about twenty minutes. Ryan's originally planned interview with Prince William was cancelled at the last second due to a ribbon cutting ceremony in London, and since Ryan's had so many requests for Mikayla, he figured he'd give it a shot. He couldn't find her number, but someone told him that she's at this hotel. And that's how I ended up here."

He sounds like the nerdy type, the kind who just keeps talking. I like him. This anonymous stranger slash Ryan Seacrest's minion is now my favorite person on the planet.

I roll over onto my stomach and stand up. My middle section hurts. Who says that you have to do a million sit-ups in order to be fit? I'm probably more toned now than if I had done five hundred. It's about quality, not quantity.

Kurt looks over his shoulder. "Micky, honey, this man here is from Ryan Seacrest's radio show. They were wondering if you could do a five minute interview with Ryan today. It'll be in about twenty minutes, but you can just call in from here."

I love the radio. This means I won't have to look glamorous or smile fakely when I really want to barf.

I look ceiling-ward and mouth a quick thank you to God. He got me out of sit-ups.

Incredible.

"Definitely. I definitely could do that."

The anonymous minion is grateful. He whips out a cell phone and punches in a number and says in that same nervous manner, "Yes, Mikayla Rivers has agreed to do the show. She'll call in about fifteen minutes so you can connect with her and make sure the speaker volume is okay and all that jazz. Yup. Yup. 'Kay. Bye." He hangs up. "Thank you so much, Miss Rivers. And just for the record, I am your hugest fan. For real."

I grin awkwardly, feeling uncomfortable that my hugest fan has seen me in an exercise bra and tight pants and nothing more except a sheen of sweat covering my aching body.

Kurt gets me a glass of water. I drink it and sit down.

Kurt and the guy are talking about the fashion mistakes and triumphs of Lady Gaga. I hear the words "meat dress," "beef jerky," and "bubble wrap." The guy keeps looking at his watch and finally he nods. He rattles off a phone number that I dial on my cell.

A woman answers. "KIIS FM. Thank you, Mikayla, for calling in."

Wow. I wonder how she knew it was me. "Hi," I say awkwardly.

"You're on in three minutes. Remember just a couple things: This is radio, so make sure that you talk. No awkward pauses. And have fun and be yourself. Any questions?"

"Uh, no, I don't think so."

"Great. I'll put you on hold and then you'll be counted in and then Ryan will begin the interview. Thank you very much."

Click.

Tanned, Toned and Totally Faking It

I hear the Black-Eyed Peas newest song begin to play. Nice hold music. So much better than when I have to call the bank and am put on hold for hours and all they have playing is a lone flute, slightly off-key.

A voice says, "Five, four, three, two, one."

And I hear the most familiar voice. My heart races. Anyone who's watched American Idol faithfully their entire life (like me) would recognize this voice.

"Mikayla Rivers' CD has gone platinum five times. She's the newest, hottest thing in Hollywood and we have her with us today. Welcome, Mikayla Rivers, calling in live on KIIS FM. This is Ryan Seacrest. How are you doing today?"

"Wow, Ryan Seacrest! I'm a huge fan!"

Ryan laughs and replies, "Well, I think I should say that I'm your biggest fan, not the other way 'round. We play your music all the time and I must say that there is something about your songs that just relates with people. A lot of people love your music. So tell us, what music do *you* love? Where do you get your inspiration?"

I lick my lips and say quickly (no dead air!), "I love music of every kind. One of my friends loves oldies and jazz, so I've started liking that kind of music lately. And then of course I grew up in the Spice Girls and Britney Spears and Christina Aguilera era and so I love that poppy, girl music. I love it all."

"So you would say that they are the inspiration for your current hits?"

"Well, not exactly. I mean, I write all my own music, and so of course some of it kind of stems from what I hear and what I grew up with. Those are huge influences in my life, so I'm sure they do inspire some of the things that go into my music." I don't know if that sentence even made sense. I must sound totally illiterate.

"But you're not trying to be Britney Spears?" Ryan says.

"No. No, I will never dance with a snake, if that's what you're wondering."

151

It's easy to talk to Ryan. And since it's just me and the phone, I don't feel nervous. I think I could really get into the whole radio thing.

We talk for a few more minutes and then Ryan says, "Well, Mikayla, thank you so much for joining me today. Your new CD is out in a few months and so hopefully we can get you back in the studio before it hits the stores. It's been a pleasure. Now let's hear the original breakout song of Mikayla Rivers – *Break Up*."

There is the tinny sound of music as it comes through the phone. Ryan says to me, "Thanks again, Mikayla. I'll have to get you back for another show in the next month or two. See you."

I say goodbye and hang up. That was awesome!

Kurt gives me a hug and points to the headphones around his neck. "I heard the whole thing. You were great!"

The anonymous angel of mercy shakes my hand and leaves.

"Kurt, that was so fun!" I say, jumping around the room.

Kurt jumps around with me for a minute and then stops abruptly. "You almost had me distracted there, Micky. I believe you have four hundred and eighty nine sit-ups left to go."

My eyes widen in horror. That wasn't the deal I made with God! It wasn't a momentary reprieve. It was supposed to be a forever kind of thing!

Kurt points to the floor like a drill instructor from the movies.

"Let's go, girl." He chuckles. It's an evil, Cruella DeVille laugh.

I groan and ease myself down onto the carpet.

Stupid Kurt.

Chapter Twenty

A few hours later my body is in excruciating pain, and I am hobbling toward the elevator on my way to see Jordan.

I'm sure that abs of steel are worth it for some people. Just not for me.

I knew a girl once, in college, who had an eight-pack. Everyone called her Eight-Pack Girl. She showed it off a lot. She'd lift up her shirt and kind of flash her abdominals around. Boys loved it. Girls hated it, but guys definitely liked it.

It's not worth it. Eight-Pack Girl must have had a really crappy lifestyle, doing sit-ups morning and night.

I somehow managed to do all five hundred. The last few Kurt had to pull me into the sitting position, but I'm sure that my muscles got the benefit of it. Plus it gave Kurt a workout, so it was a mutually beneficial endeavor. Shortly after, I had a hot bath and then Kurt and I got ready for our respective evenings, doing each other's hair and makeup. In a fit of generosity, I even let him borrow my Calvin Klein blazer in case it gets chilly when he's out with his friends tonight.

I leave the hotel, and the doorman hails a cab. As the cab pulls away into traffic, I lean back and focus on what has been quietly nagging on my mind all day. How am I supposed to meet Jordan's mother today without having my entire cover blown?

It's a good sign that Jordan wants us to meet, of course. It shows he wants our relationship to progress and move forward and… and I'm a little panicked about it. Don't get me wrong. If I was just me, I would love to meet her. But me being, well, *me*, I *can't* do it. She most likely follows the Hollywood scene and knows who's who. She might shriek or faint or something when I walk in with her son.

Not to sound arrogant. I mean, I'm not like Jennifer Aniston or Johnny Depp. She may not know me. But the odds of that are slim.

I have to get out of this.

I don't want to lie to Jordan again. And even if I did lie, it would have to be a massive one to get out of this.

I should have stayed home and told Jordan I was sick. But then, knowing him, he'd want to come over and make me soup. And then as soon as I was better, he'd reschedule our meeting.

This is such a mess.

The cab pulls up to campus, and I climb out. My cut off jeans and baggy sweater blend in pretty well. I hurry to the apartment building and go upstairs to Jordan's door. I knock and he instantly opens the door.

He gives me a big, warm hug. "Hey Micky!" I lean into him and feel his heart beating in his chest. He smells so good.

I smile up at him. "Hey you."

He leans down and his lips brush mine. "So I have good news and bad news."

I raise my eyebrow. "Okay, let's hear the bad news first. Get it over with."

Jordan steps back and motions for me to come in. "My mom's car broke down so she can't come over tonight."

I feel guilty at how instantly joyful I've become. I am a bad person, rejoicing in other's misfortunes.

"That's too bad. Hope her car is okay." I try to sound convincing and struggle to keep my mouth from bursting into a huge smile. "So what's the good news?"

"The good news is that to make up for it, because I know you wanted to meet her, she said we can chat on Skype. Cool, huh?"

I pause for a moment to process it. Skype? I wonder if I can distort myself enough so that she can't recognize me.

Or I wonder if Olga can return for one night. I look contemplatively at Jordan. I am about to ask him when I realize it's futile. He's not going to let me assume a foreign identity in order to deceive his mother.

"Sure." I say, feigning a smile. "Yeah, we can do that. Sounds great."

Crap.

I tell Jordan that I need just a minute and I rush into the bathroom. I look in the mirror. Alright. What can I do with limited resources to make myself look like I'm not me?

I don't have a hat. But maybe I can re-comb my hair across my face a bit more. Like that. I fumble with the brush for a minute and step back, surveying the results.

Not too bad. It's kind of like bangs, sweeping across half my face. And since I can only see half of me, maybe she won't recognize me. I take another calming breath and walk back into the living room.

Jordan is on his laptop. He looks up. "You look beautiful." He reaches out an arm. I walk over to him and he gives me a side hug. "So I'm connecting with my mom right now. And I already called for the pizza. I figured that would be okay with you."

He knows me so well.

I smile. Pizza. Love pizza. Love Jordan for being the provider of pizza.

I make a mental note to only eat two pizza slices so that I won't have to do another killer ab workout ever again, and then I hear a voice coming from the computer. Jordan grins at the laptop and says, "Hi Mom!" I strain my neck so I can see around Jordan's shoulders. The woman on the screen has bleached blonde hair, frizzy from being colored too many times. She is deeply tanned and has profound wrinkles across her face. She looks like she was once beautiful. She's sitting on a faded, orange couch that looks like it belongs in *That 70's Show*.

"Hi Jordan." Her voice is raspy. A smoker's voice. Deep and throaty and thick.

"How's your car?" He asks in concern and I feel my heart well up.

"It's probably out of gas again, now that I think about it."

Jordan frowns at her. "Are you drinking?" His voice is sharp.

I think about my angel mother. I don't think she's ever had a drink in her life. She is good and pure and sweet and beautiful, inside and out.

"I'm not drinking right now." Her words are slurred.

Jordan is still frowning. He glances over at me, and his eyes show embarrassment.

"It's okay," I mouth. "It's okay."

He looks like he's in pain and turns back to the screen. "Mom? I'm glad your car isn't broken down. But remember to fill it up with gas next time. Deal?" His voice is patient, like he's a parent dealing with a difficult child.

She makes a noncommittal sound.

Jordan sighs. The sound penetrates my heart. My poor boy! He says, "Mom, I have someone I want you to meet, remember? My girlfriend, Micky."

He beckons for me to come over, into the view of the screen. I walk over, biting my lip. Even though she's drunk, she may still recognize me, so I keep my head slightly tilted away from the screen. I smile and give a half wave, feeling a little stupid.

"You are as beautiful as Jordan described you. Just beautiful." Mrs. Baker blinks at me.

Tanned, Toned and Totally Faking It

I breathe out. Can it be that she doesn't recognize me?

We talk for a minute more. She makes a few comments and asks a couple questions, but Jordan carries the conversation. He talks about me, about how I'm from Canada. He tells her about my interests and what I took in school. He makes me sound like I'm the most incredible, interesting person in the world. He talks briefly about law school. I rub his back gently with my right hand. His mother is fidgeting and looks bored, playing with her brittle hair and coughing loudly.

Finally, Jordan starts to wrap it up. As we are saying goodbye, Mrs. Baker says, "You look like that singer. You know that singer. That Mikayla singer. She's famous."

I look at Jordan in panic, my hair whipping my shoulders. I half expect him to jump up and say, "You're right! It's her! I've seen her on a magazine." But of course he doesn't. Instead he says lightly, "Mom, you think every pretty girl is famous."

Mrs. Baker nods her head once and says it was good to meet me. Jordan tells his mom that he loves her and that she should take care of herself.

And it's over.

I survived the whole meet the parent thing. And my respect for Jordan has skyrocketed. I reach out and put my hand on his shoulder. "Are you alright?" I ask him.

He looks down at his hands. "Yeah. It's just a bit of a downer to see her when she's been drinking. I should have known that her car was okay. She often forgets things like gas and stuff like that. She'll go a month without buying groceries and end up with nothing but sour milk and expired yogurt. And yet she always remembers her booze."

He sighs and turns to me with a hurt expression in his eyes. I can just picture that little ten year old– fatherless, alone, coming to LA with his mom and ending up homeless.

I pull him into my arms and stroke his head. "You're an amazing person, Jordan. I really mean it."

He hugs me back, clinging to me. "Thanks, Micky," he says

157

heavily. He pulls back and looks into my eyes. "You mean the world to me. I hope you know that."

I do, actually. I can tell every time he looks at me.

We stay like that for a few seconds, and then there is a knock on the door. Jordan gets up. "Pizza."

I watch him walk across the room and wonder how many people would still make so much of their lives after growing up in his situation. I can't help but feel like I am the luckiest girl in the world to be with a man like that.

Chapter Twenty One

I get to meet Ellen DeGeneres today!

I am bouncing around my hotel room, while Cheryl tries to give me instructions. "Now, Mikayla, no 'yes' or 'no' answers. Be talkative. Be candid. Ellen doesn't interview just anyone, you know. You need to take advantage of this. Be sweet, be funny, and don't you dare be quiet!"

"I know, Cheryl!" I try on a pair of pink high heels and look at my outfit in the mirror. "I like being interviewed. I'm not stupid; I know how to run my own life, thank you!"

Okay, so I forgot about this interview, although I will never admit this to Cheryl. Things have been going so well with Jordan that I haven't thought about much else. I went with him to one of his law lectures on Monday afternoon. I wore thick, eighties-style glasses (without prescription) and a brown wig that I told Jordan was just for fun.

We've been so busy having fun that I've had a hard time focusing on my music; nor have I had the chance to tell Jordan about my celebrity status.

But it's bound to come into conversation sometime. We'll be having a romantic candlelight dinner and Jordan will look at me and say, "So, Mikayla, tell me. Do you have any secrets you've been scared to tell me?"

I will smile in a self-assured way and say, "As a matter of fact, I do." I will tell him that I'm famous, and he'll be so blown away and impressed that he'll kneel down and propose to me on the spot.

So maybe he won't propose yet, since we've only known each other for a few weeks. But theoretically, if he did, I wouldn't exactly say no.

I'll tell him. I just need to find the opportune moment.

Now is not the time to think about telling Jordan the truth. I need to focus on Ellen. I am so stoked about being on her show!

Cheryl burst into my room this morning, demanding to see what outfit I was going to wear, and I asked her "For what?" She freaked out and reminded me that I was interviewing with Ellen today and could I stop being such a moron and—

Anyway. Not important. What is important is that I am going to be on her show.

I can't calm myself down. We head over to the studio in the limo that Cheryl arranged.

Cheryl monologues to me the whole way, which effectively kills my enthusiasm. She's a genius when it comes to destroying happiness and joy. I try to block her out, but the words come through, no matter how hard I try to not listen.

"Told Reese Witherspoon that I can't help being beautiful, it just comes naturally—"

"Had to turn down Brad Pitt, but I didn't feel like hurting Angelina's feelings—"

"Probably going to create my own CD. I hope you won't mind when I stop being your manager to launch my own successful—"

Is she that delusional? I'm positive that Brad doesn't even know who Cheryl is. I doubt he knows who I am! And as for the music career? If she wants to stop being my manager, I won't be upset about it.

Just when I think that I cannot take one more word from Cheryl, the limo pulls up in front of a building and the driver says, "Here you are, ladies."

We get out and I am mobbed by people squealing my name. Cameras flash. Cheryl elbows me in the ribs and mutters, "Smile."

I'm pretty sure I was smiling already. But just to appease my Nazi manager, I paste an even bigger, toothier smile on my face and wave as we walk into the building. I sign a couple of autographs that are shoved in my face, and by the time we get inside I think I am about to go blind. I look around for Cheryl and see her posing and waving at the crowd in the doorway.

Could she be any more embarrassing?

Finally Cheryl comes inside and a lady approaches us. She welcomes us to the show, leads us to our dressing room and tells us that we have about an hour. She says that Ellen will come see me shortly and that I can refresh myself in the bathroom if I need to.

Cheryl sits down in front of the mirror and starts primping herself. I have to get away from her, or else I might get violent. I walk into the bathroom. I'll breathe in there and splash some water onto my face and try to calm myself down. Stupid nerves, acting up all the time.

Suddenly, something big and fast lunges at me from behind the door. I shriek and cower in fear, pulling my hands up to shield my face.

This is it. I'm going to die. A crazed fan somehow got in here and is going to kill me.

I hear laughter. Laughter? I peek around my hands and see Ellen DeGeneres standing in front of me. She gives me a big hug. "I'm sorry, Mikayla! I couldn't help myself."

I feel so stupid. I should have been expecting this. I've watched the show enough to know that Ellen tries to freak people out by jumping out at them or having huge stuffed creatures sneak up behind them.

I laugh nervously. "Wow, hi, sorry, I was just, uh, not, well, hi!" I cannot make a coherent sentence.

Ellen seems to understand. "Don't worry about it. Now, when you come out for your interview, walk right across the stage and sit on the couch across from me. I'll talk to you. You can look at the camera and the audience. Don't get nervous about it. And we'll chat. I'll ask you questions. You answer them. It'll be about ten minutes total, and then you will perform *Drowning* and that's it. How does that sound?"

I nod. I only hear a little bit of what she's saying, but I get the gist of it. It'll be okay. And she's so nice! She's as kind in real life as she is on TV. She pats my shoulder and says she'll see me later.

She leaves, still chuckling about freaking me out.

I sit down in the dressing room to calm my panicked heart. I pick up a magazine from the coffee table and flip through it. Taylor Swift found a new love. The *Twilight* actors are confirmed to be dating. Jennifer Aniston found a new man; will he be The One? Mikayla Rivers is still single, despite some of the most eligible bachelors throwing themselves at her. If only they knew. Having a secret love with Jordan makes me feel special.

There is a knock on the door. "Ready, Mikayla?"

I follow the guide down the hall and stand in the wings. I hear applause and laughter. Ellen says, "And now, please welcome Mikayla Rivers!"

I take a quick breath and walk out onto the stage. It's gorgeous and huge and everything is a deep mahogany. I can't see the audience for the shining lights, but I hear them screaming and clapping. I wave and smile and look around in panic for Ellen.

Where's the couch? I see it. I walk over and Ellen is standing there. She gives me another big hug and turns me around to wave again at the audience. I feel more natural now. Ellen makes

Tanned, Toned and Totally Faking It

me feel like everything is normal and nice and that I'm not standing in front of millions of viewers. The intense butterflies in my stomach calm down a bit.

The applause dies down and we sit. Giving me that familiar grin, Ellen says, "Mikayla Rivers is fairly new on the Hollywood scene. Seven months ago she was a college student, now she's got Grammy nominations. Her first CD, *Break Up,* has sold millions, and her latest single, *Ransom,* has been on the top 100 for the past six weeks. Plus, she's just accepted a role in a new Peter Jackson film, and we're so happy to have her with us today!"

Everyone claps and Ellen turns to me. "So Mikayla, tell us. You have a new CD coming out and a tour scheduled." She says it flatly, not like a question, but in a way that a response is required.

I nod, brushing a stray piece of hair out of my eyes. "Yeah, I'm in the process of recording the last few tracks for my new album. And I start a new tour in about two months, I think. We're going all across Canada and the US and so it should be a lot of fun."

People clap and Ellen nods. "And you also have been nominated for some Grammy awards."

My cheeks hurt from smiling. "Yes, three of them. I can hardly believe it!"

"Well, I think you're remarkable. You're also one of the sweetest girls I've met," Ellen says.

That's really nice of her to say. I have nothing to say in response. I feel ridiculous.

"So, Mikayla, we are very happy for you. Now, tell us about you before you got famous. This happened very quickly for you. Are you the same person you used to be? Who *did* you used to be?"

I feel myself flush. How do I explain this? How do I describe me? Everything is so different.

Think, Micky, think. You have to say something!

"Well, I used to be a normal college student, you know, studying, skipping class whenever I felt I could get away with it, checking out the hot guys and going to campus football games. I ran a lot, I was big into running. I went to the track three times a week. Just normal."

I hope that was a good enough answer. I already forgot what the original question was. I hope that answered it, or else I'm going to feel quite stupid.

"So are you different now?" Ellen leans forward and rests her hand on her knee.

Right. That was part of the question. Am I different than I was?

I shrug. "Honestly? Probably a little. I think I would be lying if I said I hadn't changed a bit. Every experience in life changes you one way or the other. But overall, I hope I am still very much the same person. When I'm alone with myself, I think I'm still me, you know?"

Ellen seems happy with that answer and leans back a bit. I wiggle in my chair, trying not to look at the audience. This is just me talking to Ellen, I tell myself. I am alone with her. Nobody is watching me.

My palms are getting sweaty.

I hope she doesn't want to shake my hand. Although why she would shake my hand right now, I have no idea.

"How do you handle the fame? You can't go anywhere without being mobbed and having your secrets splashed on the tabloids. Do you like people knowing everything about you, or are you a more private person?"

I bite my lower lip. "I think it's a bit of both. When I was a kid, I sometimes dreamed of being a star. I thought I'd like for people to know my name and praise and adore me and all that stuff. And I get a lot of free things from companies who want their products to be seen with me. So sometimes it's pretty cool. I get to meet a ton of people I never would otherwise. I mean, look at right now! I'm being interviewed by you! This is awesome. Except you are making me sweat profusely."

Everyone laughs and Ellen chuckles. "I'm making you sweat? Are you calling me hot?"

I laugh. "No, see, this is what I mean. It still makes me super nervous when I'm in front of people."

Ellen smiles at me. "Fair enough. Well, I think you are a wonderful famous person, so don't change. Stay the way you are." The audience claps. "But enough of this fluff, it's time now to get down to the nitty gritty. You sing a lot about hating men. Is this inspired by one guy in particular? Are your songs true to life?"

This is at least familiar territory. I've been quizzed about this before. "People should write about what they know, and I know from experience how messed up love can be."

"So who is this young man who inspired so many hit songs?" Ellen questions. "What is his name, his social security number, his address? I would love to write him a letter to thank him for inspiring you to write so many awesome songs!"

"He doesn't deserve thanks. But if you want to write him to bawl him out, then maybe I can hook you up," I say and everyone laughs again. "He was my boyfriend for a year in college and then he turned out to be a two-timing scum bag. So we aren't together anymore, which makes sense, considering."

Ellen grins. "Do you think you will love again? Is there anyone in your life now?"

I flush as Jordan's face pops into my head. "Um, yes, of course I still love and am in love and all of that." Suddenly I realize what I said and I begin to stutter. "I mean, no, not that I am in love right now, but I will. One day. I will love again one day, just not right now."

I hope that Ellen doesn't latch onto my obvious attempt to backtrack on my answer, but she is clever and immediately jumps onto it.

"You say that you still love and are in love right now. Does this mean that there is a potential Mr. Rivers out there right this moment that we just don't know about and that you are desperately trying to hide?" Her tone is joking and the audience is riveted. Everyone wants to know.

I laugh in embarrassment and say, "I don't think I'm going to answer that."

"What is his name?" Ellen asks me in a cajoling way.

I shake my head again and can't help but laugh at the hopeful look on her face. "No way, I'm not about to say that either. Just leave it with I'm happily positive about love and about my future at this moment."

Ellen kindly changes the subject, smirking at me in that cute Ellen way. The other questions she asks aren't as awkward, and I'm actually having fun. I grab my guitar and play an acoustic version of my song and everyone claps and Ellen hugs me and we dance in that funky way that Ellen always does, and then it's commercial break and we're done.

People applaud, and I wave and leave. Cheryl is standing in the wings and she gives me her brittle smile. "Well done, Mikayla. I especially liked how you made up something about a new love. That will get interest and the tabloids will start going crazy about you again, which is exactly the publicity we need. Well done."

"I didn't make it up," I mutter.

Cheryl looks at me sharply. "So you are dating someone then," she muses, nodding slowly. "I thought you were, especially since you've been disappearing so much lately. Who is he?"

I shake my head. "No way. I'm not going to tell you yet. This is my secret. Maybe later."

Cheryl shrugs. "Whatever. Not like I even care."

She cares. I can tell because she keeps giving me sidelong glances as we walk. As if she thinks that if she gets me off-guard that I'll spill and suddenly tell her everything.

Not a chance, Cheryl. Not a chance.

We leave the Ellen building and sign more autographs. Back in the limo, we drive to the Monsoon Café for lunch. I love this little place. It looks like a funky Asian temple with high ceilings

Tanned, Toned and Totally Faking It

and gold columns. The food is delicious. Not that I get to try the food, but what's at other people's tables smells pretty awesome. Cheryl and I have a salad. Cheryl has wine, while I sulk my way through an orange juice.

If it weren't for Jordan supplying me with meals on a daily basis, I would starve. I had no idea how much I missed food until I started hanging out with Jordan.

The salad is good, I have to admit. And Cheryl seems quite pleased with the cameras and fans and how the *Ellen DeGeneres Show* went. She doesn't say anything mean or arrogant to me while we eat.

If she weren't so horrible, I wouldn't mind being her friend. And if she didn't always threaten to tell my mother on me. It's hard to be friends with a blackmailer. It's the principle of the thing.

After we finish lunch, Cheryl drops me off at the music studio and I spend the next few hours in practice with the guys.

It's not a bad life, really. I'm fairly positive that tonight I will tell Jordan the truth. Or maybe tomorrow. But sometime soon I will bite the bullet and tell him who I am.

Chapter Twenty Two

The keys fly across the room and hit the wall with a thud. Cheryl shrieks and looks around for something else to chuck at me.

"Kurt knows. Your sister knows. Everyone knows but me!" Cheryl shouts. I peek over the top of the bed that I am cowering behind. Cheryl is standing with her arms crossed by the door, pouting. She looks angry, but also kind of hurt. I feel a twinge of guilt.

Maybe I've been too hard on her. Plus, yesterday after the *Ellen Show* she was pretty decent.

I should tell her. I raise my hands in a sign of truce and stand slowly, ready to leap back behind the bed if she makes the slightest movement.

My day had been going well up to this point. I had been reading the *Twilight* series for the third time, happily sitting on my bed eating potato chips that I had sneakily gotten from the vending machine down the hall. Band practice had been cancelled because Johnny had a dentist appointment, and so I had the whole afternoon to just relax and chill before going to hang out with Jordan tonight.

Then suddenly Cheryl walks in and demands to know who I am spending so much time with every day. I responded that it was none of her business, which inspired her to throw a tantrum. And her keys.

I think they dented the wall.

Cheryl is glowering at me and trying to look pitiful at the same time.

"Fine, what do you want to know?"

"What's his name? Is he famous? And how serious are you about him? In that order." She rattles it off so fast I can tell she's been planning this for a while.

"His name is Jordan. He is not famous at all. And I love him."

Cheryl frowns. "Not famous? How is this going to boost your publicity?"

I shrug. "Cher, I really don't care about publicity. I'm famous, but I don't care about it. If people suddenly hated me tomorrow, I'd go back to Okotoks and be done with it all. I enjoy playing music, and it's been awesome to get paid for doing what I love, but the whole celebrity thing is getting to be a bit much."

Cheryl glares, and her tone is icy. "You're speaking foolishly, Mikayla. Fame matters. Fame is the only thing that does matter."

I shake my head, trying to stay calm. "But it doesn't matter to me. It really doesn't. Some days it's kind of cool and all, but I've found what I've been missing in Jordan. I don't need anything else."

I can tell that Cheryl is furious, but she tries to hide it. She smiles at me but it looks more like a grimace. "Fine. That's fine. I'm happy for you. I was just a little… shocked."

She sits down on my bed and pats the mattress beside her. "Let's talk, okay? Tell me more. What are you guys doing tonight?"

I am suspicious. I hesitate. I don't know if I can trust her. I don't know if I should tell her anything.

Cheryl is watching me. She bites her plump lower lip and says silkily, "Micky, I've known you for your entire life. We've lived together for a year and a half. We're friends. I just want to know about your life."

Well, it can't hurt, can it?

"We're going to hang out at his place, maybe order in some dinner and then have a dance party in his apartment. Crank up his stereo and have some fun."

Cheryl smirks. "You need to get out more." She rolls her eyes. "Is he that ugly that you don't want to take him out in public?"

I feel a little hurt. "I would take him out, but he doesn't know that I'm famous yet, and so I don't want to go anywhere that a paparazzi will find me." What if Jordan thinks I'm ashamed of him? Jordan must know how proud I am of him and that I would love to be seen with him. I need to just tell him the truth.

Or not.

Cheryl examines her plastic nails and says in a bored voice. "Meh, there are plenty of places you can go that don't involve paparazzi. Go to a little night club in the suburbs and I doubt anyone will find you there."

I think about it. That's true. I bet we could go somewhere a little farther out. The thought had never occurred to me. And if I wear a hat or wig, I could get away unnoticed.

"Where could we go?"

"I know just the place," Cheryl says. "I went on a date with a married Oscar winner a month ago, and he didn't want to be seen. We went to a little place near Magic Mountain called The Pitt Stop and had a fabulous night. The crowd there isn't really into mainstream music and movies. They won't even know you exist."

A married man. "Do you have no morals?" I ask her in disbelief. "A married man?"

Cheryl waves my accusing look away. "Everyone does it." She touches her breast (Okay, I seriously need to tell her how disturbing that is) and then says, "Anyway, do you want me to get you an address for the club, or not?"

I think about it. It would be fun to go out with Jordan somewhere that isn't a dingy pizza place. Feeling like I might regret this, I agree.

Cheryl jumps up and hurries out of the room. I watch her go, feeling a rising sense of foreboding in the pit of my stomach. I push it away and get up. I might as well do my hair nice tonight since we're actually going out.

And I can't help it... I'm excited!

*****

"How do I look?" Jordan asks, coming out of the bedroom like a model on a runway. He's strutting toward me, wearing khakis, a gorgeous, black-collared shirt I've never seen before, and his hair has gel in it.

"You look great!" I say, getting up from the couch. I'm wearing a slinky black dress that I've been dying to show off to Jordan. My hair is long and wavy down my back. I kiss him lightly.

He puts his hands on my waist and says, "We could stay in, you know."

I mock swat his hands away. "No way! This is going to be awesome!"

Jordan sits down on the couch and ties the laces on his black dress shoes. "What gives? Normally I have to drag you out with me, but tonight you're all pumped up to go out to some dance club. Why the change of heart?"

I was afraid he'd ask something like this. I plop down beside him on the couch and put my legs into his lap and think quickly. "I like going out. I'm not, like, completely anti-social. It's just that, usually, it's been a long day and I like to, um, relax and stuff."

I don't look at Jordan and instead play with my watch,

unsnapping and re-snapping the band onto my wrist. Jordan finishes tying his shoes and leans into me, going slightly limp. "You're cute," is all he says.

Phew. Dodged another bullet. I really do need to tell him sometime. Just not today.

"No more dawdling, let's go dancing!" I jump to my feet and pull Jordan up with me.

He puts his arm around my shoulders and says, "Okay, but I'm a fairly brutal dancer. When your feet are all bruised, don't say I didn't warn you."

We head down to the curb. The taxi I came in is waiting for us, as I had requested. We climb in, and I give the driver instructions. The cabbie tears away, dodging cars and slamming on his brakes. Jordan and I snuggle down into the back seat.

We talk about random things we saw today, the people we met, and well, pretty much everything and nothing.

The cab ride takes longer than expected due to heavy traffic. After an hour we pull up in front of a club that looks gritty and dank. This isn't right. The way Cheryl had described it, I imagined a funky, out of the way club, where artists and visionaries would hang out.

I doubt anyone would hang out here, unless they were trying to catch hepatitis.

"This isn't exactly what I had pictured," I say in disappointment. I had told Jordan it would be cool and trendy. This is definitely not either. I am annoyed with myself. This is what I get for trusting Cheryl.

Jordan senses my frustration and reaches out for my hand. "No worries. This will be fun. It's an adventure. Let's go check it out."

As we approach the building, we can feel the beat pounding through the concrete. It's loud and fast, and I don't recognize the artist. Taking one last breath of fresh air before entering the gloom, Jordan opens the door and we walk inside.

Once our eyes adjust to the dim light, I draw in a breath.

Tanned, Toned and Totally Faking It

It still looks a little manky, but it's manky in a groovy way. Lights beam around the dance floor, where hundreds of bodies are gyrating to the beat. A bar along the wall is packed with people. There is a rebellious energy in the air. I like it!

I can picture someone like Lenin standing up on a bar stool and hollering and leading the people to revolt. Maybe Lenin isn't the best example. Martin Luther King. This is exactly the place where he would jump up and say, "I have a dream."

A bouncer stands beside us, arms crossed. He doesn't ask for ID. Underage drinking must not be a top concern here. The beat is getting into my head, and I grab Jordan's hand and pull him onto the dance floor. I sway to the beat, moving my hips. Jordan follows my lead.

After dancing madly for a while, I take in the people around us. Everyone here looks goth or artsy, new-age and hip. They are all ages, from about fifteen all the way up to a gnarly old man in the corner who looks like he might keel over and die any second. Cheryl was right. I doubt whether anyone here has ever heard of me. It's the perfect place to have a night out without being mobbed.

You know that one song, the one that says something about two people dancing the night away? That's us. Jordan and I dance the night away. We grab some bar food from the counter (yummy chicken wings and quesadillas) and dance some more.

At one point, as a song is wrapping up, Jordan wraps his arms around my waist, leans in and whispers "I love you" in my ear.

I am so in love that I feel tipsy.

Chapter Twenty Three

$\mathcal{I}$ stare at the newspaper, half hoping that if I look long enough, the picture on the front will fade and somehow morph into Jessica Simpson or Cameron Diaz.

I look away and then glance back.

No luck. It's still me. I'm wearing the slinky black dress that I wore last night. And Jordan is wearing his khakis and that incredibly sexy black button-up.

Somebody followed me. I wasn't sneaky enough, I wasn't careful enough. I feel a rising mountain of dread looming in my chest.

I look at the smaller picture. It's of me and Jordan, right after we kissed. It's such a cute picture. He's holding my hand and we're lost in each other's eyes. We look so happy.

We were happy, I think bitterly. We *were*. Why do people have to interfere?

Cause now Jordan is going to know I've lied to him for the past month. Front page news is hard to miss. Even if he doesn't read it himself, someone is bound to recognize him and tell him.

Tanned, Toned and Totally Faking It

And he'll know I lied. I haven't meant to, but the opportunity to tell the truth just never really arose. Sure, I didn't try too hard, but still.

I feel like I am going to throw up.

Cheryl walks into the room. It's time for another Botox treatment. Her lips are starting to sag a bit.

"Oh, good, Micky. You're up." She touches her chest implants briefly, and I make another mental note to talk to her about that. It's getting to be kind of disgusting, this little anxious tick of hers.

"Cher, did you see this?" I try to sound cool, but my voice is shaking. I wave the newspaper in front of her.

"Oh, yes, you and your mystery boy are exposed. Well, honestly, Mikayla, you didn't think you could keep it a secret forever, did you?"

I remember the talk we had yesterday, and how Cheryl had acted too happy for me. This is Cheryl. Who was I kidding? She's not my friend or my confidant. She is only happy for me when it will benefit her.

And then I know. I can see it all. I know how they got my picture. The sudden realization makes me go cold. She called a magazine and betrayed me. She saw a way to make a quick buck. She knew that I hadn't told Jordan who I was. And despite that, she would betray me and make a killing.

I jump up from the bed. "How much did you make?" I say accusingly, glaring at her.

My suspicions are confirmed when Cheryl opens her eyes wider than normal and says in a false, high voice, "What do you mean? What do you think I made?"

I roll up the paper and throw it at her. It bounces off her fake chest. I doubt she even felt it hit. "You called the newspaper and you told them where I was. Or you took the pictures yourself and sold them. You betrayed me!"

My voice is rising with each word, and before I know it I am screaming at her. Cheryl's face is losing color and she is backing away from me, her hands raised in front of her.

"Mikayla, they were going to find out anyway. If I told them, I would make some money, as opposed to them getting a tip from someone else and me getting nothing. You're a public figure. Of course they were going to find out! It was simply a matter of time."

Tears are streaming down my face, and I start throwing everything within reach at her. My shoes. A pillow. The book I had been reading last night before bed. (Sorry, Harry Potter. No offense.)

"You sold me! You knew I hadn't told Jordan yet, and now everyone in Los Angeles is reading the paper, seeing his face! Everyone in his classes will talk to him about it. Front page news is hard to miss."

I glance around for something else to throw, but nothing else in reach. My rage begins to abate and I feel crushed. Empty. Like I've lost my best friend. Which maybe I have, technically. My shoulders are shaking uncontrollably and I feel weak. I have no energy. I sink down onto the floor and curl up in a fetal position.

That's it. I've lost him.

My Jordan. The first boy who I've given my heart to since Matt. The love of my life.

Cheryl comes and stands in front of me. "It's your own fault, you know. If you hadn't lied, there wouldn't be a problem here. You're the one to blame for deceiving him all this time."

I know that she's right, and it kills me. I want someone to blame. I need someone to blame. But I know that she's telling the truth. If I hadn't lied to Jordan, this wouldn't be such an issue.

I only wanted to be normal, to have a normal relationship.

And besides, if he had known who I was, we would never have had anything. He wouldn't have been casual around me. He wouldn't have asked me on the first date.

My heart hurts, and I am scared. I've never felt this afraid before. Because I have to call him. I have to talk to him, to explain and to make him see.

There is a knock on the door and then it makes a little beep as the keycard is inserted and Kurt walks in. He looks at the ransacked room, sees me on the floor and Cheryl standing over me. Understanding dawns on his face and he gives Cheryl a death look. He hurries over and puts his arms around me.

"My poor little darling, I saw the paper. I'm so sorry."

His hug feels refreshing and good and safe. "It was her," I say shakily, pointing at Cheryl.

Her face expressionless, Cheryl turns away, and without a word leaves the room.

Kurt pulls me half into his lap and starts rubbing my head. "My poor Micky. I'm so sorry. I knew she had it in her, but I didn't know she would actually, you know, do anything that evil. I always thought slightly better of her."

The tears are flowing again, streaming down my face. I know I look a mess, but I don't care. I can barely speak, I am crying so hard.

"It's my fault though. I lied to him," I sob.

Kurt shakes his head. "No, you didn't lie. You just didn't tell him everything. Which is fine, sweetie, don't worry about it. He'll understand. He told you he loved you, didn't he? And if he loves you, he'll understand. You did it so you could have a stable relationship for the first time in months. He'll understand."

I look up at Kurt. "Really?" My voice breaks and I wipe my nose on my hand.

Kurt wrinkles his nose but ignores it. "You need to phone him right now. Before he finds out on his own."

I nod. Kurt's right. Jordan needs to hear it from me.

I crawl onto my hands and knees and Kurt hands me a Kleenex. I blow my nose and wipe my tears and then get up and walk to the bathroom. My head feels like it will explode. I hate crying. It feels good at the time, but afterward you just feel crappy. I splash some cold water on my face and slowly my head begins to clear.

Kurt comes in and hands me my cell phone. "Go ahead, darling."

I'm scared. Now that the moment of truth has arrived, I'm petrified. Living a lie is so much easier than having to face the truth.

I sit down on the edge of the Jacuzzi tub and dial his number. With a trembling finger, I hit send and the phone begins to ring. One ring. Two rings. Three rings. Then I hear his lovely voice say, "Hey, you've reached Jordan's phone. I can't take your call right now, but if you leave a message, I'll call you back."

I take a shaky breath and say, "Jordan, hey, it's Micky. Um, I need to talk to you. As soon as you get this message. Please call me back, despite what you may or may not think of me right now. Please. Love you!"

Kurt tells me to put some jogging clothes on and we'll go for a quick run. I agree, knowing that I have to do something to take my mind off this. We leave the hotel room, but as soon as we get out of the lobby, I wish I hadn't.

Photographers are everywhere, snapping pictures and asking questions. Kurt politely tells them "no comment" as we make our way through them.

"How does Jordan feel, dating such a celebrity?"

Great, now they know his name. That didn't take long.

"How long have you been dating? Why did you keep it hidden?"

"Does it make him uncomfortable knowing you earn so much money?"

"Will your romance survive when you go on tour?"

Kurt puts his arm around me and as soon as we break through the crowd, we begin jogging. A few of them jog beside us for a hundred yards, but when they see that we aren't answering questions, they stop.

Tanned, Toned and Totally Faking It

We run in silence, the only noise our shoes hitting the pavement rhythmically. It's a therapeutic sound, and soon I am feeling better.

Kurt's right. Once I explain things to Jordan, everything will be okay. It's a gorgeous day and there is nothing to be upset about. Sure, Cheryl betrayed me, but I was dumb to trust her in the first place. And now Jordan and I will have a fully open relationship and we won't have to sneak around and I won't be terrified every time we go out in public.

Yes. This is good.

My phone vibrates inside my bra, making me jump.

I stop running and reach down my tank top to get it out. It's Jordan.

Trying to slow my breathing, and calm my erratically beating heart, I hit accept. "Hello?"

"Micky, hi, it's Jordan." He doesn't sound angry. Just normal. Does that mean he's cool? Or that he hasn't heard it yet?

Breathe.

"Hey, Jordan. Um, thanks for calling back."

"No problem." He sounds amused. Good sign? "You seemed quite upset on the phone. I called as soon as I got out of class."

He pauses and I realize that he's waiting for me to explain. I take a deep breath and open my mouth.

"Okay, so you may already know this, and I hope you do, well, except I kind of hope you don't so I can explain before you get mad or something, and if you don't then I really hope you understand when I tell you," I say with trepidation. I'm rambling.

I can't do this, I think in dread. I can't do this over the phone.

"I need to meet you. Can we meet right now? I'm out jogging with my personal uh, Kurt, my personal friend, but I can be at campus in like twenty minutes."

I've talked about Kurt before, but Jordan's always been under the impression that Kurt is someone at my work.

Which is sort of true.

"Meet me at my place. I have a couple hours before my next class, so I'm heading home for breakfast. Want some pancakes?"

"Sure, that would be great." I pray silently that Jordan will go straight home, that he won't see anyone and that he won't look at a newspaper.

"Can't wait to see you, sweetie," Jordan says and my heart melts.

We say goodbye. I look in panic at Kurt. "How far are we from UCLA?" I ask.

Kurt shrugs. "Probably five or ten miles. Why?"

"Cause I have only twenty minutes to get there!"

Without even missing a beat, Kurt pulls out his cell phone. "We need a car right now," he says into the phone then snaps it shut. He reaches into his back pocket and pulls out a small comb and a powder compact. "They'll be here in five minutes. You'll get there on time."

"Seriously?" I ask in amazement. "You carry makeup and a comb when you go running?"

"I always need to be prepared. Isn't that the Boy Scouts' motto?"

I gratefully take the powder and dab it on my face until I no longer look blotchy from crying and sweating. Meanwhile Kurt is poking at my hair, brushing things out and shaping it with his fingers to frame my face. He stops only when the limo silently appears at the curb.

We climb in and head toward campus, with five minutes to spare. I look around to make sure that Jordan is nowhere in sight, give Kurt a hug, and climb out of the car.

"Call me," Kurt says, holding his hand up to his ear in a phone motion, and the car smoothly sails away.

I hurry through the now-familiar campus and get to Hilgard apartments just as Jordan comes walking up.

"Hi!" I say, giving him a hug.

He looks normal. Happy to see me. He may still be oblivious.

Tanned, Toned and Totally Faking It

Jordan kisses me lightly on the lips and puts his arm around me. "Wow, you look pretty good considering you were jogging." We walk inside, out of the sunny morning and into the gloom of the lobby.

There are a few people wandering the halls, but nobody looks at us twice. We get to his apartment, he unlocks it and we step into the familiar, comfortable space.

We sit down on the couch. Jordan holds my hand and kind of massages my fingers and says, "Okay, so what's the big emergency?"

I look into his beautiful brown eyes and gulp. Here goes nothing. "I have to tell you something. I haven't been completely honest with you." I hesitate because he is frowning now. I don't want to make him frown!

"Are you married?" he asks, apprehension in his eyes.

I breathe out a laugh. "No! No I'm not married or anything." I'm glad that was his first thought. Maybe he won't think that me being a secret celebrity and getting his face in the papers without telling him and having everyone know his name isn't that big of a deal.

"Okay, then what's wrong?" Jordan asks quizzically.

"I've never really told you about my job," I say tentatively. "But I think it's time that you know everything. Alright? See, I'm actually a singer. I have a CD and am working on another one. I've been nominated for a couple Grammy awards. I've made, well, millions of dollars in the last seven months, and I'm kind of, like, famous."

I bite my lip and watch his face.

His expression is unreadable and then he laughs. "You're hilarious, Mikayla! You have no idea how much I love you. You always make me laugh."

I stand up, dropping his hand that is still holding mine, and say, "Do you have today's newspaper?"

He points through the open kitchen door to the counter, where a newspaper is lying beside the sink, rolled up and unread.

I walk into the kitchen and grab it. I hesitate. Jordan hasn't seen it yet! Maybe I could hide the newspaper and laugh the whole thing off and pretend like I was just kidding around.

I place the paper on the counter and look into the living room where Jordan is watching me curiously. No. I can't lie this time. Now that we're so close to having the truth, I have to be strong. Brave. I lick my lips and pick up the newspaper again. This time, before I chicken out, I toss it gently into his lap. "Take a look." I sit down beside him again.

He opens it up and stops. 'Mikayla Rivers and her Secret Love: Who Is He?' Jordan stares at the picture of himself, plastered over the front page of the paper. The amusement leaves his eyes. He looks up, his expression guarded.

"Mikayla Rivers. Famous Celebrity." He stares in disbelief at the paper in his hands. "Why didn't you tell me?"

The disappointment in his eyes is too much to bear. A tear trickles down my cheek and I brush at it angrily. This is it—the moment of truth. I need him to believe me, to comprehend why I did it.

"You have to understand. I didn't mean to lie to you. I just..." I shrug and blink back tears, trying to regain control of myself. "I didn't want you to treat me differently. Everyone treats me different when they realize who I am. And the first time I met you, I really liked you. I knew immediately that you were the kind of boy I wanted to get to know. Not the Mikayla that everyone sees in magazines or on the television set. But the real me. I wanted us to have a chance at a real relationship."

The tears keep flowing and I stop, begging him in my mind to say something.

Jordan's face is still expressionless. He glances at the paper again. "I can understand you wanting to keep the truth from me the night we met in the library, or maybe on our first date. But we've been dating for four and a half weeks! I've asked you outright what your job is, and you've lied to my face."

I reach out my hand, wanting to touch him, to calm him

down, but he jerks away. He shakes his head and looks at the ceiling, as if he is trying to figure out what to do next.

"That night on *Letterman*. That was you, wasn't it?" He runs his fingers through his hair. "And all the nights you wanted to stay inside, it wasn't because you were tired, was it? You didn't want to be seen in public."

He stands and begins to pace the floor in front of me, like a lawyer questioning a witness in a courtroom. "I thought I knew you. But I don't know anything about you! Is your name even Mikayla Rivers, or is that a stage name? Are you actually Canadian, or was that a lie too?"

"No!" I scramble to my feet and try to reach out for him, but he turns to me and there is so much anger and hurt and confusion on his face that I step back, afraid. "Look, I can explain everything, I—"

Jordan cuts me off. "Tell me the truth, Micky. Tell me!" His voice rings through the small apartment, commanding me. His words are biting, and I feel as though I'm naked in front of a crowd of strangers, exposed and alone. I open my mouth to explain, but he doesn't give me a chance.

"Did you even go to college? What about your job? Where do you go every day? Why have you never let me come over to your place?"

There are so many questions; my head is spinning and tears are pouring down my face. I try to speak but my words are garbled and incoherent. "I, no, yes, I mean, Jordan, please."

He points a finger at me and says, "How *dare* you let me think we had a future together. How *dare* you lead me on. I thought we were going somewhere, Micky. I loved you. And I was stupid enough to believe that you loved me back, that you were telling me the truth."

"Jordan, I do love you." I reach out for him again. I wipe at my eyes, but the tears are still flowing, and it's getting hard to see. "I only lied about my job, that's all."

"That's *not* all!" Jordan waves the newspaper at me and then with a violent movement tears the front page picture of us in two. "It's not just a 'job,' it's everything you are! No celebrity has a nine-to-five job. Celebrity is their life. It's who they are. It's who *you* are! Don't try to say that it's like you work at McDonalds and that's it. It's completely different. *You* are not who you said you were."

He tosses the newspaper pieces onto the floor, and I stare at them. My smiling face. Jordan's smiling face. Torn in half.

"Being a celebrity doesn't define me. *You* define me." I pick up the pieces of newspaper and clutch them to my body.

"If I defined you, you wouldn't have lied to me repeatedly. I saw us growing old together, Micky. If that's even your name! You better go. Just leave."

My heart hurts so much I think it could break in half. "Wait, Jordan, please!" I beg. "Please, don't make me go. I need you! You need to let me talk to you! Please."

He shakes his head, looking hurt and confused. "I need to think."

I want to caress his head and hold him. I want to make all the hurt and the sadness disappear.

"But I love you! That should be good enough!" I cry, the words catching on my tongue and then tumbling out all at once. Why can't he see? I didn't mean to lie! I love him!

"Love without trust is not love."

"Jordan, this can't be it!" I grab his arm. My world is spinning, and I'm pretty sure I'm going to throw up.

"I need time to think." He removes my hand from his arm and says flatly, "I'm leaving. Lock the door behind you when you go." With that he steps out into the hallway.

"I'm so sorry," I call out to his retreating form.

I try to reach out for him, to touch him, to help him see, but the door is closing. The last thing I see is Jordan's face, his eyes full of anguish as he looks over his shoulder at me.

The door clicks shut.

I stand there in the empty apartment, feeling like my entire world has crumbled around me.

I can't stay in here, not here, where everything reminds me of him, where everything smells like him. I unsteadily walk to the door and open it. Jordan is nowhere in sight. I feel battered and bruised, as if Jordan had physically taken a club and beaten me.

People are walking by and a couple of them look at me curiously. I look like a wreck, I know. My face is probably swollen, red and blotchy again. I have no makeup on, and I am still sweaty from my run. I'm in my scrubby jogging clothes. I lift my head defiantly and somehow manage to walk out of the apartment building. When I get to the front lawn, I take out my cell and dial Kurt's number.

Kurt answers on the first ring. "How did it go?"

I can't answer. Kurt listens to me sob incoherently. "I'm on my way, Micky. I'll be there in five minutes." He hangs up and I walk to the curb, sink down and put my face in my hands.

I can't believe it. I want to disappear. Or fast forward my life to the end of the movie to the happily ever after. But this isn't a movie and I don't think there's going to be a happily ever after. If this were a storybook, Jordan wouldn't have shut me out. He would have reached for me and hugged me and made everything better. If this were a movie, there would be a happy ending right now.

Chapter Twenty Four

I thought chocolate had healing powers. I've eaten three boxes of the most decadent chocolate that Kurt could find, but I am not healed. I am broken. Wasted. Empty.

It's been three days, and I haven't heard from Jordan. I've left him four messages, texted him seven times, and emailed him twice. This is an absolute nightmare.

I love him. And not having him love me back is an acute pain in my chest.

I haven't left the hotel since Kurt brought me home three days ago. Cheryl is furious with me because I'm not recording my new songs or practicing with my band. But I have no energy. I am a wreck.

Kurt is lying across the foot of my bed, reading the latest issue of *Celebrity Magazine,* the one with me plastered on the front, smiling and looking joyful and vibrant and young. Because when they took the picture I *was* young and joyful and vibrant. That was before my entire world was turned upside down and torn apart.

I stare blankly upward. I know I should get up. I know I should eat something. But food has lost its appeal. And I have lost all desire to go out. I just want to stay in bed. It's easier that way.

My phone vibrates on the night stand. I groggily turn my head, hoping it is Jordan, but knowing in my gut that it won't be.

My gut is right. I hate it when that happens.

It's Rachelle.

I debate not answering, but know that if I don't pick up, she'll call our mom to see what's wrong, and then Mom will get involved. So far nobody in my family knows. And I want to keep it that way. I don't want my mom worrying about me.

I reach over, using all my strength just to pick up the dumb phone. "Hello?"

"Micky? I was just reading on the internet that you've had a secret boyfriend for the past month? Is it that guy Jordan who you met at UCLA? You didn't tell me! Why not?" She sounds hurt that she had to read about my life on some gossip blog.

"Why didn't I tell you?" I echo in disbelief. "Why have you been keeping secrets from me for the past month? Ever since I told you about Jordan, you've been hiding something from me."

Rachelle is silent for a second. "I'm sorry, Micky. I was only trying to help. But I promise, I'll tell you everything. Right now. But first you tell me the truth about this boyfriend."

It seems like a fair trade.

"Deal." Alright. Where to start? "Rach, I don't know where to begin. I just…" I trail off and decide to start at the beginning and give her a two minute overview.

"We went on a bunch of dates, and he was perfect. The most smart and funny and beautiful boy ever. And really humble too, just genuine, you know? And he made me feel like the most important girl in the world. No, he made me feel like I was literally the only girl in the world. He didn't see anyone else when he was with me and it was the same for me. He was everything to me. The only thing is I didn't exactly tell him who I was. He didn't recognize me when we met and so I thought that if he knew, he'd treat me differently. So I didn't tell him. And we've been dating a month. And I am in love. Except Cheryl just spilled it to a newspaper on the weekend, and Jordan got really mad that I had sort of lied to him, and now he won't return my calls, and I think he hates me."

I sniff, aware that I am crying again and hating myself for it. Kurt reaches over and places a Kleenex in my lap. I take it gratefully. I wipe at my eyes and feel the now-familiar stinging from too many tears.

"Oh, Micky, I'm so sorry. I had no idea! I didn't know! I wish you had told me, but it's okay."

Her concern and sympathy are more than I can handle. Rachelle lets me cry, putting a word in every now and then and telling me to let it all out. In about five minutes my eyes run dry. I'm all cried out. My head is painfully pounding and I lie there, exhausted.

"So that's all I got," I say choppily. "Now your turn. What's your big secret?" I sniffle.

Rachelle clears her throat. "Okay, but you can't tell anyone. Not a soul. Not even Kurt! Promise?"

I am intrigued despite myself. What could possibly be so confidential that I can't even tell Kurt? "I can't promise that," I say, my voice catching. "I won't promise to not tell Kurt. Especially since he's in here right now, listening to me say his name."

Rachelle sighs. "Fine, just promise not to tell anyone other than him."

I promise and Rachelle continues. "Well, I saw Matt. About a month ago. And pretty much daily since then. See, he told me that he had made the hugest mistake ever when he dropped you and that it just happened so fast. Anyway, he is really sorry and he wants to make it up to you. He's going to LA. He'll actually be there tonight, I think. Or maybe tomorrow. And I gave him your number. He wants to meet you. To see you again." She sounds almost apologetic. "Please don't be mad at me."

I can barely process what is happening. "Rachelle, why did

you do this?" I can't believe she would go behind my back. She knew how badly Matt hurt me. Why would she help him get back with me?

"I just… I believe him, Micky. He seems so sorry and I couldn't help it! At first I liked that he was talking to me. I mean, you remember how charming he is. So when he first wanted to talk to me, I let him. I didn't know that you were dating Jordan. I wanted to make you happy!"

Her words hit my ears but nothing is computing anymore. I don't want to see Matt. I don't. Only there is a tiny part of me that does. I try to block it out. But I love Jordan, and I have to get him back. I can't focus on Matt right now.

"Rachelle, this is horrible. I need to get Jordan back, and I really can't deal with Matt."

Kurt looks up from his magazine as I say Matt's name. He raises his eyebrows and I hold my finger to my lips and mouth, "Tell you later."

He nods and looks back down, but the pages stop turning and I can tell that he's listening.

"Just give him a chance, okay?" Rachelle begs. "Go out to dinner with him, or something. Please? For me?"

"I don't know," I say coolly. My words come out a bit meaner than I had intended, but it doesn't matter. I don't need this right now. Everything is so confusing already without this added in to the mix. I wish I could turn back time to when life was simple and I had Jordan.

Rachelle starts crying. "Please don't be mad. I only wanted to help you."

I can't help it. I'm pretty ticked off, truthfully. I say goodbye and hang up. I can't remember a time when I have hung up on my sister. Sure, we've fought before, but I can't believe that she would betray me like this. Why would she go behind my back?

I put my head in my hands and wish I were dead.

What the crap am I going to do?

Chapter Twenty Five

"So what do I do?" I say as I lean forward to apply new lip gloss that Kurt gave me. It's a light pinky-peachy color. It's about two hours after my conversation with Rachelle, and I've actually managed to pull myself out of bed for the first time in days, shower, and blow dry my hair.

Kurt is still sprawled on my bed. At my question, he looks up from the romance novel he's now reading. "I didn't catch that? Say again?"

"What do I do?"

"Well, it depends."

"On what?" I say, using a tissue to dab a bit of the excessive lipstick off.

"On what you want to accomplish," he says. "On the one hand, you can go out with Matt on a date, make your sister happy, listen to what he has to say and kind of take it from there. Or, on the other hand, you can reject Matt the same way he rejected you and take some kind of a stand. Matt who?"

I nod. Those are pretty much the same options that I came

up with in the shower. Only I had hoped that Kurt would have some amazing master plan to make the decision easier.

"But if I go out with Matt, won't that be like, I don't know, cheating on Jordan?" Even saying Jordan's name drives another sharp, shooting pain into my chest.

"I think cheating is only defined as cheating when you actually have a boyfriend." His voice is light, but I can hear the concern in his underlying tone.

Right. Because at this very second I don't exactly know what Jordan is to me. I hope he still is my boyfriend, but boyfriends don't ignore their girlfriend's calls, right?

This seems to be the whole Matt fiasco repeating itself. At least this time I know what I did wrong.

My new rule is to not lie to a boyfriend. Especially about something as monumental as being a world-famous pop star.

I sigh deeply and put on mascara. "You're right. I should leave my relationship with Jordan out of this, shouldn't I?"

Kurt makes a non-committal sound. I want to slap him. I should hire a professional decision-maker. I mean, this is getting pathetic. First I can't order pizza on a date with Jordan and now I can't decide what to do about Matt. I wish they offered that as a university class. Decisions 101 – How to Run Your Own Life. Although, I'd probably fail.

I finish applying mascara in silence.

Kurt finally looks up from his book and says, "Look, Micky, I'm not going to decide for you. But tell me something. Do you want to see Matt again?"

I know I should be able to answer that question. It's fairly simple. Do I want to see Matt again? Well? The only thing is… I don't know. There is the stupid, forgiving part of me that really wants to see him and have him hold me and tell me that he thinks I'm beautiful. And then there is the judgmental, bitter side that wants to curse him and his future kids and grandkids and great-grandkids for all time.

Kurt clears his throat. "I am not trying to influence you at all, Micky, but just to throw it out there… you're feeling horrible because Jordan won't forgive you, right? Well, what if Matt is feeling the same way about you?"

His words are a smack in the face.

It's true. I've been hoping so desperately that Jordan will call me and talk and tell me that he still loves me and that he forgives me for, uh, misleading him, and yet here I am doing the exact same thing to Matt. Although truthfully I think Matt's betrayal is a little worse than mine.

"You're right." I walk to the closet. I'm still wrapped in a towel, but I have no qualms about dropping it on the ground while putting on underwear. I mean, Kurt is kind of like a sister. Only male.

"If Matt phones, I'll meet him for dinner. I'm only giving him one shot though."

Kurt nods his approval. "That's my girl," he responds, turning back to his book.

I want to rip the book out of his hands and make him focus on me. Not that I am selfish and needy. It's just that I need Kurt right now. This is a one-time emergency, not a lifestyle. I'm not always like this.

I can't help but feel I am cheating on Jordan if I go out with Matt. But it's not really a date. It's simply dinner with an old ex-boyfriend who I still have slight feelings for.

My phone rings. I race for the phone and experience immediate disappointment followed by relief that a) it's not Jordan and b) that it's not Matt.

It's Johnny, calling to see if I am feeling up for a couple hours of band practice today. I hesitate for only a second before I agree. It will be good to take my mind off my ridiculous love life by playing some songs.

I pull on dark blue skinny jeans and a bulky, cream-colored sweater and tell Kurt I'm leaving. He nods vacantly and cozies himself down on my bed, grabbing a pillow to make himself more comfortable. I walk outside and see a couple photographers lurking around the front doors. They take a few pictures but that's it.

Good. Let them put a picture of me in the newspaper. Maybe Jordan will see it and know what he's missing and call me!

I don't see a taxi, so I decide to walk. The studio is only a few blocks away. The fresh air will be good for me, considering I've spent the last couple days holed up in a hotel room, wallowing in my filth and depression.

I get there in about fifteen minutes and go upstairs to find Johnny and Brian already set up. Johnny is tapping out a catchy beat and Brian is plucking along, making things up as he goes. My guitar is in the corner. I take it from its case.

Brian pats me on the shoulder. "Rough few days?"

I nod. "Yeah. I hadn't exactly told that guy I was dating that I'm a celebrity. It turns out that he didn't like the fact that I kind of lied to him. So I think he broke up with me, but I don't really know since he won't actually talk to me." I can feel the raw pain lurking beneath my casual façade.

Johnny smashes the cymbals. "*Princesa,* it's his loss."

"Thanks." The sound of the cymbals gives me a much needed jolt. It's good to be back with my pals. I pull the strap over my head and strum some chords for *Hate. Love.* Johnny and Brian pick up, and soon loud music fills the studio, clearing my head and helping me vent my frustrations. When the chorus comes, I belt it and feel a much improved outlook as I do.

You lied and said you loved me
But you were full of it
Sticking to your rules
You total hypocrite!
And all because of you
I. Hate. Love.

"This album is totally going to be better than the last one." I say as the final notes drift away.

Johnny grins. "You know it!" He points out a couple minor things for Brian to change. "Oh, and Micky, I liked the rage in your voice when you got to the bridge. Be sure and keep that in for the recording next week, cause it sounded smashing."

And on that note we dive into it again and again, each time getting a bit more polished than the last.

When we finally finish it up, Johnny seems pleased. "Good." He consults his Blackberry. "I think we should jump to *Celebrate* before calling it a day, if that works for you guys."

We agree, and Johnny is tapping out the beat when my phone vibrates. I hold up my hand before walking out of the room and closing the door behind me. I don't recognize the number but think desperately that maybe Jordan is calling from his land line or possibly from his mom's house.

"Hello?" I say, putting it to my ear.

"Hi Micky." My heart skips a beat. I know that voice. I have heard that voice almost every night in my dreams for two years. He sounds exactly the same, only maybe a little more timid.

Matt.

I've practiced hundreds of times what I would say to him if I ever spoke to him again. I'd be cool and collected and aloof. I'd call him out for being a slime.

Apparently practice does not make perfect, because it's all I can do to keep a sloppy grin off my face.

"It's Matt. Matt Prince," he continues, giving me a minute to collect myself.

I frantically think of what I can say. Do I play it off and pretend like I barely remember him? Do I pretend like we're cool and that we're friends?

"Oh. Hi." Not really sure what I'm trying to accomplish with those words, but I am okay with it. I don't sound angry or hurt, nor do I sound excited and happy. Just somewhere in the middle, which works for me.

"Yeah, um, look, I'm here in LA. I took a week and a half off from school to come down and try to find you. I don't know if your sister told you, but she gave me your number. I was wondering if I could take you out to dinner tonight?"

He doesn't sound nearly as sure of himself as he used to, and I realize with astonishment that he's nervous! He's afraid I'll reject him, I think in wonder. I finally have the upper hand in this relationship! The realization fills me with pride. Look who came crawling back!

"Sure, we can meet up for dinner. I was planning on eating at six o'clock, so if you want to join me, we could hit Simon's Grill. I'll have my manager make us reservations." I take charge of the conversation. Matt's going to have to play by my rules.

"Wow, that would be great. Simon's Grill? I don't know where many places are in LA. Do you have the address for it?"

He sounds so normal. So Matt. It feels almost as if the past two years haven't happened and we're back to being best friends. But we're not, I tell myself sternly. He's not your boyfriend. You love Jordan. Matt is just an old friend.

"I will have my manager contact you. I have to run. See you tonight."

I hang up and feel like my body is going to explode on every side. I am excited. I am nervous. I am a little annoyed with myself for being excited and nervous. I want time to speed up, but I also want it to stop completely. I want to see Matt, but I don't. I want to see Jordan, but thinking about him still hurts.

I am so confused.

Chapter Twenty Six

Kurt arranged everything. He called a limo, he picked out my wardrobe, and he made the reservations; then he pretended to be my manager and called Matt with the address. We thought it best to keep Cheryl out of this.

It's five after six and my limo has just pulled up in front of Simon's Grill. It is one of the hottest celebrity hangouts in LA. I picked it to show Matt how powerful and cool and over him I am.

I make sure that I am fashionably late, enough to keep Matt waiting, and I step out of the car. Flashbulbs go off in my face; I smile and wave. Kurt has me wearing a black, tight dress with red stilettos, and a red bead necklace. My hair is a casual beach look, and I hold my head up high as I walk into the restaurant.

I need the confidence in my appearance to act as armor tonight. I am terrified to see Matt.

A waiter approaches. "Miss Rivers, welcome. Your guest is already seated." He takes me by the arm and leads me to the table Kurt had requested, private and in the back of the restaurant. I approach and see Matt for the first time in almost a year and a half.

He looks as good as ever. His hair is still shaggy and he is wearing khakis and a button up shirt that makes his blue eyes look that much bluer. I've only seen him wear a button up shirt once before, when we went to my cousin's wedding together. He must really be trying to impress me if he's dressed up.

He leaps to his feet as I approach, and it's a very awkward moment. He half holds his arms out as if to give me a hug, and I do the same, but then I stop and put out one hand as if to shake his hand, and we end up doing a slightly weird, tangled huggy, handshakey thing.

"Micky! Holy, it's good to see you again!" He looks me up and down. "Wow! You look so different. You look amazing!"

"Thanks!" I smile. "You look pretty good yourself."

The waiter pulls out a chair and I sink down into it. It is a plush velvet chair, very comfortable, and yet I am so edgy I can't relax.

"Wine? Champagne? Anything to drink?" the waiter inquires.

I don't want to drink wine with Matt. That is too much like a date. And champagne is too much like a celebration. I need to keep my head, so no alcohol.

"I'd like a cranberry juice," I say then turn toward Matt.

"Uh, probably some soda would be fine." The waiter rattles off the different soda types and Matt picks a Coke. The waiter nods and leaves.

Matt is looking around the place with interest. "Wow, Micky, can you believe this?" His voice is full of excitement.

I know exactly what he's talking about, but I don't want to make it easy for him. "Believe what?"

"This. All of this!" Matt stretches his arms out and motions at our surroundings. "You got a reservation here with a couple hours notice. You have CDs and fame and people know you in the street. It's incredible!"

I hate it when people talk about me like this, like I am someone special. I wanted Matt to be impressed and in awe at my success, but the reality of it makes me feel uncomfortable.

I shrug, playing with the fork lying on the table. "It's fleeting. All of it is. Eight months ago I was nothing and who knows where I'll be tomorrow. I just take it a day at a time."

I take a sip of the cranberry juice that the waiter has placed before me. "I try not to let it get to my head or anything, but that's easier said than done. Some days I wish things had never changed, that I had never come to LA."

It feels normal to be saying this to Matt. I realize how huge a void I've had in my life since he left me.

Matt reaches across the table and touches the tips of my fingers. It's a familiar gesture, one that he used to do all the time when we were dating. "Micky, you have no idea how much I wish I could turn back time. This is one reason I wanted to see you. I need to apologize, right now, before we do anything else."

I draw in a shaky breath, and Matt looks into my eyes. "Micky, I was wrong. Things were happening too fast and when I went to Fort Mac that summer I kind of freaked out. All the guys I worked with said how grateful they were to be away from their wives and girlfriends, to be free. They wanted to go to strip clubs and stuff, and I listened to them. I went with them and when you called, I believed what the guys said about 'ball and chain' and whatnot. I thought I would be happier living the single life."

He looks away as though collecting his thoughts. I take another sip of my juice and try to process what he is saying.

"I haven't been happy since we broke up," Matt says. "In April I tried to call your old cell because I wanted to see you and talk to you and sort this mess out, but your phone had been disconnected. And then one week in the grocery store I saw you on a magazine! I was blown away that it was you. I couldn't believe it. I went home and Googled you and read all about your incredible break through. I went out and bought your CD and holy crap, it's good!"

"Thanks." I am touched by the compliment. Matt's an awesome musician, so coming from him, that means something.

Matt smiles that crinkly half smile I remember so well. "I ran into Rachelle one day, accidentally, about a month ago. I told her that I needed to see you again. She told me no at first, but when I ran into her again, I finally was able to convince her. Look, Micky, I miss you. I miss you so bad. I have regretted my actions every day for the last two years. Please forgive me."

And with those final three words, his voice cracks and he looks away. Matt Prince is all choked up over me? I have to look away too, because I don't want Matt to see me blinking back tears. I don't want him to notice the huge swell of emotions he's created within me. If he only knew how badly he messed me up. I had hated myself, thinking it was something I did that drove him away. Whenever I looked in the mirror I resented my own reflection.

And now here he is, asking for my forgiveness.

It's everything I always wanted. It's everything I prayed for.

I finally look at him, thinking I have myself under control, but seeing his face makes the tears spill over. "It's alright," I say quickly. "You have no idea how much it means to me, you telling me all that. All this time I thought it was something I did, something wrong with me. Thanks for telling me the truth."

Matt seems horrified that he's making me cry, but I can't stop myself. "Micky, if I'd have known that you blamed yourself…" He trails off.

I reach across the table and pat his hand. "It's okay. No worries. It's old and done. I'm really glad we finally can have closure and all that." And I mean it. I love this kid. I think you never really stop loving your first true love. But I am no longer in love with him. I am over him.

At that moment the waiter appears and asks if he can take

our order. I tell him we need another minute and he leaves. We open the menus and Matt's eyebrows go up when he sees the prices. I can read him so well.

"Oh, and dinner is on me," I say.

"Thanks! I forgot about needing money when I got here. I just focused on saving up for the trip here and back."

That is so typically Matt, never seeing the entire picture. "You always were a horrible planner," I say with a small giggle. "Remember when we went to Banff that weekend and you remembered the tent and the poles and the axe, but you didn't have matches or clothes?"

He laughs. "We got there, and I had only put socks into my backpack. No wonder it was so light!"

And just like that all the tension and awkwardness is gone. It's as if the last two years had never happened.

"Remember that one time when we went to that creepy house on 17th Ave that was all boarded up and we broke in because we wanted to see if it was haunted?" Matt says. "And the cops came because the neighbors heard noises."

"And then we ran off and hid in that dumpster until they ran by?"

Once we start reminiscing, we can't stop, except for a minute when the waiter comes and takes our orders. As soon as he leaves, we start up again.

"We went caving on that school sponsored trip and you kept making bear noises in the cave and freaked me out…"

"Lying on the grass behind Res…"

"When we went on that road trip down to the States and got lost so ended up sleeping in McDonalds until security kicked us out…"

"Dance parties in our apartments…"

Our meals come and we eat, still talking. My lobster tails are amazing! The butter is warm and succulent, and I pull a piece of lobster out of the shell, dip it in the butter and pop it happily into my mouth. Matt had ordered steak, all juicy and tender.

Tanned, Toned and Totally Faking It

This is the most delicious place to eat in the entire world.

We have finished our meals and it's like we can't speak fast enough, with the words tumbling over each other as we tell each other about our lives now.

"Hong Kong was incredible! So huge! I have never seen anything that compares to it. It's kind of like New York only bigger and taller and more crowded, if that is possible. And speaking of which, I totally went to New York too!" Matt had been curious about what my promotional tour was like, and I can't tell him enough.

"What time is it?" I ask suddenly. I have no clue how long we've been in here.

Matt checks his watch. "Almost nine thirty."

We've been here for three and a half hours! I motion to the waiter for the bill, and turn to Matt. "Want to go dancing?"

I've wanted to go dancing at Saratoga's ever since I got to LA. It is the most hip, fab place, and everyone goes there. I had planned to go there with Jordan, but since tons of paparazzi hang out there, I was too scared to take him. I did go to Saratoga's one time with some Broadway actor, who Cheryl figured would boost my image to be seen with him; but he spent the whole time networking and introducing himself to every movie star he saw, and we didn't get to dance much. But this time I can go there and dance.

Although thinking about dancing makes me kind of hurt, remembering Jordan and I at that funky little club.

Not that this is a date, I remind myself. I'm only going with Matt for old time's sake, and we might as well go to a fancy place.

"Yeah, that would be fun!" Matt says.

After I sign the receipt for my Visa, we leave. My limo is parked down the street. The chauffeur steps out and opens the door for us and we climb in, laughing like two dumb college kids.

Which we kind of are.

And the rest of the night we have a blast. I feel completely like myself for the first time in months. I can just be me without any worries.

When we finally stumble, exhausted, back into the limo at three in the morning, I feel happy. We collapse on the seat and I tell the driver to take us to the Econo Lodge, which is where Matt is staying. I lean my head on Matt's shoulder and he puts his arm around me.

The limo arrives at the motel and stops. Matt looks at me and I can see in his eyes that he wants me. He's going to kiss me, I think, but it's almost like an echo, something I can barely hear. And then his lips are on mine and it feels so right. It's everything I've missed. I kiss him back, and then his hands are on my back and he's getting more passionate.

I stop and push him away.

What am I doing? I have a boyfriend (I think) and I don't need to deal with this right now.

"Micky, I'm sorry. That was out of line. I just…" He shrugs and I understand. He felt it. And so did I.

"It's okay." My mind is spinning and my words are unsteady.

"Can I see you tomorrow?" Matt's face is in shadow.

I hesitate. "Sure. You can come to my hotel, if you want. We can go swimming or play some songs or something."

He squeezes my hand and climbs out of the limo. With a glance back, Matt hurries toward the motel, and the limo whispers away, taking me home.

I am left with my thoughts in the back seat.

What the hell have I gotten myself into?

Chapter Twenty Seven

"What is *this?*"

I groggily open my eyes. Everything is blurry until I blink a couple times; Kurt's face comes into focus. He is standing in front of me with his laptop computer, waving his hand vaguely at the screen.

I stare at the screen, trying to process what I am seeing. It's a picture of a blonde, skinny girl in a black dress. There's a blonde boy with shaggy hair and a button up shirt. They are dancing and laughing and have their arms all tangled up in each other. It takes a moment to realize that it's me and Matt, from last night.

"What?" I keep my tone neutral.

"What happened to you going to a nice dinner just to hear him out and then coming home like a responsible girlfriend? Look, he's got his hands all over you. What about Jordan?" Kurt sounds upset with me.

I rub my hands over my face. Last night. Matt and me at dinner. We went dancing. The limo ride to his motel. The kiss.

I groan and sink my head back onto my pillow.

Kurt places his laptop on the corner table. It's only seven a.m. Why is he here so early?

Kurt sits down beside me and leans back against the headboard. "Okay, tell me what happened."

I sigh. Where do I begin? "Well, it just was so normal." I try to remember everything that happened. "We talked and he apologized. Said he'd kind of freaked out about commitment but as soon as he lost me his life sucked. And so he was sorry. And we just kind of started talking and reminiscing and I thought I was over him, and that we were cool, you know, just friends, but then we went dancing and at the end of the night he kissed me and I totally agreed to have him come over and hang out today." My voice is rising with each sentence and I feel more overwhelmed with each word.

Kurt rubs my head gently. Playing with my hair, he says, "It's okay. We'll figure something out. I was concerned because I felt I had pressured you into going out with him and then I log onto Perez Hilton's celebrity blog and there you are with him. I was worried that I had pushed you into something disastrous. This, my love, we can handle."

"What about Jordan?" I say in a small voice. "Do you think he'll find out?"

Kurt shrugs. "I doubt it. This isn't big news right now. Some rapper got busted for murder last night, and I just heard about a CBS star who committed suicide, so I think the media is over other news stories for the time being. I doubt this will get in the magazines, and I really doubt that Jordan reads online celebrity blogs."

I move on to more complicated problems. "So what do I do? If I go out with Matt again, I think we're going to end up dating. I just kind of feel it. And I sort of would be okay with it, but I don't know. I mean, at first I thought we were cool and I was over him. But then by the end, I felt like I was madly in love with him again. And what if I only like Matt because he dumped me and I'm trying to compensate for that? And then what about

Jordan? I mean, he still hasn't called me. So I'm not really dating him anymore, am I? I shouldn't pass up Matt if Jordan is done with me, right? I mean, this is *Matt!*"

The words are tumbling out and getting tangled on each other as I try to make sense of things.

Kurt frowns and cracks his knuckles once. "Let's pretend for a minute that both of them are equally accessible to you. Both of them want you, so you have to choose. Which would it be?"

Hmmm, I stop for a minute. Which one would I pick if all things were equal? Jordan is sweet, and sensitive and funny, and we have a great time together. He makes me want to be a smarter and more humble and generous person. He is kind to homeless people and has this incredible work ethic. But Matt… is Matt. He's been haunting my dreams for years. He was my best friend when I was eighteen. He is gorgeous and sexy and so sure of himself. And we have all those good memories together.

But, my brain nags, what about Jordan? You already have good memories, even though you only dated for a month. Remember the beach and the sand and just hanging out? Remember your first kiss? Remember sleeping on his couch and him making you pancakes in the morning? Remember pizza and video games and helping him study for his law exams? Remember him playing along with your Olga thing and how good he is to his mother? What about all that?

Kurt is perusing the menu for room service. "Want something?" he asks.

I think for a second. "Yeah, uh, bacon and eggs and pancakes."

Kurt looks shocked. "You don't eat bacon! And pancakes are bad for you. What about some yogurt and berries?"

I shake my head. "Kurt, I'm not dieting anymore. I've been breaking my diet since I started dating Jordan and I'm not going back to it. I won't eat a ton or anything, I'll limit my portion size and all, but I want to eat what I want."

Kurt raises an eyebrow. "I knew it! I knew you'd gained some weight, even though you denied it when I tried to increase your workout. And here I assumed it was just stress. Are you feeling okay?"

"I'm fine. My head is splitting, I'm exhausted, and I am torn literally between two lovers, but I know that I want some bacon."

Kurt places the order. He asks for the same as me, I notice, and I almost make fun of him but decide not to. Kurt always eats what he wants, whether it's burgers and fries or bacon and eggs or thick steaks. He eats anything, which is a little hypocritical, if you ask me.

As soon as he hangs up from room service, we decide to make a list to weigh the pros and cons for both Jordan and Matt. When it's down on paper, I'm sure everything will become clear.

Matt:

Pro – He's gorgeous and we have a long history together. Plus it gives me a higher self esteem to have him back. And he's a good dancer.

Con – He dumped me and maybe is only coming back because I'm famous. He doesn't really care about school, has no work ethic, and still acts like an eighteen-year-old kid.

Jordan:

Pro – He's sweet, charming, old fashioned, handsome (but doesn't think he's handsome) and humble. He's smart and works hard. We have fun together. I can be myself with him (even though I was hiding a little teeny portion of who I am) and he always cares about my feelings. He hates materialism and wants to become a lawyer to do some good in the world. And he makes awesome pancakes. And he let me cut his hair which was so awesome. Especially since it turns out I am an amazing hairdresser. And he didn't even get mad when I made that tiny little blip with the razor when I was shaving the ends. All he said was, "It'll grow back."

Con – He hasn't phoned me in a week and he may in fact hate me.

Tanned, Toned and Totally Faking It

Okay. So the pro and con thing clearly has its flaws. I mean, sure Matt may be immature and selfish, but he's really fun to be around, and he did drive all the way to California to see me. I'm sure there are more good things about Matt than the couple I jotted down. I rack my brain.

We have a connection, I write after a minute. Which is true. I mean, sure, it might be just because we knew each other a long time ago, but that still counts as a connection. But me and Jordan also have a connection, I think. And ours happened out of nowhere. I write the same sentence under Jordan too. Alright. So this is going nowhere.

Kurt is watching my face. "You're in love with Jordan."

"What?" I sputter, feeling heat rise to my cheeks. "No, I mean, yes, I love him, but I love Matt too. Clearly. Otherwise this wouldn't be an issue!"

Kurt shakes his head. "No, I honestly don't think you do love Matt and that's why I don't believe this is a real issue. I've been watching you make that list. Your face gets softer when you write things about Jordan. And you don't have to think about it. You just write. But with Matt you chew the back of the pen and you scratch your arm and you look around the room. You love Jordan and are just trying to make excuses so that he can't hurt you the way he has been."

Is this true? Am I so afraid of being hurt again that I am trying to minimize Jordan in my life? I think back to last night. I was sitting at the table with Matt and after he apologized I thought… how much I love him as a brother. I did, didn't I? I had thought that he was a good friend and was impressed that I finally was over him. But as the night carried on, I let myself be fooled into thinking that Matt was the old Matt, still a boy to date.

I moan. "It's true. I don't love Matt. I only love the idea of Matt. I thought that if I dated him again, I could, like, erase the past few years."

"It's alright. Things like this are confusing. I know they are.

Just don't let it get to you."

I climb out of bed. "I'm going to shower before our breakfast comes."

I stand in the shower and let the hot water course over my body. I'm pretty sure that Kurt is right. I do love Matt, but it's an old love, kind of like a fond memory. And now that he's apologized, things are normal. I can think of him without hurting myself. But Jordan, on the other hand, when I think of him I feel all flushed and happy and warm. He gives me butterflies in my stomach and every time the phone rings I get nervous, hoping it's him.

I finally know what to do. I'm over Matt. And I have to get Jordan back.

As I come out of the shower I hear Kurt talking. I wrap the towel around me and walk out into the main suite. Kurt is sitting on the bed, and Cheryl is standing in the doorway.

"Saw it on the celebrity blog. And I think it's good to have it published. I'll be phoning *Celebrity Magazine* this morning to get an article on the secret love life of Mikayla Rivers. We'll showcase both her non-famous boys and try to get her on a date with a celebrity too before the article comes out. We'll make her out to be a kind of America's sweetheart with player on the side and it will bring in a lot of cash, believe me."

I stand in shock, feeling the water drip down my neck, cold and icy. Cheryl is trying to sell me out again. She's going to crush the little remaining chance I have left with Jordan. This can't be happening.

"What are you talking about?" I hate that my voice is shaking and that I sound like a pathetic child.

Cheryl plumps up her right breast. "As your manager, I have found a way to get you to bounce back solidly into the spotlight."

"What do you mean, 'back into the spotlight'?" I ask. "It's not like I'm washed up. I've never been hotter. I am on every radio station. I am on the cover of magazines."

Cheryl sighs in a would-be patient voice. "Look, sure you're on and off, hot and cold, but if we can get a huge story, people will flock to it. You will make millions off the story alone. Trust me."

I hate the matter-of-fact way that she speaks. And I hate that she is trying to be my best friend. I hate that she used the word 'trust.'

I feel more icy tendrils of water run down my neck and as they drip, I feel a tiny bit of self-resolve build up inside me. I cannot trust Cheryl. She has ruined my relationship with Jordan, and now she's trying to make money from the ashes. She has bossed me and controlled me and tried to push me around for too long.

I've had enough.

I draw in a deep breath and speak slowly, my voice starting off shakily, but getting stronger as I go. "No, Cheryl, no. You won't call them. I won't let you. You have interfered long enough. You're done. You're fired."

I expect her to get angry, but instead she laughs. "You can't fire me. I'll phone your mother. I'll let her know that her perfect little angel has silicone lips. You've been lying to your mom, and I know you don't want her to know that."

Her words are biting, hatred and disdain spewing from her oversized lips.

I almost back down. I almost give in. I want to be the peacemaker again and let her do what she wants. She's right in a way. I am terrified that my mother will find out, because as much as I hate Cheryl, I love my mother. And I don't want her to know the truth about my lips.

I don't want my mother to be ashamed of me.

I see Kurt shake his head. Just a tiny movement, but I can read his face as if he were shouting. Be strong, Micky. Don't give in. Give Cheryl what she deserves.

I blink back angry tears and say, my voice thick with emotion, "Cheryl, you are finished. You are one hundred percent fired.

You have done enough. You whine, you complain, you backstab. You ruined my relationship with Jordan just to earn yourself more money. You sleep with married men. You are a vile, horrible excuse of a human being. And if you breathe one word of my lips to my mother, my sister, or any member of my family, or to the press, I will publicize the fact that you slept with a married man. And I will tell *your* mother about all your implants and your silicone and your collagen injections and all the plastic inside *you;* that you don't look this way because of a new diet. If you want to start a mud-slinging contest, I will be right there with you. And I've got good aim."

"You can't fire me!" Cheryl shrieks and runs toward me, her hands outstretched. "I'll kill you, you whore! I'll rip your heart out! I'll tear your head off!" Kurt leaps up and grabs Cheryl around the waist, dodging her flailing arms.

I step back into the bathroom, shut the door and lock it. I hear a crash on the other side, and then banging, as Cheryl pounds her hands against the door.

"I'm calling security!" I shout through the wood. I'm not, actually. I don't have my cell with me.

But maybe if Cheryl thinks that security is coming, she'll have enough sense to leave quietly on her own and not get herself arrested.

This is such a bad time to be without a bodyguard. Come on, Cheryl. Leave!

She doesn't.

I hear Kurt yell and another door slams. Suddenly there is a loud crash and the sound of breaking glass.

Oh my gosh, Cheryl has gone insane.

I always knew this day would come, but I had hoped I would be far, far away when she finally snapped.

I hope Kurt's alright. I hope he got out.

There's another bang on the bathroom door, and then it becomes rhythmical. Bang. Bang. Bang. She's pounding her fists against the door like a toddler having a tantrum.

"You can't fire me!" she screams. "I made you who you are!"

"You didn't make me at all," I shout back. "Charles Nash found me. Kurt got me looking the part. I wrote my own music. Johnny and Brian made my music great. All you did was boss me around and take my money. You limited me. I wanted to perform in the indie scene, you refused to let me! You only helped me when you saw a profit in it."

I am on a roll, shouting behind the bathroom door. "Sure, you were good at promoting me, but any other manager would have done the same. It's not like you went out of your way to help me. Plus you've made millions on this job, so don't pretend it was out of the goodness of your heart!"

The relief at finally telling Cheryl the truth is liberating. Empowering. I feel like burning a bra or something. Yay for woman power.

Bang. Bang. Bang.

She's still pounding away, hollering a stream of words that I can barely understand. I sit down. Kurt is outside somewhere, probably getting security. I just have to wait it out.

They come sooner than I expected. I hear voices outside in the suite. The banging stops. And there is silence except for the calm male voices talking.

I summon the nerve to open the door a crack and peek out. A security man is holding onto a squirming Cheryl. Kurt is standing by another man in uniform. Breathe. Just breathe. You're going to live through this.

I walk out of the bathroom.

"Are you okay, Miss Rivers?" The man holding Cheryl asks me.

I nod and tighten the towel around my body. "Yes." I turn to Kurt. "Thanks."

Kurt shrugs. "All I did was save you from an insane psychopath. You'd do the same for me."

"I'll have you know, Mikayla," Cheryl smirks, "that I don't

need you. I was going to quit soon anyway. I'm launching my own music career."

She somehow manages to adjust her left implant with her elbow while still having her arms held by the security guard.

Ew. If I never see Cheryl and her nasty obsession with groping herself again, it would be fine with me.

"Well, if you are planning on being a star, you might want to stop touching your implants. I mean it. It is disturbing. Just stop." There. I finally said it.

Cheryl stiffens. Her face turns a little red and she glances at the others.

Kurt nods. "It's true."

The security guards shift uncomfortably. "Let's get you out of here," one says, and they escort Cheryl to the door.

Cheryl glares at me. "I'll be more famous than you'll ever be!" She says in a last fit of rage.

Kurt walks them to the door. "Remember Cheryl, if you ever mention anything about Micky again, to the press, to her family, to anyone, we'll go to town on you. You won't be able to walk outside without having people throw sticks at you."

Cheryl turns her head and marches away, pushing her way out of the security guard's grip.

Kurt gives me a tight hug. "Honey, that was incredible. *You* were incredible. I honestly never thought you would have the courage to tell Cheryl off. It's about time you stopped letting her walk all over you."

I nod, feeling shaky and weak, but good, like there is a tiny spark of something stronger inside of me.

I read a self-help magazine once, after Matt dumped me. It said that everyone has either a fight or flight mentality, and those who choose flight end up being trampled by the fighters.

I have been a flighter instead of a fighter. I flee. I run. I pacify.

I never knew that fighting back, even as insignificant as my fight was, could be so liberating.

I look down at myself. I had forgotten that I'm still in a towel. That's awkward. The security guys kind of saw me naked. Only with, you know, a towel on.

Kurt winks at me. "Want to go running?"

I nod. Maybe running will sort things out. Cheryl. Jordan. Matt. Jordan. Cheryl. Matt. They are all spinning around in my head and I can barely concentrate.

I need to figure this out.

No more flight.

Chapter Twenty Eight

After my run with Kurt, I feel better, more stretched and relaxed.

And I'm relieved that Cheryl is gone. I know my mom will call when she hears the news. Cheryl's mother will complain. I've decided to tell my mom the truth about my lips when she calls. She's my mom. She'll love me no matter what.

Jordan loved me once.

Thinking of Jordan hurts, so I change the channel of my mind.

Matt.

I have to get out of here. I have to figure out what to do.

I turn off the water and step out of the shower, grabbing a plush bath towel and wrapping it around my shivering body. It is soft and luxurious and brightens my mood substantially.

Kurt is lying on my bed, chattering away on my cell, talking to someone.

"Good, good. Yes, oh, she's just out of the shower. One moment." He covers the phone with his hand and mouths,

"It's Matt."

I take the phone. "Hello?"

"Hey Micky, it's Matt. Just calling to see when you wanted to hang out today." His voice doesn't make my heart leap any more, and I realize again… I'm not in love with him anymore. I care for him, but that's all.

Kurt was right. I love Jordan. I wanted Matt to love me before, but now? I want him to move on, the way I have.

And I don't want to hang out with Matt. Not really. I think he wants to be more than friends. I don't think he came all this way just to hang out.

I decide to tell him, right now, over the phone. I don't want to lead him on. "Look, Matt, I had a great time last night."

I hesitate but then continue on before he can say anything. "It was fun to see you again and all that. And I appreciate you taking the time to come down and apologize for being a prick."

He begins to say something, but I cut him off and blurt out the rest really fast. "But truthfully, what happened last night, when you kissed me? Well, I've moved on, Matt. I'm dating somebody else, and have been for a while. You were a great friend, but that's all we ever will be."

I draw in a shaky breath.

"Micky," Matt says, "Micky, you little sweetheart. Look, let me come see you. We can talk about this."

He thinks I'm exaggerating. Or just kidding or something.

Don't say yes, I tell myself, just get off the phone. You need to get Jordan back. You don't need to deal with Matt right now.

Matt's voice becomes almost pleading. No, pleading is the wrong word. Wheedling? "Micky, please. I need to see you face to face. We need to talk about this. Tell me your hotel and I'll be there in twenty minutes."

Tell him no! I command my brain. Fight! Fight! Fight!

"Uh, I don't know," I hear myself say. Lousy brain.

"Just for half an hour."

215

Say no! Be firm. Stand strong! Don't let him come. Hang up and be done with it.

Although, I do still care about him. It is only fair to end it officially, face to face. "Sure, fine. You can come for a half hour, only to talk. I know I said we'd hang out, but we will just talk and then you go." I wish I could take back the words, but I've already rattled off my hotel name and Matt says he's on his way and hangs up.

Kurt looks up. "Matt coming over?"

"Yeah, I think so," I say in frustration. I flop down on the bed. "I am such a pushover. Why can't I say no to Matt? I finally managed to get rid of Cheryl. Why can't I be strong all the way through?"

"Look, he was a big part of your life for a long time. You still care for him. It's better this way, to do it to his face and not over the phone. This way you will have no regrets later. But just remember that you love Jordan. This happens. People move on and find someone new. Let Matt know that he is no longer the most important person in your life. You be that fighter I know you are. Stand strong. I know you can do it."

I nod. Alright, Matt. Let's get this over with.

Chapter Twenty Nine

There is a knock on the door. I clench my fists, tell myself to be tough and not such a wishy-washy sucker. I open the door. I can do this. I told Cheryl the truth, now I can tell Matt.

All I can see is a massive bouquet of flowers. Deep, gorgeous, red roses, probably two or three dozen of them. They are so delicate! Some even have tiny droplets of water on the petals. The roses shift and I see Matt's face grinning at me. "Hi Micky!" He holds them out for me. I take them into my arms and stagger back into my room.

I lay them on my desk, and pick up the hotel phone and dial for room service.

As the phone rings, I see Matt gaping in the doorway at the opulence of the room. I beckon for him to come in as a stiff, formal voice says, "Room service, how may I help you?"

"Hi, this is Mikayla Rivers in the President's Suite. I need like four or five vases. I just got delivered a bunch of roses and I need to put them in something."

"Miss Rivers, always a pleasure to assist you. How many roses?"

"Um, I don't know for sure. It looks like three dozen or so."

"But of course. I will have several vases brought up immediately. What design do you desire?"

Design? On a vase? Isn't a vase a vase? I would use an empty Coke bottle or a pitcher or something if I had it. "Uh, whichever you have. I don't want to inconvenience you at all."

"They will be there within ten minutes." He hangs up the phone.

Matt is watching me. "Micky, you seem upset. Come here," he says, holding out his arms.

I step back, away from him. "Matt, I appreciate you coming all the way down here. And I am happy that we finally can have closure. But honestly, I am in love with someone else. I loved you once. I really did. You meant everything to me. But that was a long time ago. I've moved on."

I am going to say more, but Matt cuts me off. He walks over and hugs me. I stand stiffly in his arms, refusing to hug him back. He isn't here to be just friends, and I don't want to lead him on.

"Micky, I love you. And if you loved me before, we can get it back." He kneels down and reaches for my hand.

I stand there in shock. Is he doing what I think he's doing? He's got to have a lot of self-esteem if he thinks he can waltz down here after not speaking to me in well over a year and propose and think I'll actually say yes.

"Micky, I know you've been upset with me. But we belong together. We do. I will help you with your music career, and we will get to know each other all over again. It was a mistake for us to break up, and I'm here to offer you my heart. We were made for each other, and I've known that since I met you. Marry me, Mikayla."

He stays there, gazing up into my face and suddenly Cheryl's face pops onto his body. Her arrogant eyes, her cruelty. Matt is like Cheryl. They used me and only liked me when it was convenient.

I feel rising revulsion as I look at him. I jerk my hand away and shake my head. "No!" I cry, backing away from him. "No, I won't marry you. You dump me and think you can come crawling back now that I'm famous? Absolutely not!"

"You think that your current boyfriend cares about you? I would bet you anything that he's using you for your money and fame. You're not going to have a normal life, Mikayla. You *chose* this."

I draw in an unsteady breath. "You're wrong about Jordan. He loved me before he knew that I was famous."

"He lied then. Everyone knows you're famous. You're blind."

Wow. This has got to be the worst proposal ever. I sigh. "Matt, please just get out. Just leave."

Matt looks angry now, and suddenly I realize that everything we've had has been a lie. Everything I thought I had with Matt, even our dinner yesterday, all of it was fake. "All the things we've done together, even last night at dinner and how we were remembering and reminiscing and what you told me about missing me every day… it all was a lie, wasn't it? You just came down here to use me, didn't you? What do you want? You want to become famous? You want my money? What is it?"

He's been playing me. He was planning this all along.

"Mikayla, you've changed."

"You aren't welcome here, Matt." I said what I needed to, and now I just want him out.

Matt glowers at me and picks up one of the bouquets. He chucks it at the wall. "Good luck with your boyfriend." The flowers crash and fall to the ground. Some petals fall off and they crumple into a heap.

I stare at them. What a perfect metaphor of my love for Matt, my life with Matt. Pretty on the outside, but leaving me wounded. Damaged.

"Get out. We're finished. I appreciate you coming. You gave me closure. But now you need to leave." My voice is firm, but inside I am turning to jelly.

I feel like my world is crumbling. Once I loved him. It had been very real to me. And yet all of it was a lie.

Matt stares back at me, his face expressionless.

And my resolve starts to crack. I am going to cry. I don't want to cry. Crying is what flighters do. Fighters don't cry.

I see on my nightstand a photo propped up against the lamp. It's a simple snapshot of Jordan and me, taken at arm's length while we grin into the camera.

Even if Matt used me, even if he never loved me, what Jordan and I had was real. I don't have the slightest doubt about that. If Jordan never wants to see me again, at least I'll know that our love was the real thing.

I walk Matt to the door, my back straight and my shoulders stiff. To my relief, he follows. I hold the door open wide. Matt hesitates.

This is it! He's going to apologize. He'll say that he's sorry for being so mean and that he knows that I'm right and –

"Do you have Taylor Swift's number?"

Wow. Fame whore.

I shake my head. "Not on your life."

"Heidi Montag?"

"She's married, I think." I point my finger toward the door. "Get out, Matt. And never call me again."

As I close the door, Matt calls out, "What about that chick from *The O.C.*?"

I shut it firmly. I sink down onto the carpet and lean my head against the door.

It's over. Matt is over.

Cheryl and Matt, both out of my life in the same day.

I should have given him Cheryl's number. They deserve each other.

Kurt walks out of the bathroom. I wondered where he had gone. He puts his hand on my shoulder. "Sweetie, you did the right thing. I mean, I would have kicked his sorry butt to the curb and then stomped on it for good measure, but you were pretty close to that. You did good."

I embrace Kurt, and he squeezes me tight.

"Well, this answers my question about whether I should go with Matt or Jordan," I say.

Chapter Thirty

Kurt and I are lying on the grass in a park, shoulder to shoulder, after a strenuous five mile run. It's a warm day for the end of October. The grass is cool and tickles my neck.

I remember me and Jordan lounging under a tree on campus, enjoying the sunshine. We bought ice cream cones that were dripping over our fingers, and we were laughing and trying not to get ice cream on our clothes. That was back when everything made sense.

Kurt and I are brainstorming ways to win Jordan back. Kurt has thought of everything from renting a sky-writer plane to faking my own kidnapping.

"Okay, what if we blow up a huge picture of you and him, and we put it on a billboard across from his apartment. And we call in the media and get this whole story going about you trying to win him back. And you go on the news and read a statement saying you are sorry and that you want him back."

I frown. "Jordan didn't like the media to begin with. Using it to publicize our relationship isn't going to help at all. Plus that was Cheryl's idea. And anything Cheryl thought was good has got to be a horrible plan."

Kurt shrugs. "True. So buy him a puppy. People always want a puppy."

Puppies and college students? I shake my head no.

"Fine. Don't go with the puppy," Kurt says. "You come up with something then."

I look up at the clouds drifting by. The sky is grey today. I think it is supposed to rain later. What could I possibly do to regain his trust? Or at least get him to let me back into his life so over time I can eventually regain his trust.

My phone buzzes, and I reach into my pocket and take it out. "If it's Matt, I'm not going to answer," I mutter.

It's a number from Calgary, but it comes up as CALLER UNKNOWN. If it's Matt calling from a different number, I think I'll scream. "Hello?"

I hear a pause and then, "Micky? It's me. I'm calling from my apartment number cause I was afraid you were still mad and wouldn't pick up."

Rachelle. "Hey Rach." I want to say I'm sorry for getting mad, but I also want her to say it first.

"Micky, I'm so, so sor –"

I cut her off. This is my sister, my best friend. I don't need her to grovel. "Rach, don't worry about it. We both were out of line."

There is an awkward moment, a heavy pause, and suddenly we both are crying and giggling and laughing. I tell her about Cheryl and Matt and she congratulates me for being so tough. She tells me about school and her latest crush. It's normal girl talk, and I am so happy to be talking to Rachelle again.

She tries to come up with a few ideas to help me with Jordan, but we got nothing. Finally she hangs up, promising to call again tonight.

I wipe a tear that is trickling down my face and say goodbye.

My life is slowly coming back together.

Now, to just get Jordan to love me again. Then everything will be perfect.

Kurt takes out his smart phone and Googles "How to get back with your boyfriend when he thinks you lied." He starts scrolling through the results, calling out an idea or two here and there as he goes.

"'Make him dinner and put a love potion in his drink.' Although I think you have to be good at voodoo or witchcraft or something in order for that to work."

"Oh, the kidnapping idea again. I really like that one."

"'Write him a song on your guitar and play it outside his bedroom window.' Very Romeo and Juliet."

We all know how Romeo and Juliet ended up. "This needs to be Jordan and Micky. Nothing to do with Shakespeare."

"My apologies. I'm out of ideas here, girl. And Google is out of ideas too."

That's it. Apologies! I need to apologize, to just tell him the truth. Here I am worrying about a plan and making it big and elaborate, but really, what I need to do is tell him the truth. Again. He's had a week to think, to cool down.

To miss me, I hope.

"Alright. Here's the plan. I'm going to go to his apartment. No, wait. He might not open the door for me. So I'll go to his class. I'll wait outside for him to come out. He can't run away from me in public. And then I'm just going to – "

"Fake your own kidnapping?" Kurt says hopefully.

"No!" I exclaim, laughing. "I'm just going to apologize. I don't need a big, fancy plan. I just need to be me."

Kurt seems to be processing what I said. "Yes, well I can see how that *might* work. I personally would go with something with a bit more pizzazz, but to each his own."

"We have to go home. I need to shower and change and get to campus stat!"

Kurt scrambles to his feet and drags me up with him. "Okay, but you have to tell me everything. Every detail. Or better yet, let me follow along and video tape the whole thing. I'll stay out of sight."

I smack him as we race to the hotel. "Not on your life! This is just for me and Jordan. I'll tell you details after, but I'm not letting you come along!"

I jump into the shower and as soon as I get out I start blow-drying my hair. Kurt has laid out on the bed a sexy little outfit from D&G, but I shake my head.

"I want to be me. I don't want to wear some designer outfit or flaunt my money. I want to be the girl he fell in love with."

Kurt goes back to my wardrobe and returns holding a long sleeved T-shirt that says "Mickey!" with a picture of Mickey Mouse on it. Rachelle gave it to me for Christmas a year ago. He is holding my favorite skinny jeans and Ugg Boots.

I beam at him. "Perfect," I call over the roar of the hair dryer.

When my hair is dry, Kurt takes over. He runs the straightener through my tresses until they are bone straight. I finish applying my minimal makeup and take a look at myself.

Other than my hair color (and those freaking lips that I still hate myself for getting) I look like me. Like the real me. The me that Jordan liked.

I go into the bathroom, where I can be alone, and kneel down. I haven't said a prayer, an honest-to-goodness prayer since I was probably six years old. God most likely hates me since I only acknowledge him when I need help, but I don't know what else to do. I need divine assistance right now.

"God?" I whisper, feeling slightly ridiculous. "I think I need your help. Please make Jordan like me again. Okay? Just make everything better, alright? Um, thank you very much."

I go back into the main suite. "Well, I'm ready." I turn slowly in a circle, allowing Kurt to critique me. He gives me a thumbs up. "You look ravishing. He'll love it."

I give Kurt a quick hug and he squeezes me tight. "You can do it, girlfriend."

I blink back tears of gratitude and with a final look at Kurt, I exit the room.

I take the elevator downstairs. There are a million lights flashing in the foyer of the hotel, and I know that someone famous is there. I walk toward them and see Lindsay Lohan and her mother and sister, holding their designer bags. Lindsay waves at me, and I smile back.

We met once, I think. It's hard to keep track of everyone; they all kind of whirl around in my head, these beautiful, famous people.

A few of the cameras stay on the Lohans and a couple turn their attention to me.

"Mikayla, where are you going?"

"Is it true that you are dating your ex-boyfriend from Canada again?"

"What is going on with you and that law student?"

I smile and stop, waiting. As they grow silent and focus on me, cameras still clicking away, I say, "My personal life is personal. I appreciate people taking an interest in my life, however due to some, uh, problems right now, I can't comment on what's happening in my love life. Thank you for respecting my privacy while I try to sort everything out."

People are all shouting at me and calling things and asking a million questions.

Right. That didn't work.

I fake a smile and walk through them, not answering anything else. I climb into the cab and we head to campus.

Let me think. Today is Monday. That would mean that he has the lecture with the boring professor. I vaguely remember where it is.

The cabbie lets me off at campus and I hurry across, keeping my eye out for Jordan. He could be anywhere.

I get to the building where his class is held. Now what? Do I stand outside? Do I go in? I think his class is over in about ten minutes.

Tanned, Toned and Totally Faking It

I decide to go in and wait outside the classroom. What if he decides to exit the building a different way? I don't want to miss him.

My stomach is fluttering, and I think I might throw up.

I sit down on the floor outside the classroom and wait.

Oh no. I feel my stomach heave and I leap up. I dash down the hall, my hand covering my mouth. I barely make it to the bathroom before my breakfast reappears.

Puking has got to be the most revolting thing in the world.

I go to the sink and splash some water on my face. Okay. Breathe. Just breathe. I feel better now; my stomach, happily empty of the granola with skim milk I had for breakfast, is now calm. I dig through my purse for some gum.

Nothing.

How can I not have gum? Great. Just when I get to talk to Jordan for the first time in a week I'm going to have vomit breath.

I hurry back down the hall, looking for a vending machine. Nothing in sight. I pass a boy playing some game on his iPod. "Excuse me, but do you have some gum?"

He pauses his game, looks up and grins broadly. "Olga! Hi!"

Olga? What the? Sudden recognition hits me. Oh my gosh, it's that guy with the buzz cut and braces from that game night.

I smile and say in a choppy accent, "You 'ave gum?"

He digs into his pocket and displays some lint, a couple of pennies and two sticks of peppermint gum, thankfully still wrapped up.

I take one, wipe it surreptitiously on my pants and say, "Tank you, but I 'ave to go now. I am late."

I pop the gum into my mouth and hurry back down the hall to the classroom.

People are leaving. What if Jordan's gone already?

I stand there, unsure of what to do. I'll go outside. That's it. I'll go out and look really quickly to see if he's there and if not, I'll come back in. I join the flow of students and go outside. I look around but it's too hard to tell with so many backs to me.

I stand on my tiptoes and am craning my neck desperately, when I hear an astonished voice. "Micky?"

It's him. It's his voice.

I spin around and see Jordan standing behind me. He's wearing jeans and a baby blue sweatshirt. His ragged backpack is slung over his shoulder. He runs his hand through his hair and stares at me.

I stare back. Now that I see him, everything I wanted to say is gone from my mind. I gape at him.

"What are you doing here?" he demands.

I reach out to touch him, but he moves back. This is not the way I envisioned it. He is supposed to be crying and hugging me by now.

"Jordan, can I talk to you?" I say in a small voice.

He gives me a long look and then shrugs. "Fine, but I don't think we have anything left to say."

He sounds so mean and un-Jordan-like. I did this to him. I hurt him and warped my sweet little Jordan into this bitter husk.

We move away from the open door and stop. We're standing by the garbage can and it smells a little funky. This is definitely not going according to plan.

"Jordan." To my horror I feel my eyes welling up. "Jordan, my name really is Mikayla Rivers. I am twenty years old and my natural hair color is strawberry blonde. I'm afraid of the dark. I enjoy playing music and performing on stage, but I generally hate people recognizing me on the street. I also was in New York that weekend when you thought I was working late, and, yes, that was actually me on *Letterman*."

I half expect Jordan to cut me off and walk away, but he stands there, watching me. I take a shaky breath and keep going. "I like shopping and makeup, but I also like camping and shooting rifles with my dad and walking in the rain as long as it's not cold out. My best friend is my sister and a close second after her is my personal trainer, Kurt. I prayed for the first time in years today when I decided to come and find you."

I can't determine what he's thinking. His eyes are expressionless.

"And about a month ago I met a boy who literally changed my life. He made me want to be a better person. He consumed my thoughts and made me happier than I ever thought I could be. And I learned that I would do anything for this boy. Anything."

I sniff and wipe the tears away with my hand, annoyed that I am crying. Some people look cute when they cry. I look like a drowned rat with puffy eyes. And I don't want to look rat-like when I'm trying to convince Jordan to forgive me.

"And when I hurt you, I felt like part of me had died. I had been trying for a month to find the right moment to tell you the truth, but I never could. It was scary, and I didn't want things to get weird between us, the way I knew they would if I told you that I am a millionaire pop star. But the truth is, Jordan, that I love you. I really do. And the person you got to know? That was me. It *is* me. I was always myself around you."

I don't know what else to say. I open my mouth to say something brilliant and witty and to make him laugh, to see those crinkles around his eyes again, but all that comes out is a pathetic whimper. "I'm so sorry." I stand there feeling lame, waiting for him to make a move.

Say something. Do something. Anything.

It feels like eternity, but it can't have been more than three seconds. My hands are shaking. My knees feel like they are turning into jelly. And then Jordan turns away from me. My heart is going to shatter into a million pieces. He's leaving. I've poured out my heart and soul to him and he's leaving. I reach out and grab onto the wall of the building. I can't physically support myself any longer.

But Jordan doesn't go. He stands there with his back to me. Suddenly he turns to face me. His eyes are wet; he runs his palm over them. He reaches out, and I fall into his arms.

"I'm sorry too," he whispers, stroking my hair. "I was so

negative about Hollywood, no wonder you felt you couldn't say anything. If anyone is to blame, it's me. And when you tried to come clean, I freaked out. I'm sorry."

I cling to him, weeping into his shoulder. "I love you," I sob, over and over.

He holds me tight and presses his mouth into the top of my head. "I love you too. Oh gosh, Mikayla, I love you too."

Maybe my life is sort of like a movie after all, because this is exactly what happens in the movies. Star-crossed lovers suddenly reunited after an emotional monologue. He is gorgeous and she… well, in the movies the heroine wouldn't look like a drowned rat. And the theme music would start to play right about now. And my nose wouldn't be running and I wouldn't be chewing gum that tastes vaguely of vomit.

But it doesn't matter.

Jordan pulls me closer, and his lips find mine.

My Jordan.

Fade to black and let the credits roll.

###

Acknowledgements

I'd like to thank all the people who helped me with my book, giving support and editing help, to just letting me run ideas off them and vent when I got stuck. Among others, thank you to my mother, who inspired me to write, my father and siblings, for not laughing when they heard what I was attempting to do, my husband, for his unwavering belief in my ability, and WiDō Publishing and my editor Karen, who saw a great story in between all my editing mistakes. Finally, I'd like to thank a university professor, Dr. Brown, who once told me that there are three ways to becoming immortal in this life: 1. Plant a tree. 2. Have a child. 3. Write a book. I'm on my way to immortality, apparently, so thanks for all your support.

About the Author

Whitney Boyd was born and raised in Calgary to parents who loved reading and shared that passion with their children. Today, Boyd loves traveling and over the last few years has lived in various parts of the United States including Utah, Florida and Idaho. She graduated from the University of Calgary in 2010 with a Bachelor of Arts degree, majoring in Spanish. Boyd married her husband, Stephen, in 2009 and together they enjoy camping, hiking, fishing and spending time together.

CPSIA information can be obtained at www.ICGtesting.com
Printed in the USA
LVOW130043070412

276528LV00001B/1/P